MATTERS OF THE HEART

Western Australia, 2019: The Bennets are a farming family struggling to make ends meet. Lizzy, passionate about working the land, is determined to save the farm. Spirited and independent, she has little patience for her mother's focus on finding a suitable man for each of her five daughters. The dashing Charles Bingley, looking to expand his farm holdings, buys the neighbouring property of Netherfield Park, and he and Lizzy's sister Jane form an instant connection at a dance. But it is Charlie's best friend, farming magnate Will Darcy, who leaves a lasting impression when he slights Lizzy, setting her against him. Can Lizzy and Will put judgements and pride aside to each see the other for who they really are? Or in an age where appearance and social media rule, will prejudice prevail?

Books by Fiona Palmer
Published by Ulverscroft:

THE SUNNYVALE GIRLS
THE FAMILY SECRET
THE SADDLER BOYS

FIONA PALMER

MATTERS OF THE HEART

Complete and Unabridged

AURORA
Leicester

First published in Australia and New Zealand
in 2019 by
Hachette Australia Pty Ltd

First Aurora Edition
published 2020
by arrangement with
Hachette Australia Pty Ltd

A catalogue record for this book is available
from the British Library.

ISBN 978–1–78782–429–4

Published by
Ulverscroft Limited
Anstey, Leicestershire

Set by Words & Graphics Ltd.
Anstey, Leicestershire
Printed and bound in Great Britain by
T. J. International Ltd., Padstow, Cornwall

This book is printed on acid-free paper

For the readers

'I declare after all there is no enjoyment like reading! How much sooner one tires of any thing than of a book! — When I have a house of my own, I shall be miserable if I have not an excellent library.'

Pride and Prejudice, Jane Austen

1

There was something magical about standing out in the open, the morning sunlight warming her skin, the scent of night lingering on the crisp air and magpies' cries so haunting they gave her goose bumps. Lizzy Bennet loved this time of the day, the sun just peeping over the horizon and the wildlife in full swing. It was as if the land hummed with energy, and she tried to draw from it because Lord knows she needed it.

Just a moment longer, she promised herself as she sat up on the quad bike watching the sky illuminate with shades of blue, yellow and golden streaks of the sun's rays. There wasn't a cloud in sight, just large gum trees nearby, their long waxy leaves glistening like tendrils of metal catching the light. It was a scene of which Lizzy would never grow tired.

A wet nose pushed into her neck and she squirmed, reaching back to pat her black-and-tan Kelpie.

'I know, Pippa, it's time for breakfast. Let's go face the noise.'

Pippa braced herself on the back of the bike as they headed for home, the cold morning air making Lizzy shiver.

Pippa suddenly barked madly, her muzzle right by Lizzy's ear. Lizzy winced and noticed a big wedge-tailed eagle circling above a white woolly body on the green pasture to her left.

'Good spotting, Pip.' She made a beeline to the ewe as the eagle flew up high, keeping its dinner in sight as Lizzy stopped the bike. She swore softly as she knelt beside the deceased ewe and sank her hand into the wool.

'I'm sorry,' she mumbled, feeling the hard, cold body under her hand. Lizzy had been out checking them yesterday afternoon. How had she missed this one? How long had the ewe struggled overnight before she died? The heavy feeling of failure weighed on Lizzy's chest. It never got any easier. Lizzy felt horrible with every one she lost.

She checked the ewe's back end and saw a tiny lamb, only halfway through birthing. At first she thought it was also dead — its ear was red raw where the eagle had taken a few bites, and its tongue was swollen — but then its eyes opened.

'Oh thank goodness.' She smiled as she reached for the lamb and gently pulled it the rest of the way out. Lizzy held it against her chest as she looked it over. Pippa watched with interest, tilting her head slightly. 'I think this one's a fighter, Pip.' Its eyes opened again and it weakly tried to move. 'Let's get you home and fed.'

She wrapped her jacket around the lamb and climbed carefully back on the bike. Pippa jumped on behind her and together they headed home at a gentle pace.

The Longbourn house sat on the edge of the farm amid two large sheds, four silos, scattered piles of old rusted machinery and a dam. The structure itself wasn't anything fancy: a faded red tin roof, wrap-around verandahs and

2

well-established trees to make it cosy. Some of the back verandah had been enclosed to make two more rooms when her younger sisters Catherine and Lydia had come along. Lizzy shared her room with her older sister Jane, and Mary had kept a room to herself as her piano-playing had driven everyone out over the years. In all fairness, she was very good now and they loved the tunes she could play, but the early years of lessons had been rough on them all.

As Lizzy headed up the garden path, past tough irises edging a struggling lawn, she heard voices, raised and giggly as if a hen's party were in full swing. Just the usual breakfast banter that came with a house full of women. Noisy Bennet women.

Inside she found her father at the table, a plate of fruit and yoghurt in front of him. He shot it a look of disdain before turning back to the newspaper.

'How's a man supposed to do a decent day's work on just that?' he asked his wife when she brought Lizzy a bowl of the same.

No one noticed the slight bulge of her jacket where the little lamb was curled up underneath.

'It's good for you, John. Stop your whining and eat it,' said Margaret.

John held the paper in one hand while he poked his spoon at the bowl with his other, his expression suggesting he would rather eat a sour lemon. 'Why should we suffer just because the CWA decided to put on a few health workshops?'

'You look nice, Mum. Quilting club today?' Lizzy asked as she sat down beside her dad and patted his shoulder. 'It's okay, I know where she keeps the chocolate,' she whispered.

Margaret wore a long soft blue skirt, dark blue blouse and a soft pink scarf around her neck, plus a full face of make-up. She pressed a hand to her curly grey hair pulled back into a bun, gently probing for any recalcitrant loose strands. 'Thank you, Lizzy I have a CWA meeting today and then we're making teddies for the Smith Family.' Margaret's voice rose an octave as she shouted, 'Lydia Bennet, get out of the bathroom now and come and eat your breakfast or you'll miss the bus!'

Lizzy squinted one eye as her mum's piercing voice went right through her. Her dad always said Margaret had the lungs of a horse; but even he would have to admit that trying to control the toileting habits of five daughters with one tiny bathroom could do that to a person.

'Hey Dad, look who I found this morning,' Lizzy said, opening her jacket.

His glasses were perched on the end of his nose, his grey hair like tufts of wire wool that thinned out towards the top of his head. He lowered the paper and a sadness swamped his eyes. 'The mum?'

Lizzy shook her head.

You can't save them all, her dad had said when she was six and saw her first mauled lamb. *It's nature; that lamb has fed a family of birds.* It was a rough way to learn about the cycle of life, but in farming there was no shying away from it.

4

Lizzy had built up a tough resolve from that moment on. She'd learned to use a gun to put animals out of their misery, including her own pet lamb when it had been torn open by wild dogs. Her dad's hand had been on her shoulder the whole time. She'd been fifteen then. There was no way any of her sisters would have done it. Sometimes she felt like she was the only one who took after their dad, the only one who truly understood life at Longbourn.

'Oh, this one is just hanging on,' said Jane as she joined them at the table.

Margaret came out and put Jane's breakfast in front of her before she spotted the lamb, practically sitting at their table. 'Poor little blighter. Was nearly someone's breakfast, I see. I'll get some stuff for its ear and then make up some milk.'

'Thanks, Mum.'

'You girls eat up while I get it ready.'

Jane picked up her spoon with long graceful fingers. 'Thank you, Mum,' she said with a wide smile.

Jane put the smallest amount of yoghurt on the end of her spoon and slipped it into her mouth soundlessly.

Lizzy touched her brown hair, hurriedly plaited this morning, as she admired the way her sister's blonde silky mane cascaded over her shoulders as if she'd spent the past two hours brushing it until it shone. When Lizzy was little she used to think Jane was a princess for her delicate ways and beauty; indeed, she often wondered how she could be Jane's sister when

5

she was so different: brown hair, sun-dyed skin and bull-at-a-gate tendencies. Her eyes were brown and her body curvy, contrasted with Jane's gorgeous features: high cheekbones, skin creamy and blemish free plus blue eyes that looked like sparkling sapphires.

Jane met her gaze and her perfect lips curled up. 'How are you today, Lizzy? Did you sleep okay? I heard you get up early.'

'I wanted to check on the lambs and see the sunrise. It was worth it,' she replied. 'I'm not sure this little guy would be alive if I'd found him any later.' Her sister's concern always warmed her heart. No matter if it was a snotty-nosed four year old or an old man who repeated himself ten times over, Jane would focus her attention on them wholeheartedly. She was a natural nurturer and perfectly suited to her role in childcare.

'Mum, Lydia still isn't out of the bathroom and I need to do my face.' Catherine stomped into the open kitchen-dining area in her fluffy pink onesie.

'Oh my god, Kitty, you're not even dressed! Here I am worried about Lydia.' Margaret pushed a bowl into her daughter's hands. 'Eat this quickly while I sort out your sister.'

Jane smiled as Kitty joined them for breakfast. Before eating she slipped the hood of her onesie up so she resembled a pink rabbit. Who would have thought she turned seventeen this year? Most days she behaved as if she were two years younger, like Lydia.

Moments later they heard banging on the door

as Margaret yelled a hurry-up to Lydia.

'Oh wow, we have a new pet lamb?' said Kitty, spotting their guest. 'Can I feed him?'

Lizzy frowned. 'I don't think you'll have time. But after school he's all yours.'

'Yay.' Kitty turned to Jane. 'Looks like we might be catching a lift in with you, sis.'

'Well, I'm leaving in fifteen minutes. Be ready.'

'Oh, did you hear the news?' asked Margaret eagerly as she re-joined them at the table with her bowl of yoghurt and fruit. She didn't wait for anyone to answer, too caught up in her own excitement. 'Janice at the P-and-C meeting last night told me that Netherfield Park has finally been sold.'

John shifted in his seat and Lizzy jerked upright, suddenly all ears. Lizzy wasn't one for gossip, but when it included the large property — worth millions — that bordered their land, she was interested. Not only that, but some of Netherfield used to belong to the Bennets, back before she was born, so she felt a vested interest in the place.

'Who would have bought that? No one around here can afford that kind of money.' It was prime farming land that had been built up by the Jones family for three generations. But last year their only son had died on the farm, leaving the family devastated. The two daughters didn't want the farm, and the parents simply couldn't bear to stay, so they'd decided to sell and follow their daughters to the city.

'Who has that kind of money? A corporate? The Chinese? I heard they bought a big farm up

7

north,' said Lizzy, again, hoping her mum had the answers.

Margaret fluffed up like one of her chooks as she relayed the information. 'The Bingleys have bought it. I was told that their son, Charles, is to take over the farm.'

'Charles Bingley is a hunk,' said Kitty. 'All the girls at school follow him.'

Everyone's eyes shot to hers.

'Follow him where?' asked Margaret.

Kitty rolled her eyes. 'On Twitter. His sister is a fashion guru, with her own blog. Charlie posted a photo just the other day of him at the front of the gates to Netherfield. Such a hottie, those blue eyes,' said Kitty as she brought up the photo on her phone. 'See?'

She held out her phone to show them all. Kitty never let anyone touch it, so Lizzy had to lean over the table to get a good look at Charlie. Sure enough she recognised the gates to her neighbour's farm and there next to them was a tall, handsome man with the said blue eyes, in moleskin pants and a patterned button-up shirt. He looked like a model advertising watches, not someone who would pull lambs from dead ewes. 'Yeah, he is a bit all right,' she said as Kitty snatched her phone back.

'Maybe if you followed some cool pages instead of all that farming and political stuff you might actually know what's happening,' teased Kitty.

'I don't have time to scroll through some random person's photos, even if you think they're famous. Why would I want to? It's not like I know them personally or ever will. Seems like a waste of time and data.' Lizzy ignored Kitty's pulled face. 'Besides, I *have* heard of the Bingleys. And I know they have the money to buy a property like that.' She turned to her dad. 'I wonder what his plans are for the place?' she said, raising her eyebrows.

'Wonder if he's found the busted boundary fence yet?' her dad replied. 'You think seeing as he's so wealthy he might fix it all himself?' John gave her a hopeful wink.

As far as this Charles Bingley was concerned, the Bennets were at the opposite end of the farming spectrum. Half of their land was leased out to Ken Collins, and the bank had been breathing down their neck for years. Each season they clung to hope that they'd have a good enough year to get through.

'Be nice to have a new young man about, and a good-looking one at that. It'll cause a stir in the hen house if he's single!' Margaret put her spoon into her empty bowl. 'Bet he's never had to worry about where his next bit of money is coming from or feel the pressure of waiting for the bank to come knocking on his door! We'll be the talk of the town soon with the way this season is panning out, John.'

John breathed out slowly as he put down his spoon. 'Margaret, I can't help it if we had a drought one year and then a frost the next.' He tilted his head slightly, his eyes squinting behind his glasses. 'Farming is a gambling man's game and I was never very good at the casino. But if the government could see fit to look after the ones feeding the country, like they do in America, then we'd not be so hard up thanks to Mother Nature.'

Lizzy smiled at her dad. 'Should go into politics, Dad, and sort them all out.'

Margaret frowned. 'Really, Lizzy, don't egg him on.' She tutted and headed over to the sink with some dirty dishes.

Jane and Lizzy shared a conspirator's grin just as Lydia waltzed in, her school uniform consisting of a very short navy skirt and a polo shirt emblazoned with the school's logo. Her long dark hair was swept up on her head in a loose knot. The girls had an hour trip to get to the district high school. If they missed the bus Jane sometimes took them in on her way to the childcare centre that she managed. Which could happen today unless Kitty planned on wearing her bunny onesie to school.

'If Mary was here she'd tell you that you wear too much make-up to school,' said Jane.

Lydia squinted at her oldest sister. 'Yeah, but she's not and I don't need you on my case too. Besides, all the girls wear eyeshadow.' She shot Jane a look to show just how much she cared before moving on to something she was interested in. 'Mum, I need a new dress for the cabaret on the weekend. Can I have a hundred bucks?'

Margaret threw her hands up in despair while Kitty left to get dressed. 'Do I look like I'm made of money? I struggle to pay our grocery bill. Borrow one of your sister's dresses.'

'No way! Not fair, Mum. You don't understand. Do you want me to be single *forever?*' Lydia took out her phone and started texting. It beeped shortly after. 'Megan says you're horrible too,' Lydia announced as she picked up her school bag and headed outside to the beat-up old ute they used to get to the end of the driveway to meet the bus.

'Maybe Charles Bingley might be at the cabaret,' said Margaret touching Jane's shoulder. 'You should make a new dress for the occasion. Use that baby blue material you have, it sets off your eyes.'

Jane closed her eyes for a moment, her white teeth pulling on her bottom lip. 'I don't know if I'll have time,' she said. 'Still lots of setting up to do at the hall.'

'I was thinking of wearing jeans,' said Lizzy and waited to see her mum scoff.

'I wouldn't put it past you, Elizabeth. A flannel shirt and your work boots too, probably.' Margaret rolled her eyes as if she'd been shown how by Lydia.

'I like the sound of that,' said her dad.

'Don't you start,' warned Margaret, handing Lizzy a beer bottle filled with milk with a black teat on the end.

'Thanks, Mum.' Lizzy moved in her chair so she had room to feed the lamb, who had been so quiet she would have thought it was dead if it wasn't for the feel of its heartbeat against her chest. 'Poor little guy is so worn out.' She opened the lamb's mouth and wiggled the teat into it, trying to let some of the milk dribble out so it could get a taste. 'Come on, you know you're hungry.' Everyone was watching, holding their breaths, silently hoping the lamb would feed. It was a long few seconds and then the lamb began to suck and Lizzy felt the room relax, including herself.

'Good, good,' muttered John.

Jane grinned from ear to ear and reached over to stroke the lamb's head with her finger.

'Well done, Lizzy,' said Margaret. She checked her watch as Kitty sped past them, dressed in her uniform and trying to brush her long brown hair as she went.

'Bye, catch you later,' she said as the screen door slammed behind her.

Jane went to brush her teeth and Margaret went back to the bedroom. Suddenly the house grew peaceful again and Lizzy almost sighed. Beside her, her dad actually did.

'Much better,' he said going back to his newspaper.

Lizzy couldn't agree more. The Bennet household at peak hour would be enough to scare anyone, let alone potential boyfriends.

2

Lizzy dragged the wire gate across the grassy paddock and tied it shut against the thick old fence post. She leaned against it for a moment, watching the ewes waddle with full udders while their lambs trailed close by. Some nudged at the teats, forcing their mother to stop while they kneeled to drink, sending their tails into a dancing frenzy. Lizzy grinned as she watched them. The one she'd rescued had begun to feed well and soon his tail would be jiggling like the rest. 'Hey Dad, I've been thinking,' she said turning to where John sat in the ute. 'We should call him Rocky.'

Pippa was already on the ute waiting for the next job, her tongue hanging out from the exertion of shifting this mob to the new paddock.

'The lamb?'

'Yeah. Like the movie.'

Her dad chuckled. 'Why not. It's much better than Kitty calling the last one after that boy singer.'

'Bieber grew into his name,' Lizzy said with a smirk before giving the mob one last look and returning to the ute.

'You heading into town now?' he asked as she drove back to the sheds.

'Yep, think I'll get those parts. What will you do?'

John scratched at his chin. 'I might tinker with that old pump motor.'

'Good luck.' It had died a long time ago, but John never liked to give up on anything. 'I'll drop by the pub and see Lottie while I'm at it.'

'Figured you might,' he said with a knowing grin.

At the shed her dad got out and whistled to Pippa, who reluctantly got down and threw Lizzy an aggrieved look.

'You can keep Dad company. Be a good girl.' With a wave she headed down the driveway.

★ ★ ★

Lizzy pulled out onto the gravel road, leaving their rusty farm gate in her dust. It was surprisingly warm for the end of June. It had been a late dry start to seeding. Many sleepless nights as Lizzy prayed for rain. If a drought came now the farm would slip further from their grasp. But luckily the rain had arrived just recently and the crop was coming to life before her eyes. Lizzy left her window down so she could breathe in the air thick with damp soil and moist straw.

Paddocks flashed past, most covered with green as new crops began to grow, some edged with shrubs or tall gum trees, others dotted with barren salt patches where grey dead sticks stuck out like abandoned old fence posts. It was hard to believe they once had been trees, before the salt killed them. It was a harsh landscape at times. During the drought it had been bloody awful but it was still home and Lizzy loved this area despite the hardships it could bring. She'd long ago — at the age of ten — decided that the farm was her place, and she'd told her dad she was going to be a farmer. They had spent the day looking over the growing crop, John answering her many questions about how it grew and what the parts of the plants were called. At one point Lizzy had lain between the rows and hidden from her dad. He'd laughed until he'd nearly cried when she pretended to swim through the green crop, her stomach pressed against the dirt as her legs kicked and her arms flailed about in an approximation of freestyle. Moments after she'd sat up with the rich chlorophyll wheatgrass scent filling the air, she'd known the soil beneath her was where her roots had set up home. 'I'm going to be a farmer too, Dad.'

His reply had been simple. 'Well, I guess I better teach you how to drive the tractor.'

She'd begun dreaming of becoming a jillaroo and by the age of thirteen she was trying to convince her dad to let her stay home from school to help with the harvest but had to concede to just jumping on after school. There was something about working the machinery, looking after the sheep, being on the land from sun-up till sundown that filled Lizzy's heart with inspiration, passion and a happiness that no one else in her family seemed to understand, apart from her dad. There were times she'd catch him just watching over the land, taking in all the details, and the appreciation for what he saw had threaded down to her.

15

Lizzy slowed to watch a large blackish-brown wedge-tailed eagle on the side of the road stand over a fox carcass, tearing at it with its sharp hooked beak. It didn't pay her any notice until Lizzy was nearly level with the bird and its dinner, when finally it opened its wings and took flight. She guessed its wing span to be nearly two metres as she marvelled at its wedge tail. They were amazing birds, even if they did like to nibble on lambs like Rocky. Lizzy had nearly come to a standstill watching it, but as it soared around in a loop she put her foot down and continued on her way.

The gravel road finished at an intersection, and Lizzy turned onto the bitumen road into town. It was a half-hour journey to Coodardy, population fifteen hundred, served by a pub, a pool, a police station, a church hall and a main street wide enough that cars could park nose in to the kerb on either side. It was an old town but the council had a full-time gardener who kept the kerb gardens green, pathways swept and the red roses around the memorial hall trimmed. On Anzac Day the local ladies and school kids covered the ground around the hall and base of the flag pole with handmade red poppies. It made a spectacular display along with the roses. Lizzy always slowed when she passed the childcare centre, hoping to catch a glimpse of Jane outside with the kids, who would be charging around the yard on scooters and little pedal tractors or playing in the sand pit.

She parked her brown ute (it was white, but with mud and gravel roads she didn't see its original colour very often) out the front of Tilly's Hardware store and ducked inside.

'Hey Bethy,' said Tyron as he restocked shelves with spray nozzles alongside the garden equipment on one of the walls; pet supplies lined another. Everything was exactly where it had been for as long as she could remember. As a kid, when her dad came in for supplies Lizzy would help Tyron put the poly fittings back into the right-sized boxes. 'The customers always mix them up,' Tyron would say, rolling his eyes as if he were forty not eight. Lizzy was pretty sure she could find her way around this shop blindfolded.

'Your pump parts are on the counter ready.' When Tyron smiled his dimples appeared, and Lizzy felt a strong desire to press them like she had in kindergarten.

'Cheers, Ty. I'm after some camlock fittings too.'

Tyron put the last of the bags of spray nozzles on the shelf and followed her down to the back corner of the large shop.

'So, you heard about the Bingleys? Town's humming with gossip. Mum saw him and his sister in the store the other day, buying up fancy stuff.'

'Fancy stuff?'

'Yeah, no-expense-spared food and drink. They bought that hundred-dollar bottle of shiraz that's been on the shelf for the past ten years,' he said with a laugh.

'Oh no, really?' she scoffed, picturing the dust-covered bottle that sat in the glass cabinet in the wine section. 'I always wondered who would end up buying that.'

'I hope they come to the cabaret tomorrow. Mum said his sister is a looker.'

Lizzy smiled. 'It's a shame she won't find a proper man around here to dance with,' she teased. 'You'll probably all be too feral for her fancy tastes.' She tugged one of his dreadlocks.

Tyron shook his head. 'You're the feral. Will we get to see you frocked up for once?'

He looked over her jeans and checked flannel shirt, smudged with grease, dirt and tufts of spider web from her hurried search of the old shed for a belt for the tractor. But Coodardy was a farming community, filled with hard-working folk among whom her farm clothes wouldn't raise an eyebrow; well, except maybe from her mother. 'I'm sure I'll find something that will suit. What *you* wear will be the problem,' she teased as she searched for the fittings she needed.

'I'll look smashing no matter what I wear.' He pushed out his chest and pulled a supermodel pose. 'Look out, I overheard Ken in here the other day saying he was going to ask you to the dance. He still trying?'

Lizzy groaned. 'It's not going to happen. Ever!' Ken Collins was a farmer from the next town, Toongarrin, sixty kilometres away. A few years back he had leased nearly a thousand hectares of Longbourn from the Bennets at a good-enough rate to keep them afloat. It seemed to come at a cost, though, because ever since he'd been asking Lizzy out to different events. Luckily so far she'd been too busy with farm

18

business. Ken thought himself quite important in social standings, strutting around like the lord mayor of his town. He was a shire councillor but no doubt had his eyes set on the President position. Lizzy had nicknamed him Ken Doll, because his hair was black and, like a helmet, it never moved. And his skin had a waxy, unearthly shine.

Tyron laughed as he went to book up her purchases on her account. 'I'll see you tomorrow, then. Save me a dance,' he said as she was leaving.

'We'll see.' She gave him a smile and a wave and headed off down the street to the local watering hole.

The two-storey pub was made from old red brick with tall deep-set windows. A verandah, top and bottom, gave it history along with the railings and gutters painted in heritage green and white slats on the top section. In the middle, where the bottom verandah met the balcony, *Coodardy Tavern* was printed in white across the green background. The tin roof was rusty corrugated iron with two large bricked chimney stacks standing proud out the top. Bordering the pub were large gum trees and a lilac tree, along with parking for the folks staying for the night in the rooms on the top floor. Seeing as Coodardy was on a main road that went north and south through the state, it was always full of travellers needing accommodation. Which kept her best friend really busy.

Lizzy pushed open the double doors and was hit by the beer scent that was only found in a pub, as if over the years it had been absorbed into the bricks, carpet and ceiling. With the amount that was spilled on the floor after a footy wind-up it wasn't surprising. She walked up to the front bar, the carpet giving way to jarrah floorboards and scattered empty tables and chairs. When Lizzy and Lottie were little they had used those chairs and tables to make a big cubby with some sheets in the dining lounge and wanted to charge people two dollars to enter. They only managed to get Mr Peters, the delivery man, to have a look. They'd spent their earnings on a cool drink, which they shared on the balcony while their legs dangled below between the railings as they sipped and watched the town cats and dogs roam about.

'Hey Dave, where's Lottie at?'

Charlotte's dad wore a grey singlet, chest hair exploding beneath it like wool escaping from a bale; the only place hair didn't seem to grow on him was a narrow bald patch on the top of his head.

'Hey, Dizzy Lizzy. She's out the back working on a beer order for the shindig at the hall,' he said with a grin.

He nodded to the back door, but Lizzy was already on her way. She could never resist a smile at the sound of the nickname Dave had thrown at her when she was six. *Dizzy Lizzy and Snotty Lottie. What a pair!*

Lizzy pushed through a few scratched doors and veered left to the small office identified by a tattered *Staff Only* sign taped to the door. Not clear tape; no, this was red gorilla tape four fingers wide. Dave had gone around the whole edge and said it would make people really see it.

Inside Lottie was leaning over a keyboard, the click-clack of pressed keys and the tick of a wall clock were the only sounds until she leaned back on the chair, its familiar squeak like a trodden-on mouse.

'You can't sneak up on me, Lizzy Bennet. I know the sound of your boots a mile away.' Lottie flicked her wavy brown hair back and smiled.

Her best friend's smile filled her with a familiar contentment. 'Hey you.' Lizzy pressed her finger to the crease line between her friend's eyebrows and gave it a little rub. 'You work too hard.'

Lottie almost snorted. 'Says the pot.' She pushed her chair back and stood up. 'I need a new life.'

'I know.'

Lottie had said those words at least once a week since Lizzy could remember. She was frantically saving money so she could leave and set herself up somewhere else — anywhere else. Her dad had none to give, and he relied heavily on Lottie to help keep the pub running. Her mum had died when she was nine, and Lizzy knew that it was the memories of her mum around the pub that kept Lottie tied to it. Lizzy knew how trapped Lottie felt at times but silently — and selfishly, she knew — hoped her friend would never save enough or overcome her fears to leave. Coodardy wouldn't be the same without her.

'What brings you to town?'

'Parts, but when I'm done will you be free for a drink or two?'

Lottie raised an eyebrow, her hazel eyes twinkling. 'Shall we take a few to the hill? Watch the sun set?'

Lizzy was already nodding, her plait moving up and down her back with the motion. 'Yes, let's.'

'It's a date. See you at five.'

⋆ ⋆ ⋆

'Hey, Lizzy, I nearly thought you weren't going to show up today,' said Alice, the local librarian, with a grin. She moved towards a pile of books stacked up on the library counter, her coloured bohemian dress billowing out behind her. 'Now, here they are, all ready to go. The *Animal Health and Welfare* didn't come in. Maybe next week. But the new Jane Harper book came in and I put *The Nowhere Child* in as well; you'll love it.'

'Thanks, Alice.' Lizzy picked up the top book. *Understanding Engines* and underneath that was *Plant Nutrients and Abiotic Stress Tolerance*.

Alice held up the third book, *Soil Science*, and gave her a look that Lizzy knew all too well.

'Thank you. These are great.'

Alice sighed. 'It's such a shame you didn't go to uni, Lizzy. It's not too late, you know?'

Lizzy focused on piling up the books and tried to ignore the prickle from her words. There had always been a choice. Lizzy could have left the farm, got a job and paid her way through university in order to study agronomy — but then there might not have been a farm to come home to. There still might not if they didn't get some good years behind them. But the Bennets had not been able to afford to hire a farm hand, and it had been Lizzy's choice to stay home and help run Longbourn with her dad.

She was happy with her decision. She wasn't paid a wage, just her food and board and some cash every now and then, but that was plenty if it meant they could keep the farm. She had been trying bloody hard these past four years since leaving school to help turn things around.

'I'll see you next week, Alice. Let me know what you can find on hydraulics please, and maybe some more on plant science.'

Alice sighed again as she leaned against the bench, her arms rattling with all the bracelets that adorned them. 'Okay. You take care. I'll let you know about the Learning Plant Language workshop. Hopefully we'll get enough signed up so we can hold one.'

'I hope so too, Alice. I've heard it's great. See you later.'

Lizzy balanced her books against her chest and exited before Alice could start up on some other opportunity that would be better than working on the farm. Alice was all for women advancing academically and never hid her view that Lizzy was wasted out on the land. Lizzy knew that Alice simply didn't understand — couldn't understand — just how that land had nestled itself into Lizzy's soul. Take her from the land and what would she do?

Exactly a minute after Lizzy put her books in the ute's cabin, Lottie marched out of the pub carrying a large blue esky, which she hauled up onto the back of the ute.

'Let's get the hell out of here before I get another job,' she said with a grin. 'I think Dad was hoping I'd hang out the bar mats he just washed, but I've clocked off.' As if to prove it she tapped the face on her watch. 'It's five on the dot, let's go!'

They drove out of town in silence, windows down and elbows resting on the doors. The 'hill' could be seen from town; actually, it could be seen from ten kilometres out and was in the Coodardy Nature Reserve. It was strange to see such a mound on predominantly flat land with its collection of old gum trees, gimlets and jam trees which would be covered in yellow wattle flowers and smelled like raspberry jam when cut. Some granite rocks protruded up here and there, and in winter the rock pools would fill up and home hundreds of tadpoles. As kids Lizzy and Lottie had spent many hours collecting them in glass jars and then watching them grow legs.

Lizzy turned off onto a narrow track. Scrub scratched the sides of the ute and they drew their arms inside as they weaved their way to a little parking spot. The rest of the way was taken on foot. At the start of the track, off to the side under a quandong tree, was an old garden cart on four wheels. They pulled it out and put the food and esky onto it and then took turns pulling it up the track to the top. About six years ago they'd decided to camp overnight, and with swags, pillows and food under their arms they'd started up the hill. Then halfway up, Lottie's swag had slipped from under her arm, rolled away and collided into Lizzy, causing an explosion of swags as she'd lost her balance and tumbled back down the hill. It was funny to look back on now — Lizzy could remember Lottie's scream and her shocked face as she ran down behind her — but it hadn't been fun at the time. Lizzy had ended up with scratches, a twisted ankle, dirt in her mouth and eyes and too many bruises to count. After that the cart had been 'borrowed' from her mum. To this day she often muttered about her missing garden cart.

At the peak of the hill was a small clearing where an old bench seat sat north overlooking the town and surrounding district. Ty and his cousins had brought the seat up a few years back and it had become part of the landscape. An old washing-machine liner sat behind it, ready to use for bonfires, and a collection of mallee roots was stacked back under a small gum tree.

Not many people knew about this place, so it remained how they left it. And there were rules. All rubbish was taken from the site, and any wood used had to be restocked.

'Man, I never get sick of this place. Makes me feel like a kid again when we used to come up here and sleep under the stars,' said Lottie plonking herself on the bench seat and breathing in the bush scent.

Lizzy threw her a bag of sweet-chilli chips and fished out two cans of beer from the esky before sitting beside her. 'I needed this. Cheers,' she said, crashing her can against Lottie's and causing beer to slop out the top.

'I can't wait for the cabaret. I need to find a wealthy man who can take me away from my current life.'

'You don't need a man for that, Lottie.'

She scoffed. 'Oh I know, but it would be easier driving out of town in a fancy new car. Dad wouldn't feel so bad about me leaving then.'

'He'll miss you like crazy but your dad wants you to be happy. I want you to be happy. I know you miss your mum, and that leaving here means leaving a bit of her behind, but Lottie, your mum will always be with you. Wherever you go. And so will I.' Lizzy reached for Lottie's hand and gave it a squeeze.

It had taken Lizzy a while to realise her friend suffered from depression, so well had she tucked it away deep inside her. It was a few years back that Lizzy had found Lottie in the corner of her room curled up staring blankly at the wall. Dave had called Lizzy because Lottie hadn't moved in two days and he was at a loss as to how to help her. Since then she'd made Lottie promise to talk to her about anything that was troubling her. These visits to the hill had become a form of therapy, along with the appointments Dave suggested she make with a counsellor who came to town each month.

'Yeah, I know. It's so hard. I feel bad when I can't remember Mum. Then I walk into the pub kitchen and I get a memory of her leaning over the bench, her hair dropping across her face as she makes me cookies. She looks up and says,

'Hello my darling.' In that moment I feel like I've found her and lost her all over again. It's a constant battle between leaving and staying.'

Lizzy felt a heavy weight on her heart as she took in her friend. 'I wish I could help you.'

Lottie smiled. 'You do help me, Lizzy. I'm in a better place than I was back . . . then.' She sucked in a deep breath and then exhaled.

They lapsed into easy silence. As the minutes ticked by, Lizzy glanced at the wooden box sitting in a nearby tree; they'd made it together when they were twelve for the phascogales to live in. They hadn't seen any of the brush-tailed marsupials yet but could tell they were using the box, so they'd made another four and put them in various trees around the hill. They had, however, once seen a little mouse-like dunnart with its extra-big ears and fat tail hiding under a rock.

'So, Charlie Bingley, hey?'

'Who?' said Lizzy as she watched the clouds change from white to yellow as the descending sun's rays shifted beneath them. Soon the clouds would be deep golden and red, projecting the colours of the sunset.

Lottie repeated his name and Lizzy nodded. 'Oh, him.'

'*Oh, him?* The whole town is talking about him! Charlie Bingley is loaded, he'd have to be to buy up Netherfield so easily, especially with what old man Jones was asking for it. Rumour has it he bought the whole lot, no lease in sight. Mick Jones thought he was going to have to split his farm up into bits to sell it off.'

'There's five thousand hectares at least; we don't even have half that!'

'Dad overheard that Bingley's a big farmer from further north looking to expand. Apparently they're well known around the place.'

'Yeah, they must be looking to diversify. Wonder what drew them this way?' Lizzy said, taking the chip packet and grabbing a handful.

Lottie sniggered. 'Who cares. It'll be nice to have some fresh blood about town. Must be sending all the single ladies into a tizz. I think the last new bloke in town was that German backpacker who did seeding for Mr Roland.'

'I didn't even meet him,' said Lizzy. 'You get to see them all being at the pub.'

'True, and if the pub gossip is correct — and the pub is usually never wrong — this Bingley guy is coming to the cabaret and bringing his sister.' Lottie wiggled her eyebrows, then pulled out her phone and brought up a photo of Charles Bingley. 'Not bad, hey?'

'Kitty showed me a photo.' Lizzy glanced at the phone. 'He doesn't look very old.'

'It says he's twenty-five.'

'I feel for him. He's going to be studied like a pretty butterfly in a glass jar.'

'Yeah, he will be.' Lottie tapped her phone, Charlie disappeared and her iTunes account opened. 'Happier' by Marshmello and Bastille played from the small speaker in her phone, just loudly enough for them to enjoy without it encroaching on the quiet bushland.

'We are living in the moment, Lizzy.' Lottie rested her head on Lizzy's shoulder and gestured at the view. 'This is the best part of my life right now.'

Lizzy nodded in silent agreement. Land stretched out until it connected with the coloured sky, its hues turning deeper shades of pink and gold. Beside them thin waxy gum leaves flittered in the gentle breeze, making a faint rustling sound just audible over the music. From the corner of her eye Lizzy caught something moving and pointed silently to show Lottie. Together they watched a short-beaked echidna waddle its way along the edge of the clearing. Its ivory-looking, black-tipped spikes glistened in the sunlight while its little feet carried its small brown body along.

With smiles on their faces they watched the echidna until it was gone and so was the sun.

3

'Kitty, *where* is my fuchsia lipstick! You had it last.'

'I don't know. Where are my black heels? You wore them to the school dance. I need them, they go perfectly with this dress.'

'Kitty, Lydia, *get a move on*,' Margaret's stern voice pierced through the bickering.

But they continued on unaffected.

'I need them, nothing else suits my dress!' Lydia replied, her voice reaching a glass-breaking pitch on the last word. 'I *also* need my lipstick!'

'Shoes for your lipstick?' Kitty bartered.

Lizzy, Jane and John sat in the lounge room, all reading as they waited with varying levels of patience. Lizzy was already halfway through *The Nowhere Child* and didn't want to put it down.

Margaret bustled in, red-faced and tugging at a curler in her hair. A pair of pantyhose was slung over one shoulder. 'Why are you just sitting there? Get dressed or we'll be late!' she yelled at John.

He looked up from his newspaper. 'They won't start until you arrive, my dear.'

Lizzy tried to hide her smirk, but Margaret merely scoffed and disappeared to the chaos of lipstick and shoes. She was back a few minutes later, pantyhose on and hair sorted. 'Why are you all just sitting there?' she repeated. 'Get ready.'

'We *are* ready, Mum,' said Jane quietly as she looked up from her romance novel.

Jane sat with her legs neatly to one side, her blue dress elegant on her slender frame. A wide boat neck, with a fitted bodice that flared at the hips and stopped short of her knees. Lizzy felt like a prickly pear next to her sister with fuller hips and breasts and skin that had wear and tear from a hard farming life of sun and grease.

'Lizzy, you're not wearing *that*, are you?'

Margaret's sharp intake of breath was well known in this family. Lizzy clenched her teeth in preparation for what would come next.

'Jeans and a top is not cabaret wear, Elizabeth. Now is the time to dress at your best. Show off your amazing figure, mingle with the men. How are you supposed to attract a husband when you won't try?'

'I'm not trying to 'attract a husband', especially not one who's just after a pretty wife or the farm,' she said, returning to her book.

'You need a man to help run this farm! Your dad can't work forever,' Margaret stressed. 'He should be retiring soon.'

Lizzy felt her blood begin to boil. 'I don't need a man to help with the farm, Mum. Kitty or Lydia might decide to work the farm with me, or I can employ a labourer.'

'Good luck with Kitty or Lydia; those two can't stop fighting long enough to think about their futures.' Margaret gestured to Jane. 'I'm sure your sister has plenty of dresses you could borrow.'

'I like how I'm dressed, Mum. I'm comfortable.'

'John?' Margaret squeaked.

'Aren't we running late, dear?' he said mildly.

Margaret threw up her hands and headed back to her room muttering, 'I'll be stuck in this house full of girls till I'm dead. There'll be no peace and quiet. At least a man would take them to his home.'

John shared a conspirator's grin with his girls before going back to his reading material.

An hour later Lizzy and Jane pulled up outside the busy hall in Jane's car, their parents and sisters following only a minute behind them. The parking area was packed, people mingled out the front and Lizzy could hear the music already. The cream church-like hall with its high pointed roof and old double wooden doors at the front glowed with lights.

Jane had been involved with the decoration, and the hall interior sparkled with abundant lights, draped chiffon and gold accents from cut-out stars hanging from the ceiling to the strategically placed gilt candle holders. The floor was made with wide wooden planks perfect for dancing, and someone always brought a box of Weeties to sprinkle over the floor to aid the dancing. Coodardy tried hard to uphold the tradition of their dance cabarets; they were a part of the town's history and a way to bring the community together every year.

'You've done an amazing job, Jane. The hall has never looked so good,' said Lizzy looping her arm through her sister's as they walked towards the bar in the far corner next to the stage.

'It was a joint effort with Charlotte. There she is,' said Jane, pointing as they made their way past locals who stood around chatting, all dressed up in suits and wedding-worthy dresses. Yet there were always one or two farmers who came in their best checked flannel shirt and polished-up old work boots. Lizzy was the only woman in jeans, although she had spotted one wearing soft-flowing dress pants. The cabaret was a fancy affair, but Lizzy had always opted for comfort over presentation. It may have stemmed from her mother making her wear frilly lace dresses when she was a child. One particular cause of embarrassment that stuck in her memory was a big purple puffed-sleeved ensemble Margaret forced on her when she was fourteen. She felt like a walking bunch of grapes, not helped by the fact that all the boys laughed at her. Maybe it had scarred her a little but she couldn't help feeling like being a farmer meant she had to be more masculine. Could it be why she didn't have a boyfriend? Did men only want a really feminine woman?

'You guys look great,' said Lottie, hugging each of them and then handing over drinks with an on-the-house wink.

'You look fabulous,' said Lizzy, admiring her soft yellow dress and full make-up.

'I'll try to get away later so we can catch up. What's going on over there?' Lottie said suddenly.

The crowd had gone quiet and all seemed to have crammed together like sheep at a narrow gate. Lizzy stood on tiptoe; her dress boots didn't have height like Jane's pretty heels. 'I can't see anything. Is it a fight? Or has Bert come dressed as a woman again?'

Jane smacked Lizzy's arm and shot her a look. 'Don't be mean. Bert is lovely, and I happened to like the pink dress he wore last time.'

Lydia came running to them, her short black dress far too provocative for a fifteen year old but their mother had lost the reins on her by the time she turned ten. It was as if after four previous girls Margaret was just too tired or too old to be an influential parent anymore. She had no strength to fight Lydia on most things these days, be it clothes, make-up, curfews, phone use or boys.

'Oh my god, he's *gorgeous*. He's all mine,' Lydia practically shouted as she flung herself at her sisters.

Lizzy often wondered if Lydia even knew what hushed tones were; she had come out screaming into the world and hadn't stopped.

'Who is?' asked Lizzy.

'That Charles Bingley bloke. Drop-dead honey. How old is too old?'

Lizzy glanced at Jane, and shrugged. 'Anyone would think the Queen had arrived,' she said.

Kitty came crashing into Lydia. 'He's coming this way. Do I look okay?' Kitty glanced down at her tight white dress, which resembled a snug leg warmer.

Lydia ignored Kitty and darted for the crowd that was beginning to part, her phone held high trying to snap a photo of him.

As three people approached the bar Lizzy recognised Charles Bingley from the online photos. In reality he looked just the same: handsome, lean, blond and moneyed. Beside him was a woman who looked like she belonged at the Melbourne Cup. Her body language didn't suggest she was his girlfriend; if anything, there was a resemblance to Charlie but her facial expression was stern, almost irritated. Her pinched features contrasted the bold blue designer-cut dress and matching accessories.

Yet it was the brooding man on his other side who took most of Lizzy's attention. Strong jaw, short dark hair, straight back and shoulders as if he were someone of importance. He was handsome too but in a dark, mysterious, almost dangerous way. Charlie was all smiles and sunshine whereas this man was anything but unicorns and rainbows. Something about the way his eyes flitted over the crowd, not lingering, not taking much in, made her feel as if none of them was worthy of his attention. His clothes looked expensive, from the navy shirt that looked bespoke with matching cufflinks, to the tailored fitted pants. He didn't look like a brother to Charles, but then Jane and Lizzy looked quite different: Jane was the only blonde in the family, the rest dark, but they shared similar high cheekbones and full lips.

No sooner had the three newcomers bought drinks — Coronas for the men, Lizzy noted; she almost laughed when the woman asked to see the cocktail list — than the crowd started to talk and mingle again but eyes remained on the strangers who stood together like cattle separated from the herd.

Lottie shot them a look, pushing up her nose with her finger to indicate just what she thought of the woman who'd requested a cocktail but had to settle for a gin and tonic.

Lizzy was suppressing a smile when she felt a stomp rattle the floorboards. She turned to see her mum coming at them from across the hall, dragging their father behind her. She was a big woman, solid and a fraction taller than their father. The glasses perched on her head almost resembled horns as they reflected under the lights, and when Margaret reached them huffing and puffing Lizzy couldn't help but picture a raging bull.

'Come girls,' Margaret huffed. 'We must introduce ourselves. We are their new neighbours, after all.'

She eagerly shepherded them all towards the newcomers, not noticing — or intentionally ignoring — the dragging feet and embarrassed faces. Lizzy had learned over the years to just go along with her mum, knowing that if she made a fuss the problem would only escalate. Margaret Bennet had no qualms about making a scene, which explained a lot about Lydia and Kitty.

Lizzy glanced at Jane, who appeared equally horrified. 'Dad, *really?*' whispered Lizzy.

John shrugged and followed his wife as if caught in a rip he knew he couldn't escape. Lizzy had no choice but to follow, her heart racing as the Bennets drew closer to the Bingleys, wondering how awful this encounter would be.

'Mr Bingley, so lovely to see you here tonight,' said Margaret thrusting her hand at him. 'I thought we should come and introduce ourselves seeing as we are to be neighbours. Margaret and John Bennet of Longbourn Farm, and these are our girls Jane, Elizabeth, Catherine and Lydia,' she said as the two youngest came barging in front of Jane to ogle Charles and the man next to him.

'Oh, the Bennets from the south side of Netherfield? Wow, you have a lot of daughters,' Charles said, his eyes finding Jane.

'We have one more, Mary, who is away at university,' said Margaret as she surveyed her girls proudly.

Lizzy watched Charlie's blue eyes settle on Jane amid the awkward silence. The woman in the stylish silk dress had her phone out and began to type intently.

'Oh yes, this is my sister, Caroline, and my best friend, Will Darcy.'

'Nice to meet you both,' said John shaking the men's hands. Caroline glanced up from her phone upon introduction and hardly cracked an acknowledgement smile.

Lizzy held out her hand and shook hands with Charlie and Will. It was a habit formed from years of greeting bankers, chemical reps and various salesmen. She was the only Bennet woman to do so, the others opting for a wave. Charlie shook her hand graciously, his grip soft whereas Will, who shook with a nice firm strong grip, looked at their entangled hands. Lizzy drew her hand back quickly, embarrassed over its dry, calloused condition. At least she'd managed to scrub most of the grease from under her short nails.

Her father was flushed red, maybe from the warmth in the hall or due to the fact of this forced meeting. Kitty and Lydia were preening themselves in front of the two handsome men, their phones in their hands as they tried to take sneaky photos. Caroline watched them with acute horror that she didn't bother to hide. Lizzy couldn't blame her as she watched her sisters' peacock display.

'Are you a Darcy from the Pemberley Holdings Darcys?' asked John pleasantly as if unaware of the behaviours around him.

Lizzy's ears pricked up. Pemberley Holdings was a name familiar to any farmer. The company — the family — owned vast tracts of land. Much more than even the Bingleys — in fact, more than this whole district put together. Darcy was a name cemented in farming royalty.

Lizzy looked Will Darcy over carefully and could see it now, the expensive clothes and the stance of someone important, it all fit. His eyes seemed locked either on the wall behind them or on Caroline. The hand at his side clenched and unclenched as if he were itching to move on to somewhere else.

'Yes, Will is. He's here to help me with the changeover,' said Charlie when his friend had offered nothing but silence in response to the question. 'No one better to help me with setting up Netherfield properly. I value his opinions and guidance immeasurably.'

Will's dark eyes landed on Lizzy. He looked her up and down and then frowned. She could see the crinkle in his forehead beginning to take shape before he glanced away. Did he not approve of her attire? Or her face? She bit down on her lip and tried to keep a glare off her face. At least Charlie seemed happy to talk with his new neighbours.

The conversation was interrupted by some banging and crashing as the local band, In Debt, took to the stage to warm up their instruments. Everyone turned to watch the boys — a couple of local farmers who got together on occasion to play — as they started their set with 'I've Got a Lovely Bunch of Coconuts' and the crowd started to separate, the younger ones moving to the walls while the older guests partnered up and headed to the middle of the dance floor for the Gypsy Tap. Lizzy saw Will Darcy's brow crease as if he were in pain.

'Do you dance, Charles?' said Margaret. 'Our Jane knows the old dances well, if you'd like her to show you.'

'I can help you,' said Lydia breathlessly, rolling her shoulders back to show off her chest. Lizzy put her hands over her face and breathed deeply. She was going to need some fresh air very soon.

'I actually know a few of the dances.' Charlie held out his hand to Jane. 'Shall we?'

His crisp white button-up shirt hardly moved with the gentle motion, and Lizzy could smell the most alluring aftershave. Was it from Charlie or his friend, Will? She glanced between the two and found her eyes lingering on William Darcy.

Caroline tilted her head away as if she disapproved of her brother's actions.

'You know the Gypsy Tap?' Jane asked him as she slipped her hand into Charlie's and glanced back at Lizzy, her eyes shining with pleasure as he led her to the dance floor.

'Oh lovely,' said Margaret. 'How about you, Will? Lizzy is great — just don't let her lead.'

Lizzy moved away as her mum reached out to draw her forward. Inside, her body screamed to be sucked into a black hole and vanish. 'Do you dance?' she asked to be polite.

'No,' he said abruptly, then cleared his throat. 'Not if I can help it.'

'Well, it seems to me that you're in the wrong place tonight,' she retorted.

'Don't I know it,' he muttered as he glanced around the room with barely disguised disgust.

His expression alone made her temperature rise. 'Well, I suggest you work on your refusals,' she bit out. 'Aiming for a base level of courtesy would be a good start. If you can't manage that, then maybe you should just leave,' she added with a huff.

His head snapped back to her, his eyes pinning her to the spot. He didn't say anything, just stared in a way that both annoyed and unnerved her.

Caroline fake-laughed and turned to Will, snaking her arm through his. 'Let's go, Will. The air here is rather . . . stale.'

'Oh,' said Margaret in a disgusted tone, glancing at John. 'Well, I never . . . '

'Dance, darling?' said John, taking her hand

40

and guiding her to the floor before she could begin her tirade.

Lizzy sighed with relief and made her way to Lottie at the bar.

'He's very good,' Lottie said as they watched Jane and Charlie dance. 'Jane is so lucky.'

'Do you want me to stay behind the bar, give you a chance to get out there and dazzle everyone with your moves?' said Lizzy.

Lottie pressed her hands together as if in prayer. 'Would you? You're the best.'

'Of course.' Lizzy laughed as she scooted behind the bar. 'I'll be happier here, believe me.'

'Let me know when you've had enough,' said Lottie. With a wave she vanished into the bustling hall looking for a dance partner.

'Hey Lizzy, thanks for giving my girl a break. We both appreciate it,' said Dave as he wiped down the counter.

'I'm more dressed for this anyway,' she said with a grin. It was fun being behind the bar: she got to see most people and fit in a quick chat. Some stayed longer, and Lizzy loved soaking up the local farmers' knowledge; she'd known many of them all her life, and different methods had been tried and tested, making their findings invaluable for the future of Longbourn.

Lottie was whizzing around the hall, the progressive barn dance had her circling past different partners from men old enough to be her granddad to some fifteen year olds as 'Click Go the Shears' and then 'Waltzing Matilda' played. That was the beauty of these cabaret dances: everyone got to mingle. Jane was in the mix still, Charlie Bingley not far away. When it changed to a waltz Lizzy noticed he had Jane back in his embrace, and Lizzy could hear Jane's angelic laughter over the music. The band eventually took a break, heading to the bar as the iPod took over with the likes of 'Proud Mary' and 'Bad Moon Rising'. Some guests still danced, while others took the break to get drinks, which meant Dave and Lizzy were suddenly swamped with thirsty dancers.

'We've run out of Bush Chook, Dave,' said Lizzy as she passed over the last red can of Emu Export.

'There's more out the back,' he said with a nod to the portable cool room. Sweat beaded on Dave's bald patch as he handled the busy bar with expert ease.

Lizzy ducked outside and paused for a moment, letting the cool night air lick across her damp skin. The air was fresh and crisp, and the music quieter. She let her ears adjust to the familiar night sounds, from the breeze whistling through the leaves to the creaking of moving branches, a car engine humming in the distance and some voices from others who had gone outside for a breather or just a place to talk without having to yell over the music. Fairy lights were strung up outside the hall where bench seats, crates and plastic chairs had been scattered. The night sky was black and clear, making it possible to see the stars and Milky Way. Lizzy was tempted to lie down on the ground and watch them, but bringing her eyes back to the task at hand, she spotted the white cool room, parked alongside the back of the bar wall. With a sigh she headed towards it, but she paused mid-step when she heard voices and saw two tall figures not far away.

'Can we leave, please?'

'No, we can't go home yet.'

Lizzy realised it was Will Darcy and Charlie Bingley.

'What better way to meet all the locals?' said Charlie in a hushed tone.

Lizzy found she had quietened her steps and held her breath, and she frowned at her sudden eavesdropping. But this was a Darcy and a Bingley, two wealthy farmers — anything they had to say could be interesting.

'This really isn't my thing. I've got a few reports I'd like to go through,' said Will.

Wool reports? Grain prices? Stock market? His deep, almost gravelly voice portrayed his eagerness to leave.

'Always the worker. We're here to have fun, remember? Come on, Will, why don't you dance with someone, there are lots of nice girls here. What about Jane's sister? Lizzy?'

'The plain one? I think you've taken the best there is here tonight.'

If Lizzy was going to move, she couldn't anymore. Will's words had struck her cold, frozen. *Plain?* She reached up, running her fingers against her cheek and across her lips.

'Now that's not fair! She's a farmer, so Jane tells me. She's still pretty, she just might not like make-up and the things you're used to,' Charlie said teasingly.

'She's opinionated, and she may try to look like a farmer but she can't possibly be one — just look at the dire state of that farm.'

'That's a bit harsh,' said Charlie.

'I did the research. Longbourn has been on a downhill slide, with sections sold off and leased. Should be perfect pickings to extend your Netherfield holdings,' he said matter-of-factly.

Lizzy reeled back on her heels as if hit by a bomb blast.

'Don't give me that look! You asked me to investigate it all thoroughly before you went through with the purchase,' added Will. 'And I did.'

'I know, but . . . I like her sister,' said Charlie. 'I really like her. So we can't go home yet. I've got a few more dances left in me.'

Will grunted and Charlie laughed. 'Relax, my friend. You work too hard.'

He slapped Will's arm and headed off inside the hall. Will remained and pulled out his phone.

Lizzy swallowed as quietly as possible and then carefully finished her few steps to the cool room, where she almost slammed the door and held it in place with her hands splayed across it. She stayed inside for a good few minutes, until the cool air tempered her fire and her breathing settled. Her mind was alight, Will Darcy's words rotating around at a dizzying speed.

When she finally came out with the carton of beer she saw with relief that Will had gone. Stomping back to the bar, she unpacked the carton with such vigour that Dave commented: 'Steady on, Lizzy, you'll have 'em all shaken up.'

44

'Sorry Dave,' she said, stopping and taking a breath.

Her blood was pumping through her body so fast she could hear it pound in her ears. Her jaw was sore from grinding her teeth as she stewed about what she'd overheard. How *dare* he call her plain and opinionated? Just what kind of women did Will Darcy associate with? Upper-class snobs like Caroline Bingley? Was it difficult for him to even be near someone beneath his social standing? His comments about her had struck a nerve, but nothing scraped at her heart like the idea of her home being ripe for purchase. How arrogant he'd sounded, as if he'd just made an amazing find, land for the taking. Even worse, stating that Lizzy wasn't a farmer! She swallowed the lump in her throat, blinked back tears and tried to quell the rage. She *was* a farmer! She had worked bloody hard to earn that title, and it had taken a mere instant for one rich, conceited man to make her feel like a failure.

'Dave, would you say I'm plain looking?' she suddenly asked. 'And a crap farmer?' It was the last question she really wanted the answer for, but she couldn't stop the words.

Dave frowned. 'Random questions, but I'll go with it. No, Lizzy, I wouldn't say that at all. You're stunning, and you're one of the hardest-working farmers I know.' He ran his hand over his head. 'You have those gorgeous big dark eyes, long eyelashes and all that lovely hair when you let it free,' he said with a warm smile. He reached over and gently tugged on the end of her hair, just like he used to do when she was a kid with pigtails. 'And no one knows just how much you do at Longbourn, but I do. Lottie tells me,' he said, nodding.

Lizzy's blood stopped thundering through her body as she felt the anger subside. She stepped forward and hugged Dave. 'Thank you. You're a good dad and mum, Dave.'

'Maybe you should take a break. It's quietened down a bit — go have a dance,' he said, putting a cold beer in her hand and gently pushing her towards the door into the hall.

Lizzy leaned back against the wall sipping her drink and watched Jane spin with Charlie while her mind raced just as dizzily. Dave had made her feel better, yet Will's words lingered in her mind as if on repeat.

'Lizzy, would you like to dance?'

Suddenly Jane and Charlie were standing in front of her, Charlie with his hand out. He repeated his question.

'Oh, okay, sure. Thank you,' she said.

Jane took her beer. 'Charlie is a wonderful dancer,' she said as Lizzy was tugged towards the dance floor.

Charlie tucked her against him as they set off in a waltz. It took a moment for Lizzy to remember the steps but with Charlie leading so well she was soon in time. It was nice to be held by a strong young man, spinning across the floor and feeling invincible. She laughed as Charlie twirled her out into a spin and back again. 'Jane was right,' she said a little breathlessly. 'You *are* good.' Charlie winked and twirled her again. Lizzy could see that though Charlie was dancing with her, his eyes knew exactly where Jane was at all times. At one point she spotted Will watching them from the wall but she pushed down the flaring resentment and focused on the nice moment with Charlie.

'Jane's a very good dancer,' she said.

Charlie grinned. 'You both are,' he replied politely. He dipped his head towards her ear. 'Is your sister seeing anyone?' he asked.

Lizzy felt a swell of excitement for Jane. 'No, she's single.'

'I'm glad to hear that,' he whispered as the song finished. He put his hand on the small of her back as he guided her from the dance floor.

'Thanks Charlie, that was fun,' said Lizzy, slightly out of breath.

'You're welcome. I've had a great night. Haven't danced like this since high school.' His words were directed to Lizzy but his eyes remained on Jane.

'Charlie, we want to head off.'

Lizzy turned at the sound of Will's voice. Caroline was by his side, but scrolling through her phone.

'Just a little longer. Come on, you two, you haven't danced yet.'

'No one's asked me to dance,' Caroline bristled.

'Maybe because you've been on your phone for most of the night,' said Lizzy sharply. When Caroline scoffed, Lizzy shrugged in reply. Then she turned to Will. 'And why did you come if you don't like to dance?' she added perhaps a little too sarcastically.

Will cleared his throat, his hands clenching into fists at his sides once more. 'Charlie wanted to meet the locals, and most of them seem to be here.' He glanced around before his eyes settled back on her.

'Well, to meet the locals would mean actually talking and dancing with them,' said Lizzy. She caught Jane's expression, the one she always gave Lizzy when she was too outspoken. Lizzy imagined it would be the same expression she'd have witnessing an accident she couldn't prevent.

'She has a point there, Will,' Charlie laughed. 'He isn't very good at mixing with people, are you, Will?'

'I find that hard to believe,' said Lizzy. 'Someone with your empire — I'd imagine you'd have plenty of people you need to mix with.'

'Work is fine,' he said, screwing up his face. 'It's the social scene that has me at a loss.'

'Well, this is the perfect place to practise.'

'You think my social skills are lacking?' he asked frowning.

Lizzy tried not to smile at the rise she'd drawn out of him. 'Quite frankly I do. Can you name one person you've met here tonight?'

His eyes narrowed. 'I've met you, Lizzy,' he said, challenging.

'Wow, I'm surprised you could remember someone so . . . *plain*. Can you name anyone else, besides members of my family?' she asked, cocking her head slightly.

His hands continued to clench and open,

48

clench and open while he maintained eye contact.

'Dean Radcliff. He has the farm on the other side of Charlie. Runs SAMM Merinos,' he said measuredly.

Lizzy felt her sister's hand on her arm, a gentle warning, while Charlie watched them as if at a tennis match. Caroline was staring open mouthed.

'I hope you greeted Dean with more interest than you did us,' Lizzy prompted. 'But then again Dean is a well-known and respected farmer, and Liberal Party leader.'

'So, you think I'm a snob too?' he shot back, brow creasing.

Lizzy shrugged. 'If the shoe fits. In fact — '

'Ah, another waltz. Shall we all dance?' cut in Charlie as a song started up.

Lizzy glanced to him and then back to Will, who was watching her with dark eyes that gave nothing away. Even in this full hall she could smell his expensive aftershave. It only made the gap between them seem wider.

'Well, I guess that counts me out,' said Lizzy, meeting Will's gaze with force. She shot him a smile that didn't reach her eyes before spinning on her heel and walking off.

It wasn't until she had lost them in the crowd that she realised how clammy her skin was and that she'd forgotten to breathe.

'Hey, I found you.' Lottie bumped next to her.

Lizzy smiled, glad for the interruption from her mental warfare.

'You only just left the bar?'

She shrugged. 'I didn't mind. I almost prefer working in there than dancing with some bloke who doesn't want to dance with me.'

'Come on, loads would love to dance with you. Tyron asked where you were, said you owed him one. I'd like to dance with Charlie but he hasn't let Jane out of his sight. It's not fair.'

Lottie pouted and Lizzy chuckled. 'Try being her sister.'

'The worst thing is she's so lovely that I'm totally happy for her. Just wish it was me.'

'Don't worry, your knight will come.'

Lottie reached for her hand and squeezed it tight. They looked at each other as the band started playing 'Running Bear' by Johnny Preston.

'I hope you're right. And I'm sure there's a perfect man out there for you too. One who won't change you but inspire and love you as much as I do.'

Lizzy sighed. *If only that were true.*

4

So, you think I'm a snob too?

His words rang through her mind like a relentless mosquito. It wasn't so much the words but the way he'd said them, as if he thought he was far from being one. What irritated her even more was that she was letting him play on her mind when she should have been enjoying the sun's rays lighting up the morning sky in hues of pinks, as she went to feed Rocky before breakfast.

The feel of the soft earth under her boots was as familiar as her bed at night, and the lamb's soft bleat made her smile. 'Hey little guy, you sound hungry.' Lizzy leaned over the fence of the small enclosure in the back yard and held the bottle out for him. To her left in the closest paddock she saw Nelly, who was once her pet lamb a few years back. Now Nelly was a big woolly ewe.

'Hey Nelly. How are your bubbas?' she asked while Rocky sucked and tugged on the bottle, jerking her arm. Nelly slowly stepped towards her and lowered her head, waiting for a pat. Her lambs stayed by her side, their milk warm and at the ready. The moment Nelly stopped they decided to drink.

'Hey girl,' Lizzy repeated. Nelly had been out with the other sheep for a while now and had mothered many lambs but she still came to Lizzy on occasion. 'Still miss me, don't you?' Lizzy smiled as she ran her fingers through Nelly's top knot of wool. 'Not like Snowflake; she never visits us anymore. Happy enough just being one of the mob.' Lizzy glanced out into the green paddock trying to see if she could spot Snowflake's green tag. But most of the mob were down the back of the paddock. Only Nelly liked to stay close to the house she'd once called home.

As she surveyed the familiar scene she couldn't stop her mind returning once again to the cabaret. She hadn't told Jane about what she'd overheard out by the cool room. She didn't want to ruin Jane's memories of the night, and she also didn't want to give voice to Will Darcy's words. Those very words that niggled at her own self-doubt and fears.

Rocky started sucking air, so she pulled the teat from his mouth, while pushing her thoughts away. 'Look at you, coming along in leaps and bounds.' She rubbed his head and across his mauled ear, which had healed nicely. He would always be distinct from the others but Lizzy knew she would spot his cute face in any mob.

His bleat was accompanied by a rumble from her belly, reminding her that it was still early and she had had neither food nor coffee.

Back at the house the only person up was her dad, relaxed in his favourite chair with the *Farm Weekly* and a cuppa. He was dressed for work — jeans and checked red shirt — but on his feet were his fluffy wool slippers.

'Kettle will need re-boiling,' he said, glancing up.

Lizzy ducked across to the blue and wood kitchen bench to flick on the kettle before heading to her room. It wasn't the cleanest house, it certainly looked lived in and that's the way Lizzy liked it. It was a busy home to a lot of people and she could see their stamp in every nook. Papers and magazines piled up on benchtops, discarded clothing littering chairs and tables and even the floor, and piles of clean washing on the side table. She often wondered what the house would be like if her sisters all moved out in future years. Her dad wanted to retire on the coast one day if he could afford it, which would leave Lizzy with this house all to herself. She'd like to think she would fill it with a family again because, despite all the noise and chaos, this house just wouldn't be the same without it.

Lizzy walked past the pile of mail on the hall table, but she didn't give it a look through; she knew there were bills that needed to be paid and no money to pay them.

Lizzy had confided to Jane, after a meeting with the bank years earlier, that they were close to having it sold from under them. Her father had been ignoring the bank manager's letters, but Lizzy couldn't. If they couldn't make the farm viable, then the bank would take action to recoup its money. Amid her panic Lizzy had begged James, the bank manager, to give her time to formulate a plan and to go through the books.

'I admire your passion and enthusiasm,' had been his reply before asking her to prepare a budget and map for future plans for the property. It had been a life vest thrown towards a sinking ship but Lizzy latched on and promised she'd make it work.

'Dad!' she had scolded John. 'You can't just bury your head in the sand and pretend everything will work out all right.'

'I was counting on a good year,' he'd replied.

'You know that in farming we can't count on anything. Every year is a big gamble. We have to make changes, we need to make plans and I need your help to turn the farm around,' she'd told him. 'Will you let me?'

'Are you sure you want this? It would be easier to let the bank take it than try to save it. I'm not sure I want you handling all this debt and stress. You're young, your whole life is ahead of you.'

And that was when Lizzy knew for certain that this was what she wanted. 'I want this, Dad. It's all I've ever wanted, to stay here and work on our farm. This is my dream life,' she'd said.

'You dream of having a massive debt?' he'd replied, still unconvinced this was the right choice for any of his girls.

'If that's what it takes, then yes.'

John had smiled proudly. 'You've always been my strongest girl. Stubborn but courageous. You're the best of me and your mother. If you think you can turn this farm around, then I'll back you and support you any way I can.'

And he'd done just that.

The door to their room squeaked a little but

there was no movement beneath the crumpled doona on Jane's bed. The farm debt was one of the reasons Jane still lived at home. This way she could help out by bringing home food and necessities with her earnings without her parents having to ask for help. One day Lizzy hoped to manage Longbourn to the point she could buy back land, leaving her sisters and parents well cared for. Any of them would be welcome to stay on the farm, and her parents could retire to the coast. For now it seemed a long way off, but Lizzy was young and she was determined.

Lizzy lifted up Jane's yellow striped doona and half-climbed in, snuggling up to her sister with her feet hanging out.

'Oh my god, you're so cold,' she mumbled as she tucked Lizzy's cold hands around her.

'Thanks for warming me up. Do you want a cuppa? I just put on the kettle.'

'Please. I'm parched,' she croaked.

'Well, that happens when you stay out all night dancing with a handsome man. Do tell . . . did you get a kiss goodnight?'

'Lizzy,' she growled.

'Come on. I haven't had any action in forever.' She sighed. 'Is he nice?' *He certainly seems nicer than his sister and that William Darcy.*

Jane turned around, her vibrant blue eyes sleepy. 'Oh Lizzy, he's so easy to talk to. I'm so relaxed in his company.' The doona ruffled as she drew her hand up. 'I got his number and . . . ' Jane's face blushed pink. 'We had a very steamy kiss goodbye.'

A smile spread across her lips and Lizzy

grinned back at her. 'I'm glad, Jane. I hope he hangs around.'

'Me too. He's the first guy I've felt I can be me around, you know? I didn't feel anxious at all, maybe because there were no expectations. Anyway, he wants to see me again, so I'm looking forward to it.'

Lizzy huffed. 'Not sure I'm keen to see his mate Will again any time soon.'

'You two really didn't hit it off,' said Jane with a grimace. 'I thought you were going to start throwing punches,' she teased.

Lizzy rolled her eyes. 'I wish. But I'd be lying if I said I didn't enjoy rubbing him up the wrong way. And that Caroline — what a piece of work! So different from her brother.'

Jane pressed her lips together and mumbled her agreement. 'Charlie is so open and friendly yet she's . . . less so.'

'Exactly!' said Lizzy heartily.

'Charlie sent me a text last night.' Jane's eyes were wide and bright.

'Really? I thought I saw phone light in the wee hours,' she said. Quite a lot of phone light before she'd managed to get to sleep.

'Hope I didn't keep you up.' Jane frowned until Lizzy shook her head. 'Okay. Good,' she said with a yawn.

An impatient whistle from the kettle reached their ears and Lizzy extracted herself from the warmth. 'Right, I'll go make our cuppas.'

'Did you say breakfast?' Jane looked up, like a starving puppy.

'Yeah, I guess I did. Pancakes?'

'Thanks, Lizzy, there's fresh blueberries in the fridge. I know it's a splurge but they looked so perfect I couldn't help it.'

They shared a smile.

'Love you.'

'Right back at ya, Janey,' said Lizzy as she closed the door behind her.

★ ★ ★

The next few weeks passed in the usual blur of work and bill avoidance. The wheat price was still terrible and she'd been holding out for a better price for last year's grain but the bills were mounting and some couldn't be put off, so this morning after she checked her grain app, she called the office and sold it for the current price on offer. Then she set about deciding which bills needed to be paid first. It was a task that always left her drained and grumpy, aided only by the emergency stash of salted-caramel chocolate she kept in the bottom drawer. After eating a row she collected some mail — cheques took longer to clear than the online banking — ready to post.

'I'm going into town. Anyone need anything?' she called out as she headed for the door.

Margaret looked up from the mountain of sewing that sat on the dining table. Her glasses were perched on the edge of her nose as she tried to thread cotton through a needle. 'Just some more milk please, honey.' She sighed and rolled her neck before attempting to thread the needle again.

Lizzy's work jeans had been mended three

times and a patch was sewn into the back where she'd ripped the bum out of them climbing over a fence. New jeans were a luxury; they were the only new thing she owned.

It wasn't just the family's clothes Margaret fixed; she did any from people around town as cash jobs, though most people preferred to go to Target and buy a cheap replacement than pay to have something fixed. But luckily some had favourite items they didn't want to part with. The money was saved for special treats, like their once-a-year trip into Toongarrin to dine at the popular Italian restaurant, as well as helping with Mary's living costs while she attended university.

Even Kitty and Lydia worked to earn spending money. They sold the excess eggs from their chooks and raked and sold the sheep poo that collected under the shearing shed. The yabbies in the dams were a good earner, too. But the youngest Bennet sisters were also very good at spending what they earned, and binge-watching TV.

On her way to the ute Lizzy spotted her dad in the workshop, his favourite spot, where he was tinkering with an old motorbike motor. She'd told him already it wasn't worth fixing but he never discarded anything, even if it was a poor use of his time and not cost effective. 'Less landfill, Lizzy,' he'd always say when she tried to change his ways. 'It's such a throwaway society today.'

She would let him win the argument, and to avoid another one now she just gave him a wave.

'I'm heading into town, Dad. Be back soon,' she yelled.

Pippa, who'd been by John's side, sprinted across and jumped up on the ute.

'Oh, if you must. But stay on the back, even if Mrs Cartell is out with her yappy Jack Russell, and no bailing up any town cats, promise?'

Pippa's expression brightened and remained focused on Lizzy, her tail wagging energetically from side to side.

Town was quiet for a Thursday and she had no problems parking in front of Tilly's Hardware. With a last warning glance at Pippa she ducked inside and almost ran into Tyron.

'Hey you. Gracing us with your presence?' he said, moving out of her road where he'd been sweeping the floor.

'I thought I better come pay you before you cut me off.' She gritted her teeth and pulled a face. 'Sorry it's late and, um . . . maybe don't bank it until next week, please?'

'This,' he said taking the envelope with the cheque in it, 'is okay. But what's not forgivable is the fact that you reneged on our dance.' Ty frowned.

'Oh. I — '

A loud repeated bark interrupted their conversation. 'Oh shit, that's Pippa. Gotta go.'

'You owe me two at next year's cabaret!' he yelled after her.

Fearing the worst, Lizzy darted out of the shop and glanced down the street, left then right, waiting for the moment she caught Pippa harassing a cat, but what she didn't expect to find was Pippa barking at a man crouched near her ute. What she noticed first was the perfect backside encased in a pair of dark denim jeans. *Hello stranger.*

'Pippa, that's enough. On the ute,' she demanded as she hurriedly walked to the man to apologise.

She pulled up abruptly as he stood, tall, well shaped and very familiar. 'Oh.' She felt the hairs on her neck prickle up.

He raised an eyebrow at her greeting. Dark eyes watched her carefully. They stood looking at each other for a moment, he seemingly calm, portraying no emotion and yet she noticed his fingers twitching by his side.

He pointed to her back tyre. 'You have wire hanging out.'

Lizzy leaned to the side to have a look, then stood upright again. 'Got another forty k's at least,' she said with a nonchalant shrug.

He frowned, head tilting slightly. 'Your dog?'

Lizzy's teeth were gnashing together. 'Yes, my dog.'

Pippa sat on the back of the ute watching them obediently.

'She wanted to tear my arm off,' he said, giving Pippa another glance.

'Pippa was protecting my ute. She's a brilliant dog.' Lizzy's nose twitched as a rich resinous scent of spice wafted around her.

'It needs abandoning not protecting,' he said with a straight face.

It took her a moment to realise he was talking about her ute. Had it come from Tyron, Lizzy

60

would have laughed, but coming from Will it felt like a personal attack, making her feel small and stupid. Another thing to add to his 'wannabe farmer' list. Lizzy was breathing heavily through her nose and started to feel a little light headed.

'Must be nice to buy everything new,' she said, yanking open her ute door. 'To have everything handed to you. Never having to struggle and hang on by the skin of your teeth.'

She got in before he could see that the springs in her seat were exposed from wear and now half-covered by an old towel.

'It's more a safety concern,' he said dryly, towering by her window, cutting off the sun.

'Safety doesn't pay the bills,' she shot back, turned the key hoping it would start first go. *Thank god.* It fired into life and when she stuck her head out the window she saw Will standing in a thick grey cloud of her diesel smoke.

Oops. Sorry not sorry.

She shot him her biggest grin while Pippa gave him a last bark as they drove away.

It took a minute before Lizzy realised they were going the wrong way, but instead of turning around and having to pass him again, she drove around the back blocks of town.

Will was still bothering her as she drove home, window down to help blow him from her mind but a loud bang like a shotgun blast disturbed the peace and sent a heap of galahs in a nearby tree flying off at a fast pace. Her ute shuddered as she gripped the steering wheel and brought it to a standstill on the side of the gravel road, only five kilometres from home. Lizzy leaned forward, resting her forehead on the steering wheel, and breathed out. She didn't need to get out and look to know she'd just blown a tyre. 'Damn you, Will Darcy.'

★ ★ ★

'Did a good job,' John said as he inspected the twisted black remains of the tyre dumped unceremoniously in the ute's tray, only the smallest amount of rubber left clinging to the rim.

'Mm,' was all Lizzy mustered as she stepped out of the ute back at Longbourn. She was not in the mood to discuss tyres. It was bad enough that Will's smug, annoyingly handsome face had filled her mind as she'd forced off the wheel nuts and changed the tyre on the side of the road, all the while praying he didn't come cruising past to gloat. Thinking about Will again now would mean spending the rest of her day angry and frustrated, and she had better things to do.

'I think we should start work on the headers, Dad,' she said. 'The bike can wait.'

'I've finished with the bike, it's back running. And yes, I guess we better or harvest will be on us before we know it.'

'Oh, nice job on the bike. Kitty'll be pleased.' Lizzy's sister would be out on it for a ride after school once she found out it was working again. She loved to go fast, on motorbikes, in utes, on her bicycle. The opposite of how she moved in the morning.

'Oh look, Jane's home.' John waved and then

tottered off inside the shed.

The little blue Gemini came to a stop next to Lizzy. When Jane wound down the passenger window Lizzy stuck her head in. 'Hey you. Good day?'

'It was okay,' she said with an epic grin.

'Do tell. What's brought that sparkle to your eye?' Lizzy asked, suddenly curious.

'Charlie's asked me over to Netherfield tomorrow for a little tour.'

'Wow, an invitation. Go you. How long were you talking on the phone last night? I'm pretty sure you didn't get in till around midnight.'

Jane blushed a little but her smile remained. 'Yeah, I was outside on the verandah. I got so cold I borrowed Pippa's old rug. But it was worth it. We just connect, you know. Talked about everything: being kids, growing up, school, the future.' Jane sighed.

'Bit like that, hey?' Lizzy smiled; her sister's glow was infectious.

'I can't wait to see him again.'

Lizzy laughed. 'I can tell.'

Since the cabaret Charlie had taken her out for lunch a few times and they were now officially dating. The disappointment was still fresh in her young sisters and the rest of the single ladies in town.

Jane's blush deepened. 'He's away a bit, still back and forth between farms.'

Lizzy nodded. 'I can't even imagine what it must be like to have so much land all over the place.'

'I better go, I've decided to make a pavlova for

our dessert tonight,' said Jane as Lizzy stepped back from the car. 'Charlie loves his desserts,' she added.

'Nice. Looks like we all benefit from Mr Bingley's attentions.'

Jane smiled and drove off towards the house. Lizzy held her loose strands of hair back as she watched her sister, smiling at Jane's newfound happiness. Before she could switch to more practical thoughts about making a start on one header at least, something hit her head and then another landed on her nose. Glancing up at the sky she saw thick dark clouds moving overhead. She took out her phone: her weather app was still predicting a lot of rain for them tonight and tomorrow. On the horizon the sky was building up, black like a mass of burning tyre smoke slowly heading their way. As it moved it was choking out the last blue of the sky and cutting off the sun's rays. A breeze was picking up, blowing dust into her eyes and swirling dead leaves across the barren yard as if they were puppets on a string. Nearby gum trees bent and swayed, leaves shaking like cheerleaders with pompoms. The bottom of her shirt flicked up and pressed against her belly as the scent of rain brought a prickle to her skin. In the distance lightning dashed across the dark sky like a camera flash followed by a rumble that took a while to reach her ears. A few more spots of rain descended from the sky landing on her phone. Giving it a wipe on her flannel shirt, she tucked it back in her jeans. Best she get a wriggle on.

When the rain started it didn't stop. It was like

background music as they worked.

An hour later the heavy drops sounded like hail on the shed's tin roof, so loud she had to shout at her dad just to ask him to pass a hammer.

'This is ridiculous,' he said. 'Let's knock off.'

Lizzy wanted to roll her eyes but her mum had been telling her off for this for years, so they were internal eye rolls now. 'You just want a beer,' she teased. It frustrated her at times when her dad took a more relaxed approach to work, but he'd been working the farm since he was thirteen and now in his fifties he was dreaming of retirement. They had both worked hard these past couple of years, her dad even leaving the farm in the quiet months to drive trucks for a local contractor. It wasn't uncommon for farmers to have to find an income elsewhere during lean years.

'Too right. I'm not young and energetic like you, Lizzy. I wish I had your zest still, you're like an energiser bunny.' He picked up an old newspaper and gave her a few sheets then held up his own as he ran to the ute parked by the shed.

'You move pretty quick for an old man,' she teased before following suit.

They drove to the house, the ute sliding in the wet clay and leaving skid marks as they pulled up by the house gate. Margaret Bennet had a decent-sized vegie garden down near the chook and dog pens, and after the rabbits mowed it all down early on, a big fence with pine log posts and rabbit-proof wire had been erected around the whole house area. It also meant that they could let the chooks out to roam through the house yard without worrying about foxes carting them off. Lizzy loved watching them scratch through the dirt among the vegie rows. Being self-sufficient was something they all liked to work towards.

The gate squeaked as they darted through to the verandah and then stood shaking off the drops while the gutters overflowed around them. The lawn — which suffered drainage issues — was already looking like a lake.

'Chance of a flood,' her dad said staring out at the blanket of rain.

He would know. John Bennet had kept rain records since he was a kid and was constantly reading the weather reports, from any source.

'The crops should be okay,' he added quickly when he saw her face. 'Only the low-lying bits will end up waterlogged. Not sure how we'll get the spraying done if it's boggy, though.'

Lizzy hadn't been thinking about the crops this time, only Jane and her visit to Netherfield.

There was a reason the Joneses used to have a dinghy parked in the shed at Netherfield, and it wasn't because Mick Jones was a fisherman.

5

'Best you call Jane and tell her to head home quick smart,' said John as he stood by the back door, water running off his wide-brim hat and raincoat. 'It's raining cats and dogs. Just checked the gauge: fifty millimetres and counting. Jones Road'll be too deep for Jane's little Gemini to cross very soon.'

Lizzy sat on the verandah, the best place to hear the rain on the tin roof and the splash as drops fell into the puddles now surrounding the house. She was reading up on humates on her phone. Her mum was just inside the door, listening to the rain as she sewed.

'Oh no, John,' said Margaret as she stitched away. 'It's not a bad thing if Jane gets stuck there — it means more time with Charlie,' she finished with a wink.

John had shrugged off his raincoat and hung up his hat but he remained outside the door, talking through the flywire to his wife.

'Now Margaret, you just keep your nose in the mending and not in your daughter's love life,' he said with a grin. 'Besides, no one can fix my pants like you.'

Lizzy smiled at her dad's teasing. Her mum fell for it every time.

'Oh John, I can't do this forever. My eyesight is going and my arthritis in my fingers flares up. I want to never see a sewing needle ever again.'

She put her sewing down with a huff and looked at him over her glasses. 'Besides, I don't think your pants could take any more mending,' she said giving the patchwork pants an appraisal.

'You're not even sixty yet, Mum.'

'Yes, you don't even have the matching fleece tracksuit set yet, dear, nor the slippers.' John shot Lizzy a grin.

'You two are awful.' Margaret huffed again. 'I'm going to put the kettle on.'

Lizzy's phone went off, a text from Jane. 'Oh no, poor Jane. She can't come home. She's started vomiting and feels awful. She's asked me to come help her.'

Her dad frowned. 'It's those little ankle biters she looks after, all number of bugs going around the day-care centre.' John screwed up his face. His glasses were starting to fog up and his face was red from the cold.

Margaret came running to the door. 'Jane is sick, did you say? Oh, now she'll have to stay there overnight.'

'Mum, don't look so happy. Poor Jane is throwing up at her potential new boyfriend's place. She'll be mortified. I have to go to her.'

'Yes, yes, you're right,' agreed Margaret.

'I don't think you can, Lizzy.' John was looking down at his phone, his glasses perched on the end of his nose either to help the fog disperse or to see a message. 'I just got a text from Merv. They've had way more than us, which means it'll be flooding down towards us, and Jones Road will be impassable now unless by dinghy.' John was staring at his phone screen. His lips twisted to the side as if he was working out the actual depth of the crossing in his head, just to be sure.

'I'll go the back way on the quad bike. It's the only way in, and Jane needs me. I don't care if I have to walk the rest of the way. I can't leave her there like that.' Lizzy was already preparing it in her mind: she'd take the bike and use the specially made bridge that her grandfather had put in before she was born, back when the Bennets used to own that part of Netherfield.

'I'll get you a bag. She'll need nice fresh clothes, toiletries and I have some medicine that might help gastro.' Margaret shimmied off down the passageway.

Lizzy kitted up in an old yellow raincoat and hat and pulled on her big wellington boots that were used only for washing down machinery or at spraying time.

'Here's some things for Jane. Give her my love,' said Margaret handing a medium-sized overnight bag, double wrapped in plastic bags, to Lizzy.

'Thanks, Mum, I'll keep you updated.'

Lizzy went through a side door from the verandah to the garage, which usually was home to Jane's car and Margaret's old white Ford Falcon. The quad bike — which Lizzy had first learned to ride as a five year old — sat to one side next to the yabby nets and dog food. Lizzy strapped the bag onto the back of the bike, then checked the fuel and started it up. As she headed out into the rain the back wheels spun over the wet, sloppy dirt more like an ice rink than a road. It didn't help that the bike tyres had lost most of their tread over the years.

She tried to tilt her hat down enough to shield her face without compromising visibility but still the rain belted at her, like darts into a board. She rode along the track to the southern part of the farm trying to dodge the big puddles and going slowly enough that she didn't drench herself in muddy water. The track turned to the left around the corner of a paddock and followed a bush section where Lizzy saw the normally dry creek rushing at full speed, the water foaming at the edges. Her hands were starting to go numb in the rain as she pulled her legs in tighter against the bike, enjoying the warmth from the motor.

The track grew narrower and rougher as she reached the last section, usually left unused where it turned towards the creek. Ahead stood the small bridge that had lasted the test of time, made by her granddad a lifetime ago. The collection of tree logs, cut and laid across the narrowest part of the creek, used to hold a vehicle back in the day, but now only enough logs remained to get the quad bike over. White ants had eaten into some, and age had made the rest brittle. When they were bored kids they'd ride over it for fun, but that was a long time ago, and she would have to take it carefully, especially in the wet.

'It's just a walk in the park,' she muttered to herself as rain spilled over her lips. Putting the bike into first gear she started to cross, leaning forward to watch for any rotting sections. It was harder than she'd thought in the rain, and all of a sudden she realised just how dangerous this was. What if it gave way and she and the bike fell into the raging creek? They couldn't afford to lose the bike. Maybe she should have walked the bridge first? *Too bloody late now.* She was almost halfway.

Suddenly one of the logs moved, lurching her to the left. *Oh hell!* She braced herself, waiting for the crack and the fall, but it didn't come. The log held and allowed her to scoot across. She sighed in relief as she glanced back at the angry rushing water. Sticks and leaves churned through the whitewash, making her visualise herself drowning in the creek. Her skin prickled with goose bumps as the close call unsettled her. 'Well, that could have been interesting,' she muttered to herself before pressing on.

Safely on the other side she gunned the bike into life as she followed the old unused track, swerving around shrubs and dodging fallen limbs and low-hanging branches. One smacked across her face, bringing tears to her eyes and an ache to her cheeks.

Soon the track came to an end and Lizzy had to open and close a few gates, narrowly avoiding getting bogged in a clay patch. A blur of white caught her eye and she glanced back: a sheep in rising water not far from the creek. With a grunt Lizzy turned the bike around to have a closer look. She couldn't live with herself if the animal was in need of help. Her gut feeling paid off as she found the ram caught in old fencing wire being thrown about by the rushing water.

'You're a silly boy, whatcha doing in there,' she

crooned as she stepped closer to the animal. His eyes were wide and there was blood on one of his legs from straining to get free of the wire.

Her boots squelched through the mud and as she hit the water the ram's nostrils flared and he had another go at breaking free. 'Settle, boy, before you do some serious damage,' she cooed as water splashed about like a spin cycle. She took two more steps. 'Oh, you *are* a nice boy.' He certainly wasn't a Longbourn ram; this guy was top of the bidding list, his make-up worth a pretty penny — she'd bet good money on it. 'I'd like to take you home. Have you jump the fence for a little while even,' she said as she reached him, sinking her fingers into his damp wool. The scent of lanolin was strong.

The next few minutes probably looked like a mud-wrestling match — Lizzy wasn't sure who was winning — but somehow she managed to unbend some of the snagged wire around his leg while he tried to fight her off. Lizzy ran a hand down his leg to check for breaks but it seemed like the cuts were the only injuries. With the wire free she tried to pull him from the water towards high land but now he wanted to play statues; she slipped trying to budge him but luckily remained upright until, suddenly, the ram with his expensive, perfectly weighted balls, realised he was free and took off. Lizzy yelped as gravity pulled her into the muddy water. She crashed onto her hands and knees, cold water ran into her boots and she cursed in frustration. 'Some thanks I get.'

Her hat had fallen off in the tussle, and she

plucked it from the water before it floated away. Covered head to toe in wet mud she squelched towards the quad bike. As she emptied the water from her boots Lizzy watched the ram trot off. Even wet and muddy — no part of her was dry — she was happy that he wasn't damaged or distressed. With a sigh she headed towards the Netherfield homestead and her sister.

★　★　★

Lizzy parked her quad bike beside one of two new-looking Land Cruiser utes in the large homestead carport. She couldn't get any wetter but she was thankful to no longer have water pounding against her face as she made her way around to the front door and rapped the metal knocker three times.

She looked down at the muddy puddle she was making on the wooden verandah. Her jeans were dark with water and brown mud up past her knees. She took off her hat and felt mud crusting on her forehead. The solid wood door opened on old creaky hinges, and Lizzy put on her biggest smile, hoping Charlie would overlook her state and still be glad to see that some help was here for Jane. But it faltered when she caught sight of the tall figure with the haunting dark eyes.

Why was Will Darcy around every bloody corner? 'Oh, it's *you*. Again.' She couldn't stop the words slipping from her mouth.

An eyebrow rose as he looked her up and down, slowly. 'Well, I think it's *you* but I can't be too sure under all that . . . mud. You're a bit of a sight today.'

She looked to his hands to see what they were doing, but he had them tucked behind him as if he were about to address a room full of conference attendees.

'Not so plain today. Just trying to look after my skin,' she smiled sarcastically as she wiped at her face and felt the dirt smudge further across it. 'I guess you'd like me to strip and get clean before you invite me in?'

The side of his lips tugged slightly, so slightly she almost missed it. She thought back on her words, her eyes narrowing as a weird feeling niggled in her belly.

He looked like he was about to reply when a blond mop of hair suddenly appeared behind him. 'Will, who is it?' He pulled up short when he caught sight of Lizzy. 'Oh, dear. Is that you, Lizzy?'

'Hi Charlie. Yes, it's me. I've come to help Jane. I'm so sorry about my state.'

'Don't be. I'm glad you're here,' Charlie replied, his easy manner and natural exuberance starkly contrasting the manners of his best friend. 'I feel awful for Jane. She's so sick. She won't let me help.'

'Well, you're sweet to try.'

Charlie tilted his head and looked intently at Lizzy. 'How did you get here? The road out is flooded. We're cut off. We couldn't even get through with my ute and it's been lifted.'

Lizzy smiled. 'You'll find a dinghy in the left-hand shed next to the header — that's what

Mick used every time the road flooded. That's why there's a shed down the driveway. He used to keep the old Merc in it for moments like these so he could get to town or the kids to school.'

'Ah, yes, I did see that the other day. Nice to know there's a plan in place for moments like these. But that doesn't explain how you got here?'

Lizzy was feeling a chill start to set in but didn't want to show any kind of weakness in front of Will. 'Part of Netherfield used to belong to my grandfather, and he made a bridge across the creek. I came that way on the quad bike. It's a bit old but I had to come and help Jane.' She tried hard to stop her teeth from chattering.

'Did you fall off the bike?'

The question came from Will, his voice smooth and deep like dark chocolate. Did she detect a hint of concern in his tone or was that wishful thinking?

'No,' she said bluntly. 'I saw one of Charlie's rams down in the north paddock, he was tangled in some stray wire in the rising water. I managed to get him free. I don't think there's any damage to his leg, just a few cuts, but all the same you might want to check on him later.'

'Oh thanks, Lizzy. We only just had my rams delivered three days ago.'

'Nice Poll ram he is, very big correct ram, extremely bright white crimping waxy wool,' she said. 'He looked too important to leave. And I do like him even if his manners are somewhat lacking.'

'Not even a thank you?' Charlie said with a grin.

'No. But I'm sure he thought I looked hilarious splashing about in the mud.'

Will's brow creased as he cleared his throat.

Charlie was smiling. 'Well, he certainly was expensive but hopefully worth every penny. You know your rams, Lizzy. We must chat. Come inside, please. Gosh, you're shaking. I'm so sorry. We should have invited you in first.'

He stepped forward and took her hat and Jane's bag, hanging the hat on a hook by the door. Lizzy shook off her raincoat and hung it by her hat, then stepped back onto the verandah and pulled her feet from her boots. She peeled off her dripping, leaden socks and stepped to the edge of the verandah to squeeze the water out. 'Sorry,' she said as she hung the socks over her boots. 'My pants are horrible.'

'Don't worry. Come inside and you can have a hot shower. I'll take you to Jane.'

Will stepped back, so crisp and clean in his T-shirt and jeans, he smelled like he hadn't lifted much more than a pen all day while sitting on a leather couch sipping coffee.

She followed Charlie who started to point out rooms but then paused. 'Sorry, you've probably been in here more times than I have.'

Lizzy nodded. 'We used to play with the Jones girls when we were kids.'

'So, you knew Jason?'

Lizzy didn't reply, just nodded. Charlie's expression changed to sadness. 'When Mick told me the story of his son's death, it was . . . full on.

I don't imagine he'll ever really recover from it.'

Lizzy couldn't trust herself to speak. It wasn't that long ago that Jason had got caught under his loader while fixing it; his jack slipped, and he was crushed. She cleared her throat. 'Mick finding him . . . like that, already gone, was hard. It wasn't easy to get him out. The Fire and Rescue blokes came out, and they all knew Jason; he was one of the volunteers on the truck.'

'Oh no. Something like that really affects the whole community,' said Charlie. He swallowed then glanced away, scratching his head and looking a little off colour.

'Um. Anyway . . . ' he said eventually. 'I've got Jane in the guest room. There are loads of towels in the en-suite, so please help yourself. We'll be having a cuppa in the kitchen soon, feel free to come and grab one. Or anything.' He handed over Jane's bag. 'Please let me know how Jane is.'

The concern in his voice was real and it warmed Lizzy's heart. 'Thanks Charlie. I know Jane will be feeling awful for putting you out but we're both grateful. I'll pop out and let you know how she's going soon.'

'Thank you.'

Charlie walked off, in his slim-fit jeans and navy polo shirt with the little green alligator. Lizzy smiled at the effort he had made for Jane's visit.

With a deep breath she knocked on the door of the guest room. 'Jane, it's me.' She spoke softly, in case Jane was asleep. The door was silent as it brushed across the plush carpet. The room was dark and held a faint scent of eucalyptus. On the bed was Jane's slim body, curled up on her side. A bucket was by her bed and a bug spray on the side table with a jug of water and a glass. Charlie had thought of everything.

'Oh Lizzy,' Jane whimpered as Lizzy moved to see her. 'Thanks for coming.' There were tears in her eyes.

'I'm here. I've got some clothes, and Mum packed medicine. How are you?'

'Rotten. I'm up to the dry-retching stage. My ribs hurt, my throat's sore. I just want to be at home. Poor Charlie. I'm so humiliated.' Her words were so softly spoken that Lizzy had to lean closer.

'I'm here now, rest up.'

'I didn't feel great this morning but I really wanted to see Charlie. I hope no one else catches it.'

Lizzy felt Jane's skin, which was hot and clammy, then brushed back her hair, damp with sweat, and stroked her head until Jane closed her eyes in sleep. Lizzy snuck off to the bathroom to peel off her dirty clothes, but there was no time for a shower because Jane sat up to vomit and Lizzy darted back to help her reach the bucket even though she had nothing to give it.

'Oh Jane,' she said brushing back her hair again and feeling her hot forehead. 'Let me get you a damp flannel. Here, sip some water.' Lizzy played nursemaid in her underwear until Jane was settled back into bed and looked to have dozed off.

Lizzy risked a quick shower, washing her hair

and scrubbing off all the stray bits of mud, and then opened Jane's bag in the hope of a spare outfit she could borrow. What she saw made her sigh. 'Oh geez, Mum.'

Pretty dresses. Delicate shoes. With a sigh Lizzy picked a soft blue V-neck dress that was made to fit Jane's slim frame rather than Lizzy's curves, but somehow she managed. It would have to do, she thought as she brushed her hair out.

She checked on Jane again and felt a wave of relief to see she was sound asleep, albeit looking pale and worn out. Maybe this was the end of it?

Tiptoeing out the door, she headed down the jarrah passage with its high ceilings and fancy cornices, towards voices in the kitchen. It was a strange scene: Charlie, his sister, Caroline, and Will sitting around the table having coffee and cake in a room Lizzy used to play in as a girl. Will was about to eat a biscuit but his hand froze, the biscuit suspended in mid-air as he stared at her.

Charlie turned around and smiled while Caroline attempted one. She was wearing a pretty lilac dress and her hair looked as if she'd just come from a salon. But no amount of make-up could hide the annoyed expression on her face at their unexpected guest.

'Come in, Lizzy. Would you like a coffee? Just press the button on the machine. Cups are beside it,' Charlie said, gesturing to a professional-looking coffee machine.

'Cool, thanks.' She saw the questions he was dying to ask glinting in his eyes. 'Jane's sleeping.

She's very worn out but hopefully she's at the end of it.'

He visibly relaxed and went back to sipping his coffee. Caroline glanced at Will, who was watching Lizzy.

'That's a lovely dress,' said Caroline.

Lizzy wasn't sure if Caroline was being sarcastic or serious. 'It's one of Jane's. I didn't think I'd get covered in mud and need a change of clothes.' She resisted the urge to tug down on the hem and instead focused on making her coffee. 'Now Charlie,' Lizzy continued, grasping for a change of topic as the coffee machine began its process at the touch of a button, 'after seeing your gorgeous ram, maybe I shouldn't tell you that our border fence line isn't up to scratch.'

He laughed. 'Which fence would that be?'

She smiled. 'Have you got a farm map?'

He jumped up, helped her into her chair as she came back to the table with her coffee and then left the room in search. Lizzy suddenly felt like a deer in a lion enclosure. Will and Caroline, who sat close together, were watching her as if waiting for her to make a run for it so they could give chase and hunt her down. Or at least shoo her from the house.

Small talk, small talk, say something . . . anything. 'Decent amount of rain.'

She almost had to laugh at herself. Neither Will nor Caroline saw fit to reply. Caroline just smiled tightly and then picked at her dress.

'So, what do you do?' asked Will. 'For work,' he clarified.

Lizzy frowned. 'I'm a farmer,' she said.

His eyebrows raised but he remained quiet as Lizzy stared him down.

'Nothing else?' asked Caroline.

'No. I farm from sun-up to sundown and everything in between. Dad handed over the reins to me not long after I left high school. It's all I've wanted to do.'

'Oh,' said Will as if suddenly everything made sense. 'I just assumed it was only your dad, and you helped out.'

'And that's why I told you I wouldn't be able to buy Longbourn, Will,' said Charlie as he came back and placed a large map on the table in front of them.

Lizzy frowned at Will. 'You want Charlie to buy our farm?' Suddenly her chest was constricting as if the removalist vans had already arrived at their home demanding they leave. She knew he'd spoken about it under the cover of darkness at the cabaret but to hear the words out loud, face to face, made her stomach churn.

'No,' he said leaning back in his chair. 'Well, yes,' he corrected.

'Which is it?' Lizzy demanded leaning forward and glaring at him. 'You were going to try to buy our farm from under us?' It was taking all her effort to keep the tremble from her voice.

Will put his hands up but Charlie cut in.

'It wasn't like that, Lizzy.' His words were soft and calming.

She took a deep, slow breath and waited for Will to explain exactly how it was.

Will's adam's apple bounced. 'When Charlie was looking into buying this place I helped him see what was possible for the future, and your farm came up as an option. *But,*' he stressed, 'that was only because we heard the family only had daughters and . . . '

He paused and looked down at his hands.

'We'd heard the farm wasn't travelling too well.'

Lizzy tried not to let the hurt show on her face.

'I'm sorry, Lizzy,' said Charlie. 'Will was just looking out for me and he's a very good businessman. I trust him.'

Lizzy gave him a half-hearted smile. Charlie she could forgive. 'I understand you need to see if your investment is viable, and you have to consider growth for the future.' She turned her eyes to Will. 'But Longbourn is *not* a business transaction, it's my life and you'll take it over my dead body.'

Charlie laughed. 'Jane said the same thing. She said you bleed Longbourn blood. I admire that, Lizzy.'

'Well, now I know it too,' replied Will. 'And for your information, our land dealings may seem like business transactions, but to Charlie and me, our home farms, the ones we grew up on, will never be sold in our lifetimes either.'

His dark eyes swirled with a passion that reinforced his words.

'Great, now we have that sorted,' said Charlie brightly, 'where is this fence?'

Lizzy shot Will a cynical glance, uncertain if

she could trust him, and dragged the map closer to her. 'Right, so this here is our boundary. This fence is old and the kangaroos have forced holes in a few places along it.' She took a deep breath. 'To be frank, we can't afford to build a new one, so I've just fixed what I could when I came across busted sections of rotted old fence post. And this here is the track and the crossing. If ever you need another way off the farm without a dinghy, this is your spot. Although, you might want to help me replace some of the logs,' she added. 'I thought it was going to collapse under me today.' She moved her finger across the map, suddenly aware of her short, dirty nails.

'What happened to your hand?'

Lizzy looked up at Will. Was that a note of concern or mere curiosity?

'Just a scratch from a bit of wire.' She shrugged and looked back at the map. 'This paddock gets a bit waterlogged, and in this one Mick had an issue with cockchafers. I'd keep an eye on that one.'

Charlie then asked her all sorts of farming questions, at first some regarding Netherfield and what she knew about Mick Jones's farming style, and then the discussion moved to the best chemicals to use and then on to soils.

'Did you study at uni?' asked Charlie.

Lizzy laughed. 'No. We couldn't afford it, and I couldn't leave the farm. But I read a lot and love talking with other enthusiastic farmers. I've found some great forums online. I grew up watching my dad manage the farm, but I had to learn all about budgets when I took over. It was a tough few years but I've got in the swing of things now.'

'Do you speak another language too?' asked Caroline as she shot a look at Will.

'Um, no. I wish I did. Why?'

'I just remember a few years back, Will recited a list of attributes his ideal woman would hold. Remember Will? She had to be truly accomplished to attract your attention. Have a vast knowledge, especially on farming and markets, skills not just in the kitchen, speak another language, be a reader and pretty on the eye,' said Caroline, dancing her fingers along his tanned forearm.

Suddenly Lizzy felt far too exposed as his eyes watched her, even though he was clearly uncomfortable with Caroline's choice of topic. 'I'm surprised you know anyone with all those qualities. Surely you'd be married to her if there was such a woman,' she said.

Will frowned while his lips pulled tight. His hands went to rest on his lap, leaving Caroline's playful hand alone on the table.

Caroline waved her hand as if needing something for it to do. 'Will isn't very good at being teased. Are you, darling?' she said, gazing across at him.

Lizzy could see the longing in her eyes; she'd seen the same look mirrored in most of the single ladies at the cabaret, including her two youngest sisters.

Lizzy's eyebrow rose. 'Are you too proud?' she asked, pushing him again. There was something therapeutic about saying what she thought of him and watching him squirm. She already knew what he thought of her, so it wasn't as if she was losing a great friendship by being frank.

'I wouldn't say that,' he said, flicking an annoyed expression Caroline's way. 'I just don't beat around the bush, I don't suffer fools and I don't forgive easily.'

'Yes, never get on the wrong side of Will,' warned Charlie. 'But he's loyal to a fault.' He chuckled awkwardly, while watching them both with concern.

'Life is too short, I believe, for seriousness,' countered Lizzy. 'There should be laughter and enjoyment, along with the hard work.' There was fire in his eyes, yet she thought she saw a hint of amusement, as if he might actually be enjoying this sparring match.

'Your sisters have that down pat. I'm not sure how they go at hard work, though,' said Caroline with a sneer. 'Well, if you'll excuse me I think I'll go finish my blog,' she said standing up. 'Come find me soon, Will. Let's do something . . . fun.' With a smile just for him, she left.

The conversation returned to farming, and Charlie and Lizzy discussed chemicals while Will sat and listened, not once looking like he was going to get up and follow Caroline.

'I always find it interesting to see what others spray with,' said Lizzy.

'I think you'll find that metribuzin will assist better in barley grass and broadleaf weed control,' Will said, taking Lizzy by surprise.

'Yes, no doubt you're right, Will,' said Charlie. He nudged Lizzy. 'That's why I love having him around. Some days I feel like I'm a leech trying to learn what I can from Will, and sometimes he's just my best mate who'll bring me a beer on a hot day even when he's four hours away.'

Lizzy didn't love having Will around. His judgmental gaze unnerved her, so she preferred to focus most of her attention on Charlie. 'I've been doing a lot of research on humates,' she said with a sigh. 'If I won Lotto I'd get a decent seeding set up with liquid and I'd put some goodness back into the soil.'

'What's your theory on that? I've been curious about it myself,' said Will. 'We use liquid but mainly with trace elements, no humates.'

And on their talk continued, as Lizzy shared her views. Eventually Charlie sat back and smiled. 'I've never come across a woman who knows so much about farming. And I mean all the nitty-gritty stuff. It's not just driving tractors.'

Lizzy couldn't help the smile that twitched on her lips. She tucked her hair back behind her ear. 'Funny, because some seem to think I'm just a pretend farmer.'

When she glanced up Will was watching her again, but he remained silent.

'Thanks Charlie. That means a lot. I'm trying to be the best farmer I can. If ever you want to talk shop, you know where I am.' Lizzy looked at her watch. 'But if you'll excuse me I'd like to go check on Jane. Hopefully when she's up to it we can return home.'

'Please, Lizzy,' said Charlie, reaching out to

take hold of her arm before she left. 'Stay until tomorrow. Let Jane get some rest and let this rain clear first.'

'He's right. Best you both stay,' said Will.

Lizzy frowned at Will's firm tone, but she knew Charlie was right. Jane had to come first. 'Okay, you win, Charlie. We won't rush off.'

He smiled with relief and from the corner of her eye she saw Will's shoulders relax. He glanced at her, saw her watching him and turned away as he cleared his throat and started to clear the table.

I will never understand that man, she thought as she headed back to Jane's room.

6

'Oh Will, do you remember that time we spent in Venice?' Caroline crowed that night at dinner, an affair made awkward by Jane's absence and Caroline's desperate attempts to monopolise the conversation and Will. 'There was the most gorgeous view from our room that overlooked the Rialto.' She turned to Lizzy and continued. 'We got home so late we watched the sun rise and had the bridge to ourselves.' Followed by a tinkling laugh that, Lizzy suspected, fooled no one at the table. She was rather enjoying seeing Caroline's frustration grow the more Will's attention wasn't on her.

'Yes, and that man with the old broom came along to sweep the bridge,' said Charlie.

'You were there too?' asked Lizzy in surprise.

'Yeah, the three of us went for a month. Best times.'

'Right, I see,' she said with a smile. 'Sounds like an awesome trip.'

'Have you been overseas, Lizzy?' Charlie asked curiously.

She sighed, resting her chin on her hand. 'I'd love to. I haven't left the state yet, though, or even been in a plane. But I think if I had the chance I'd love to see Italy too, for the history. And to visit a farm in America would be great, to see how farming is done in another country. I'd love to travel to a place I can learn something new that I could bring home to try here, farming wise.'

'A working holiday? Doesn't sound like much of a holiday,' said Caroline.

'Growing up I dreamed of being a jillaroo on a station, after I'd seen a TV documentary. Going out on a muster on horseback seemed so romantic.'

'You should do it one day, it's an experience you'd remember,' said Will, watching her closely. 'It's amazing.'

Lizzy turned and looked at him. 'I'd still like to do that one day, but that dream soon faded when I realised I could help Dad on our farm. From that moment on nothing else mattered.'

'How old were you then? When you knew you wanted to be a farmer?' asked Charlie.

'I was ten,' she said, remembering it fondly. 'I was out in the paddock, the dirt fresh after a rain and the deep green crops a foot high. My boots were buried in the soft dirt and I felt like a new sapling growing roots deep down into the ground as I stood there.' She smiled; closing her eyes she could still picture that moment.

'That's beautiful,' said Charlie quietly.

'I dreamed about being an actress,' Caroline said quickly and a little loudly. 'Had a few small parts in some shows but you boys keep me busy enough.'

'You don't have to handle our social lives, sis,' said Charlie with a smile.

'What are your thoughts on drones?' asked Will suddenly. 'Do you think we'll eventually be able to use them to spot-spray?'

When he spoke farming she saw a light in his eyes that softened his usually rigid features. He was less stern, more expressive, and once or twice Lizzy found herself mesmerised by his lips as he spoke so passionately and expertly. Then she would realise and shake it off. It was almost unnerving that they had similar views and passions on farming.

'I can't see how they could carry enough chemical, being so small, but the parts for them could be cheap so maybe there's the possibility of having lots of drones to share the workload; it could work out.'

'It makes you wonder,' replied Will as he scratched at his chin.

'My whole life has been spent listening to you two and non-stop farming talk,' said Caroline with an exaggerated sigh as she picked at her salad. 'Even Georgie would be bored by this.'

Lizzy frowned in confusion as Will's face lit up. She'd never seen him smile so wholeheartedly. It was a little dazzling. Lizzy had to look down at her empty plate, counting the prongs on her fork.

'Ha!' he said with spark. 'Georgie would love it. I wish she was here.'

Lizzy pressed her lips together, wondering about this mystery girl, then scowling at herself for even giving it a thought.

'How about we all finish up and head into the lounge room for a bit, watch a movie even?' suggested Caroline. Her eyes darted to Will.

Lizzy glanced at her watch. 'You'll have to excuse me. I'm going to head off to bed,' she

90

said getting up and taking her dishes to the sink. 'I think Jane will be feeling better tomorrow and I can take her home.' She turned to Charlie. 'Thanks for dinner and your hospitality. You cook a mean steak, Charlie. It's been a while since I've tasted meat so good.'

'Thanks, Lizzy. I've loved having your company and I feel much better knowing Jane has you here too.'

'My pleasure,' she replied, and she meant it.

'Will the flood waters be gone by tomorrow?' Will asked, as he stood up.

'No. They'll probably be passable in a day or two but Jane will want to get back to work before then, and I have sheep to check. We can pop over later for her car if that's all right?'

'Of course, any time. It's fine here,' Charlie replied. 'Night.'

'Good night, all.'

Will smiled warmly and waved her off. Lizzy returned his smile and went to raise her hand but suddenly felt self-conscious so she turned on her heel and tried not to run to the safety of the guest room.

Inside Jane was awake with a bedside lamp on. 'Hey, you look a bit more colourful,' said Lizzy.

'How was dinner?' asked Jane as Lizzy stripped off the dress and climbed into bed in her underwear.

Lizzy waited until she'd set her pillow right and was comfortable before replying. It gave her time to think about it. 'Not too bad. Better than I thought it would be. How about you? Crackers stay down?'

91

Jane's big blue eyes peered at her as she lay with the doona pulled up to her chin. 'Yes, I'm feeling much better. I'm ready to go home. I don't want to face Charlie tomorrow. I don't want him to see me like this.'

'He's not the sort of bloke to be bothered by that, Jane. I really think he's a genuine guy.'

She smiled. 'I think so too.' She watched Lizzy for a moment before speaking again. 'What about Will?' she asked.

Lizzy sighed and stared up at the ceiling. 'Jury is still out.'

'So, you didn't stab him with a steak knife?'

It was nice to see the humour dancing in Jane's eyes, a sign she was truly past the worst of her sickness. 'It was tempting to start with but . . . ' She exhaled slowly. 'Turns out I didn't need it.'

Jane's eyes were heavy as she reached an arm out to switch off the light.

'Good, I'm glad it wasn't too bad,' she murmured half-asleep already. 'You've already done so much for me by coming here.'

Jane's hand found Lizzy's and gave it a squeeze, and it stayed there until they were both sound asleep.

★ ★ ★

In the morning they cleaned up the room and crept out of the quiet house.

'Trying to sneak off without saying goodbye?'

They both turned. 'We didn't want to wake anyone,' said Jane softly.

92

Charlie came towards them wearing track pants and a white T-shirt, his hair still skew-whiff from sleep. He was carrying two jackets and held them out. 'Please take these, it's cold.' He smiled at Jane. 'Feeling better?'

Jane slyly tried to smooth her hair out. 'Much better, thanks Charlie. I'm sorry — ' she started but he moved to her and pulled her into a hug.

'Don't be.'

Lizzy smiled as Jane hugged him back. Charlie snuck a kiss on her forehead, which made Jane lean into him more.

'Text me when you get home,' he said as Jane moved to join Lizzy by the quad bike.

'I will. Bye.' Jane watched him until he was no longer visible and then tightened her grip around Lizzy.

'This takes me back to when we were kids,' she said. 'It's been ages since we went riding together.'

It was a beautiful day after the rain, the sun was out and the trees looked bright after their wash. All was nice except for the muddy earth beneath them, which had them sliding from time to time. They made it home without incident, the bridge holding up with the extra weight as Lizzy took the time to navigate the safest way across.

'Oh Lizzy, is that who I think it is?' said Jane tapping her on the shoulder and pointing to a silver dual-cab Land Cruiser parked beside the house as they drew closer.

Lizzy let out a groan. 'Can we go back to Netherfield?'

Jane was still laughing as Margaret met them

at the door. 'Oh, my girls are home. Jane, you look so pale.' Margaret drew her in for a hug. 'Come on inside, we have a guest.'

The man standing by the fire with their father made Lizzy almost shiver with repulsion.

Ken Collins was shorter than Lizzy by half a head, and his hair was thick and black, resembling that of a Lego-man. He wore a leather belt with a shiny buckle as if he'd been a rodeo champ in his day. If you let him talk long enough he'd tell you about the time he rode a bucking bronco. That was an hour of her life Lizzy would never get back.

'Ken is here, say hello,' Margaret said in a stage whisper. 'Lizzy and Jane are back,' she said to Ken. 'As I was telling you, poor Jane fell ill while visiting Charlie Bingley. But she's much better now.' Margaret shot a glance at Lizzy, nudging her to speak.

'Hi Dad. Hi Ken. I hope you don't mind but Jane and I need to go and change.'

Ken had taken a step towards them; each time he saw the Bennet girls he tried to give them a kiss on the cheek, and each time they tried to find a new way to avoid his lips.

'Oh yes, you must be worn out. Hope you feel better, Jane,' he said.

Lizzy saw Jane hold her stomach and nod, feigning a little more sickness than she felt, and immediately tucked her arm around Jane and led her to their bedroom, shutting the door firmly behind them.

'I was worried he'd start to melt standing that close to the fire,' said Lizzy.

Jane slapped her arm and attempted to glare at her but still she was stifling a smile.

'Lucky Mum has already paired you off with Charlie, you'll be spared Ken's devotion this time.'

'Come on, Lizzy, you know Ken only has eyes for you. Always has.'

They took their time to change, neither wanting to run into Ken again, but eventually Lizzy, dressed in her work jeans, Ugg boots and red checked farm shirt buttoned up nearly to the top, headed back to the dining room. While she walked she pulled her hair up into a messy top knot, catching snippets of conversation about a new tractor Ken had purchased.

'They gave me a great discount. Maybe because I'm on the council and they've put in an application for building additions, but one can't really tell if that's the reason,' he said as Lizzy appeared.

His face was slightly red from the heat of the fire, but he had moved a little away from it, to a non-melting point. Margaret's lemon-scented candles, which sat on the cabinet nearby, had no such luck, now resembling the Leaning Tower of Pisa.

'Oh, welcome back, Lizzy.'

Ken's enthusiasm for her return sent a chill down her spine. 'Thanks Ken, what brings you to Longbourn today?' she asked, catching the warning look her mum shot her. *Be polite!* it silently screamed.

'Just thought I'd drop in and see how you were all going. Did you hear about the rodeo coming to Toongarrin?' His chest puffed up a fraction, causing his blue button-up shirt to stretch. 'I'm on the committee. It's going to be great. Hopefully it can become an annual event to help bring some money into the area. Please say you'll come, Lizzy?'

'Of course she will,' said Margaret as she bustled over and sat on the couch closest to him.

'Yes, we'll all be there,' said Lizzy deftly. 'It does sound exciting. Cowboys and barrel racing. I heard a few people talking about it at the pub.'

Ken looked pleased with himself as his chin dropped, making his neck wrinkle. 'Fabulous. I've helped hand-pick some of the riders, from back in the day when I used to rodeo,' he said. 'We'll even have fireworks.'

After ten minutes of rodeo talk he paused and glanced at his watch. 'Well, I best head off now, I've imposed on you for too long.'

'Not at all, Ken,' gushed Margaret. 'Would you like to stay for lunch?'

Lizzy glanced at her dad, who was squinting slightly, one eye almost twitching.

Ken looked a little nervous all of a sudden, his lips twisting into a strange shape. 'Ah, no thank you. I must head off.' He glanced at Lizzy, his lips moving slightly as if he had more to say.

'Okay then, thanks for stopping by, Ken. Lizzy will see you off,' Margaret added as she motioned at John to stay put.

'Thanks Lizzy,' said Ken stepping towards her so quickly, he was up in her personal space before she realised. 'That would be great.'

On the short walk to his ute she asked how the

96

lease was working for him.

'Oh it's great, you don't have to worry. I'm keen to take it on for another three years.'

Thank goodness, she thought. 'Thanks Ken. One day I'd love to say we won't be re-leasing it,' she said with a sigh.

He frowned and rested his hand on her shoulder as they stopped by his ute. 'You know, there's another way, Lizzy. It could all be yours again,' he said hopefully, his eyes turning glassy as she felt a knot pull in her stomach. 'You . . . you know I . . . I care a lot for you,' he stammered. 'I'm a bit older but time isn't good to us all and I'm tired of being alone.' He took a deep breath just as Lizzy held hers. 'Please Lizzy, would you be my girl? Come out with me at the rodeo and see where it leads?' He reached for her hand and held it in his.

Lizzy was too afraid to look up in case he tried to kiss her, instead she focused on his buttons. Jane had warned her this moment was coming. She'd said last time Ken had visited that he was working up the courage to ask her out. Lizzy had laughed it off but inside, past the denial, was a small ounce that knew Jane was right. She had hoped this time would never come, that either she'd have a boyfriend or Ken would find someone, but finding a partner out in the country was harder than finding a needle in a hay stack.

'Oh Ken, you're such a great bloke.' What else could she say? Sucking in a deep breath she lifted her eyes and gently tugged her hand out of his. She had a few options: one, say she had a boyfriend; two, say she was gay; or three, say she just wasn't interested.

The truth won out.

'Look Ken, it's really sweet of you to ask but I don't think of you that way. You've been like this great uncle who's helped us out over the years.'

Ken winced at her word choice. 'Things could change — ' he started, but she cut him off with a shake of her head.

'I don't think they will. You've been incredible to us and I consider you a part of our family, Ken. I don't want that to change. Thank you, though. It's very sweet of you to ask.' She touched his arm then stepped back.

'I could give you everything you want, Lizzy. I'm considered a catch in Toongarrin.'

'Well, then, you'll make some lady very happy,' she replied. 'The right one will come along.' She moved to pat him on the shoulder but he stepped back.

'Right. Okay.' He stumbled as he turned and climbed awkwardly into his ute.

'Ken?'

He gave her a curt nod as he shut his door, started his ute and drove off without a backwards glance.

Lizzy gritted her teeth. 'That could have gone better,' she mumbled before heading inside, where she found her mum perched on the end of her seat watching her expectantly.

'Well?'

'Well what?' Lizzy frowned.

'You and Ken. Are you going out?'

Lizzy's face fell. Of course Ken would have

98

run it by her parents first. That was the kind of traditional guy he was.

'No.'

Her mum's expression hardened, and Lizzy breathed in ready for the torrent. She turned and headed for the safety of her room, but Margaret chased her. 'Lizzy, what is wrong with you! Ken is nothing to be sneezed at. Do you want to live alone?'

'Yes, Mum, I do. All I need is the farm,' she said, quickly shutting her bedroom door behind her.

'What if we lose the farm?' Margaret yelled through the door. 'You being with Ken could save it. Did you think of that? Sometimes we can't be picky. Love will come.' She moved a fraction, her voice sounding softer. 'John, tell her she's being too rash!'

Lizzy leaned against the door while Jane glanced up from her book.

'What's going on?' she whispered.

'John, tell her!' Margaret's voice raised again as her fist banged against the door.

Footsteps approached the door, and then her father's voice came softly, close. 'I'd think very carefully, Lizzy.'

Lizzy opened the door to see her mum's face flushed beside her dad's calmer one.

'You could be stuck with your decision for the rest of your life,' he said, glancing at his wife. Then he frowned. 'Lizzy, I would be very upset if you dated him just to please your mother or to try to protect the farm.'

Margaret scoffed. 'John!'

'You need to do what's right for you,' he added ignoring his wife.

'Oh Dad, thank you!' she said flinging open the door and throwing her arms around him.

Margaret threw her arms up and stomped back down the passage muttering to herself.

'What was all that about? Ken?' asked Jane after Lizzy re-entered the bedroom.

Lizzy sat on her bed. 'Yep. He asked me out on a date. I said no. He didn't look too happy about it.'

Jane smiled.

'It's not funny. He asked me to the rodeo.'

'Charlie just asked me to go too. I'm so excited.'

Her phone was on the bed beside her, blue light blinking. Lizzy would bet a hundred dollars, which she didn't have, that it was a message from Charlie waiting to be read.

'Urgh, what if I run into Ken there? What if he is so pissed at me that he won't re-lease?'

'Don't sell yourself for land, Lizzy. There are plenty of others who'll lease from us. Maybe even Charlie. Or maybe next time you won't even need to re-lease, you've been working so hard.'

Lizzy raised an eyebrow. 'True. Ah, Jane, you always know how to cheer me up.' She smiled at her sister. 'And just think: if you marry Charlie, then I won't need any Kens in my life.'

'Oh god, Lizzy. Now you sound just like Mum.'

Hell, I do! Lizzy slapped a hand over her mouth, her eyes wide in horror.

Jane laughed, and before long both sisters were in fits of giggles.

7

Lizzy wondered if she'd ever see Will Darcy in a place like this: a tiny local pub with worn furniture, history on the walls and the usual regulars at the bar. Lizzy paused just inside the door and had to check herself again for letting him invade her thoughts. Squeezing her eyes shut she sighed and continued on her way. She spotted Scotty, whose name had been written on the stool where he sat for as long as she could remember. Scotty, with only a handful of teeth and a head full of unkempt knotted hair, turned and smiled.

'Hello there, young Elizabeth.'

'Hi Scotty,' she replied.

He was a harmless drunk whose happy place was on that stool talking to whoever came into the pub. Would Will sit and chat with Scotty? she wondered. She doubted it.

'Hey, you looking for me?' said Lottie, appearing through a doorway.

'Well, I'm certainly not after Scotty,' she said with a chuckle. 'So, what was this emergency I had to be here for?'

Lottie grabbed her hand and dragged her back through the bar, outside and towards the back hotel room that was Lottie's bedroom. 'I need help deciding what to wear to the rodeo. Do I go a dress and boots, or jeans-and-sexy-top and boots?'

Lizzy pulled a face. 'You know I'm not the person to talk to about this stuff. I always ask Jane, and she does my make-up if I ever need any.'

'Well, I don't have a Jane, so you'll have to do.'

She opened her door and pushed Lizzy through. On her double bed three outfits were laid out.

'You're going to a lot of trouble,' Lizzy said, glancing at two dresses and tops with Lottie's favourite cowboy boots at the foot of the bed.

'Hell, yeah. This rodeo is going to bring in some new blood. I need something to happen, Lizzy.'

There was desperation in her friend's eyes and a tiredness Lizzy hadn't noticed before.

'I'm sorry.'

Lottie frowned and pushed back her long fringe. 'What for?' she said, glancing away as if she'd accidentally let something slip.

'I forget,' she said softly. 'I'm happy out on the farm and I forget that Coodardy is your cell.'

Lottie exhaled. 'You make it sound bad. It's not that awful here.'

Lizzy waited until Lottie's hazel eyes returned to hers.

'Okay, maybe some days I feel bad. It gets a bit much, you know?'

Lizzy swallowed and stepped forward to pull Lottie into a hug. 'You're my best friend forever, you know that, right? I love you, Lottie.'

Lottie hugged her tightly, tucking her head into Lizzy's shoulder. 'I love you back, Dizzy Lizzy. Always.'

She pulled back and put on a bright smile. 'Right. So . . . my white dress with the pink arrow Kader boots?' Lottie chewed on the side of her cheek as she watched Lizzy. 'Don't you want to be with someone? Strong arms around you at night, someone to share your thoughts with?'

'Of course, I'm not a nun,' said Lizzy. 'But I'm not going to dwell on the fact that I'm single.'

'So, you'll dress up with me at the rodeo?' Lottie picked up her short lacy white dress and swept it against her, swishing from side to side like she was dancing with someone.

'I don't really have any choice, do I?'

Lottie shook her head. Lizzy broke out in a grin.

★   ★   ★

'It's not fair,' whined Lydia as she watched Lizzy throw a swag onto the back of her ute. 'Why can't we camp too? My friends are.'

'We'll be the only ones *not* camping,' said Kitty frowning.

Both girls turned to Margaret, who was standing not far away hanging towels on the clothes line.

'We've been over this, Lydia: you are too young to be out by yourself for the night.' Margaret rubbed her temple as if trying to ward off a headache. 'How about you help me hang out the rest of this washing please, so we can leave on time for once.'

Lydia pulled out her phone and started texting. 'It's social suicide, Mum!'

Kitty pulled a blue towel from the basket and threw it over the line with a huff.

Lydia and Kitty had been at their mother for the past hour, and even Lizzy had a headache. The bookwork she'd been trying to get through wasn't going to happen today with those three at each other's throats. John had bailed hours ago saying something needed doing before they left for the rodeo. Margaret had asked him what needed doing and he'd replied, 'Anything.'

'Can't Lizzy watch over us?' Kitty asked, her gaze pinning Lizzy to the spot.

Raising her hands, she shook her head. 'No. I'm not babysitting you two ever again. Last time you disappeared for hours and we spent our night off looking for you. Never again,' she said and went to pick up Jane's swag.

Lydia flung herself at Lizzy, grabbing onto her leg as her face crumpled up with fake tears. 'Please, Lizzy. It's not fair!'

Lizzy shook her foot as if ridding herself of ants. 'We had to wait, now it's your turn.' With a last shake she picked up the swag and threw it on the ute alongside hers.

'I'm going inside to get dressed, Jane should be out of the shower by now.' Lydia was still in the black silk boxer shorts she wore to bed; the yellow smiley faces contrasting the pout Lydia was wearing.

'Have you two even had breakfast yet?' asked Lizzy as she headed back inside.

Lydia didn't reply, just scowled.

'Best you get a wriggle on then, unless you want to stay here?' Lizzy didn't wait for her reply, instead she headed inside to her room.

'Oh my gosh, those two are hard work! Please tell me we weren't like that?' she said to Jane. She took in her sister, sitting in front of her desk with a small compact mirror adding the finishing touches to her eyes. Her three-quarter sleeve rose-print maxi dress pooled at her feet, the white background enhancing the pretty pattern.

Jane glanced at her through her mirror. 'No, I'm positive we were never like that.'

'You look stunning, Jane. You do such an amazing job with make-up. Any chance you could do my face?'

Jane smiled, blue eyes vibrant with a touch of blue eyeshadow and mascara. 'I'd love to.' And with that she was diving through her make-up trying to find the right dusky colours.

When Lizzy had showered and finally settled on a dark green V-neck dress that hugged her figure and dropped to the ground, finished with a denim jacket to keep the chill away, Jane reached for her green and brown eyeshadows.

'Now I know the dress I can do the rest.'

Lizzy sat and let her sister play.

'Sit still. Lizzy, stop fidgeting.'

'I'm trying.'

It was like having to sit still in the summer heat while hundreds of flies crawled over her face. Lizzy was starting to reach breaking point when Jane yelled, 'Done!' and startled her. 'Come and have a look.'

Jane pulled her to stand in front of the full-length mirror in the corner of their room.

'Well? Do you like it?' Jane pressed her hands to her lips as if in silent prayer.

Lizzy couldn't reply, she was too busy gawking at herself. 'Wow.' Her eyes looked sexy, if that was a thing. No longer just a deep brown, they seemed to shimmer and her long eyelashes, expertly enhanced by Jane, encapsulated her eyes perfectly.

'You wouldn't be so surprised if you did it more often,' said Jane. 'You have beautiful features: full lips, high cheekbones and the longest eyelashes. This just highlights them.'

With a last glimpse of the woman in the mirror Lizzy grabbed her overnight bag and headed to the door. 'Shall we?'

'Yep, let's get out of here before Lydia or Kitty attack.'

In the kitchen sat their father, dressed and waiting. He was leaning back on a wooden chair, balanced on two legs, his glasses on the end of his nose.

'Mum would have a fit if she caught you,' Lizzy whispered, then bent and kissed his cheek. 'See you there, Dad.'

'At this rate I might need you to send me some photos,' he said with a chuckle just as Margaret came out in her best floral dress. He quickly let the chair rest back on all four legs.

'If those girls would get off their bloody phones we might be able to leave. Kitty isn't even dressed yet. Oh Lizzy, you look lovely. You might see Ken today.'

Lizzy didn't even bother replying.

'Jane, Charlie will just melt when he sees you.'

Margaret smiled as if she were picturing Jane on her wedding day.

'Time for us to go.' Lizzy latched onto Jane and they headed for the door.

★ ★ ★

It was a forty-five minute drive to Toongarrin, and the rodeo was set up just out of town next to the footy oval and caravan park. A big steel circular fence had been erected, yellow sand filled its centre and seating had been placed around it along with a small grandstand. Amid the trucks and holding yards were market stalls, games, food areas and rides. Flags adorned utes in the 'Beaut Ute' competition area, old Holdens and Fords mixing it with newer models but most covered in two-way aerials and over-sized bull bars. Sheep were kept in another holding pen off to one side, as well as bulls and horses, and people with floats trying to park causing mayhem in the paddock. It made Lizzy's belly tingle with the excitement of action.

'Did you know they're even showing chooks? Lottie told me, she's so excited to go and see them as well as the horses.'

'She would have been great growing up on a farm,' said Jane, watching everything out the window as Lizzy drove to the parking area. 'Remember how excited she was to collect the eggs and feed the lambs when she came for sleepovers?'

Lizzy laughed. 'She still does.'

Jane looked at her phone as it beeped. 'It's

Charlie. He's over by the coffee van near the big R.M. Williams truck.'

'I'm regretting my attire already,' said Lizzy as she climbed out of the car and saw women in jeans and patterned and plain dress shirts. It was like the cabaret but in reverse. Again she felt the odd one out.

'Most of them are probably riding in the barrel race or working with animals; can't wear a dress for that.'

They let out a collective groan when they saw the queue at the coffee van.

'Hope it's worth waiting for,' said Lizzy.

'Bound to be, anything is better than that cheap instant coffee Mum gets.' Jane pulled a face and then her eyes widened. 'Oh, there he is.'

Her grip on Lizzy's arm tightened as she saw Charlie striding towards them, only eyes for Jane. By his side was Will, and hot on his tail was Caroline. This time Caroline was in moleskin pants with fancy leather boots and what looked to be a tailor-made suede black jacket. But it was the big diamond earrings and matching necklace that caught Lizzy's eye.

'Caroline just radiates elegance and poise, does she not?' said Jane quickly.

'Hm,' mumbled Lizzy, not sure if she agreed at all.

'Jane, Lizzy, so good to see you both again,' said Charlie giving them both a kiss on the cheek.

Charlie smelled good, and in that moment Lizzy found herself a little jealous of her sister and this man who'd set his eyes on her. They both looked so happy to be together, and the little touches, kisses and hand-holding was something Lizzy thought she didn't miss, until it was under her nose.

Charlie stood beside Jane and was practically bouncing on his heels. Jane gave him a shy smile as her hands twisted together trying to contain her excitement.

'You look fabulous, Lizzy,' said Charlie, shooting a side glance at Will.

Will was standing quietly by his side. His eyes were watching her, as dark as his black shirt and jeans. If Charlie was the bright sky, Will was the mesmerising black rain clouds.

'All thanks to Jane,' Lizzy said, as she twirled some of her hair through her fingers then threw it away as if she'd just been caught smoking. She certainly didn't want to look like she was flirting but Will's gaze made her uneasy.

They shuffled forward in the coffee line, Charlie trying hard to make small talk, which only Lizzy replied to. Jane didn't talk much when she was nervous, and Will didn't seem to speak at all if he could help it. And Caroline — well, she was Caroline. Charlie paid for their drinks then led the way to the stalls.

'Come on, Will, let's visit Ned. I saw his truck back there,' said Caroline, dragging him with her before he had a chance to reply.

They left without a backwards glance.

Lizzy was relieved to have them both gone, but she now found herself the third wheel. 'Oh, I see Lottie,' she lied. 'I'll catch you around later,' she said, giving Jane a wave and darting behind one of the stalls.

She walked past some kids holding whips and dressed up like little cowboys, and she couldn't help but laugh as they tipped their hats to her. As she rounded the back of a horse float she suddenly collided with a man.

'Oh sorry, Miss,' he said.

His hands held onto her arms, as they sorted themselves out. 'My fault, I wasn't paying much attention,' she said as she looked up into the palest blue eyes she'd ever seen. Her surprise grew as she took in this handsome stranger. He was a little taller than her, slim but strong in build and tanned. His smile was cheeky as he flicked up his Akubra to get a better look at her.

'Must say I'm feeling rather lucky right now.' He gave her a wink, his hands remained on her.

Lizzy, feeling her personal space slightly full, stepped back, disentangling her arms from him, and looked the man over. 'Are you a cowboy?' she asked.

His jeans were worn and marked, his red checked shirt tucked in and a big silver buckle adorned his leather belt. The black wide-brimmed hat that perched on his head as if it lived there was worn and well used.

The man glanced down and shrugged. 'I guess so,' he said with a drawl.

Lizzy spotted the spurs strapped onto his boots and felt a rush of excitement. 'What are you here to ride?'

He tipped his hat up with his thumb, dark hair

visible underneath. He couldn't be much older than Lizzy.

'Some bull riding, saddle bronc and bareback, if I survive the first,' he said with a chuckle.

Lizzy cringed. 'That's dangerous. Have you done much bull riding?'

'A bit. You worrying about me already, Miss?'

'I don't know, should I be?' she threw back at him.

He laughed and held out his hand. 'Luke Wickham. Glad to make your acquaintance.'

8

Lizzy slipped her hand into his. It was rough like sandpaper, and strong.

'You got a good grip there, Miss . . . '

'Lizzy Bennet. Nice to meet you, Luke,' she said, suddenly feeling a lot better about today.

'Where were you headed, Lizzy. Did you need an escort?'

She smiled. 'I was just going for a wander.'

He stuck out an arm for her. 'Well, let me be your guide. Would you like to meet the bulls we'll be riding today? Hellfire is the best.'

Lizzy slid her arm through his and together they walked towards the pens while Luke explained about the bulls.

'Riding Hellfire will be great for getting a high score; only problem is, he's hard to stay on.'

'So, he's not a safe bet, then?'

Luke shook his head. 'Only the best want to ride him and prove their worth.'

'Have you ever been badly hurt?' she asked, glancing him over and earning a cheeky grin.

'Only a broken leg and collar bone.'

Only? Who was this cowboy who seemed in no rush to leave Lizzy's side? After the bulls he showed her the horses, explaining each one's strengths like he'd studied the stats book.

'You know a lot about horses.'

'Yeah, well, I grew up on a big property and have worked on many farms and stations around the place. I'm actually looking for a harvest job at the moment. Might have a truck-driving job lined up, so I might be hanging around,' he said. 'I'm seeing a lot of beautiful things out here.'

Lizzy felt her face burn as he gazed at her.

He glanced at his watch then and sighed. 'Sadly I have to go and get ready for my first event.' He flashed his eyes, like magnified snowflakes over a pale blue sky, and smiled. 'But please say you'll come watch? You'll be my lucky charm. Especially in that green dress.'

'Are you calling me a leprechaun, Luke?'

'Far from it, just that that deep green is like a clover leaf, a lucky four-leaf clover,' he said with a wink and brushed her arm. 'And I need a lucky girl to cheer me on. Say you will?'

Lizzy smiled and tried not to blush again. 'Of course I will.'

'How about a lucky kiss?' he suggested offering up his lips a fraction.

Lizzy thought about it for a moment then leaned over and kissed his cheek.

He smiled. 'Well played,' he said approvingly. 'I'll come find you afterwards. Stay around the bull pens if you can.'

He walked away before she could reply, and she was left to wander in a daze, past kids with butterflies and tigers painted on their faces and carrying fairy floss on sticks. People mingled about chatting, eating and drinking, and they were all smiling. Events like these were so important for rural communities, helping to bring people together.

'There you are! I've been looking all over for

you. Why didn't you reply to my texts?' Lottie grabbed her by the arms and shook her gently then paused. 'Oh wow, you look stunning, Lizzy.' Then she shook her again. 'Why. Didn't. You. Answer. Me!'

Lizzy smiled at Lottie, still feeling the groggy after-effects of one cute cowboy.

'I've never seen this look on your face before, it's almost . . . '

'I met a guy,' Lizzy finally said.

'Oh my god. I knew it.'

Lizzy dragged her friend towards the arena to find a seat close up to the action. 'Let's watch and I'll tell you about him. I love that white dress on you, by the way.'

They sat not far from the big steel fence while cowgirls on horses and holding big flags trotted around the arena in a parade. Lizzy smiled the whole time as she told Lottie about her encounter with the cowboy.

'Why is it that I'm the one actively looking and you're not, yet you find one?'

Lizzy pointed out a group of cowboys standing off to the side getting ready to ride. 'There's loads over there. Maybe Luke could introduce you to a few.'

Lottie tapped her finger on her chin. 'Do you think cowboys have much to offer? Not many would have farms or full-time jobs. Don't most just chase the rodeo and find in-between work?'

Lizzy shrugged. 'I haven't met enough to comment on that. But I'm sure a few would be up for some fun.'

Her friend laughed as they announced the

bull-riding event and the first rider had drawn Menace.

'I love the names they give the bulls,' said Lottie. 'Have you seen Luke yet?'

Lizzy scanned the group of bull riders again and spotted Luke's black worn hat and red checked shirt. 'Yep, there he is with the hat and spurs.'

'Lizzy, they all have hats and spurs,' she said with a laugh.

When Lizzy was more specific Lottie leaned across her squinting. 'Yeah, it's hard to tell what he looks like this far away.'

The PA crackled as they announced the next rider. Luke spotted them looking his way and waved his hat at them.

Lizzy gave him a small wave back but Lottie stuck her arm right up and waved it like she was stranded on an island and had spotted a plane flying over.

'Oh my god you're as bad as Lydia,' Lizzy groaned.

Lottie smacked her arm. 'Take that back, I'm not *that* bad. How dare you put me in your sister's league,' she said, feigning horror.

They laughed until the rider trying to stay on the bull fell off in front of them, hitting the ground with a thud before scampering up to scale the fence. Lizzy held her breath while the clowns tried to distract the bull from charging the cowboy.

'Bloody hell,' Lottie cried as the bull hit the fence with force causing the cowboy to jump over to their side. His hat fell off and Lottie picked it up for him.

'Thanks,' he replied before dusting it against his leg and wedging it back on his head.

'This sport is crazy,' said Lottie. 'I think I like it.'

Her eyes were wide and full of energy as she clutched her hands together in her lap.

'*Next up is Luke Wickham on Hellfire.*'

'Oh no!' Lizzy's heart dropped as the announcer's words sank in.

'Is that your fella? What's wrong?' Lottie frowned.

'Hellfire. Luke said he was the meanest bull here and that only the best could ride him. Oh, I hope he doesn't get hurt.'

'Oh my gosh.' Lottie leaned forward, resting her elbows on her knees.

The gate sprang open releasing Hellfire, a dark brown bull with mean-looking eyes. The bull came out thrashing, his body contorting and twisting, his nose snorting as his legs jutted about while Luke clung to his back with one hand.

Lizzy covered her face then spread her fingers to watch Luke's legs pump up and down as he tried to keep the bull's rhythm while his free arm was raised, moving around to keep his balance.

'Why isn't he wearing a helmet like the last two blokes?' Lizzy said almost hysterically. These cowboys were nuts. At least he wore a black padded vest, though if a bull did trample on him she wasn't sure how much that would protect him. The tassels on his black leather chaps danced about with each leap the bull took, up and down, trying to shake Luke free.

A horn sounded and in the next second Luke was trying to free his hand and get off his ride. He had to dart out of the way as Hellfire almost side-swiped him. He was only a few metres from where Lizzy sat and while the clowns and men on horses rounded up Hellfire, Luke took off his glove and threw it to Lizzy. She caught it quickly and he dipped his hat at her before heading over the railing to where the other cowboys gathered.

'Wow-wee, that is some cowboy,' said Lottie, snatching the dirty white leather glove from her hand and fanning herself. 'You weren't wrong. He is sizzle.'

Lizzy snatched the glove back and was watching Luke walk away when she witnessed the strangest thing. Will Darcy was coming the other way with three coffees balanced in his hand and almost collided with Luke. He looked up just as Luke was in front of him and Lizzy saw an apology ready on his lips but then it stopped. She frowned as Will's eyes widened and then his face grew stormy. Not his usual stern expression, but one laced with anger. Unbridled, seething anger. Her heart skipped a beat. This was a side to him she'd not seen, as if he were teetering on the edge of rage.

Luke flicked Will's hat and then moved on, leaving Will standing there looking like he'd seen a ghost. Her breath caught in her throat as she leaned forward, eyes narrowed.

His face had paled. She watched him glance back to Luke, his shoulders tense. Lizzy had never seen this look of disgust before, his lip curled slightly and his eyebrows pinched together. Well, this is something new, Will unable to hide his emotions. Luke and Will knew each other. There was some kind of history there. And she was dying to find out what.

Lizzy raised her hand in a wave as Will continued past them, not even glancing in their direction, which made her feel like a fool. Clearly they weren't friends enough to even get a nod; if she'd been with Jane and Charlie they would have been given a proper greeting. But this was Will. Closed-book Will. It was as if they had never met.

The rest of the cowboys rode, or tried to ride, the bulls, and at one point the crowd gasped in unison as one man was flung so far from the animal that he resembled Superman for half a second before taking a dive into the yellow sand. One of the blokes dressed as a clown rushed to his side but the cowboy got up without any serious injuries, though he did look a little sore as he limped off.

'I'm going to call it: I think your cowboy got the best ride,' said Lottie.

The announcer started rattling off the place getters as the riders walked into the arena to collect their prizes.

'*And the winner of the bull ride, with a sensational ride on Hellfire, is Luke Wickham.*'

Lottie shook her. 'He won! Must be a real cowboy,' she teased.

Luke was looking right at her and when he gave his acceptance speech she was gripping the edge of her seat.

'And I'd like to thank my gorgeous four-leaf clover for all the luck she brought me,' said Luke in his gravelly drawl.

'Oh, I see what you mean about his voice. Hey, is he talking about you in that green dress? He hasn't taken his eyes off you.'

Lizzy felt heat crawl up her neck and enflame her cheeks.

The team roping came on next and it was during the first run that Luke slid next to her on the seat.

'Hello, my lucky lady.'

'Congratulations, Luke. Great win. I'm not sure how you survived but I'm glad you weren't turned into bull dust.' Lottie was leaning forward, openly gawking at Luke and waiting for her introduction. 'Luke, this is my best friend Charlotte.'

'Nice to meet you, Miss,' he said giving her a flirtatious appraisal.

'I'm off to get a drink, would you like one?' asked Lottie standing and straightening the hem of her short white dress.

'Coffee would be great thanks,' said Lizzy even though she knew Lottie was just giving them some space.

Luke shook his head. 'I'm fine, thanks.'

'Lots of pretty ladies about,' he said as they watched Lottie leave.

'Wait until you see my sister,' said Lizzy and pointed out Jane. 'The pretty blonde.'

Luke leaned next to her and looked to where she pointed, and she saw the moment he spotted Jane and then who she was with; felt the change as his body tightened and he sat back. 'You're still prettier,' he said.

Now she knew he was lying but she let it go; it was nice to hear even if she knew it wasn't true. But that wasn't what took her interest at the moment. 'So, I take it you know Will Darcy? I saw you two earlier.'

Luke's blue eyes shifted, as if those snowflakes were slowly spinning. 'Yeah, I know him.'

Lizzy glanced over at Will and smacked into his dark eyes, which were trained on her. He'd been watching them and he didn't look happy. He quickly looked down at his coffee cup, picking at its lid with his long fingers.

'Not a happy reunion earlier, then?' she prodded.

Luke rubbed his chin, it sounded like rubbed sandpaper as his rough hands brushed over his stubble.

'You could say that.' He glanced at her. 'How do you know him?'

'Charlie Bingley bought the farm next to ours.'

He nodded as if the news didn't surprise him. 'More money than sense, that lot. Born with silver spoons in their mouths while the rest of us learn to find our own way.'

'So, what's the story between you two? It looked pretty tense.'

Luke stared at his hands for a moment, picking at an old blister. 'You really want to know?'

When she nodded he sighed and leaned close to her, his voice low. 'I was raised on the Darcy property. My dad was the head overseer. Will

121

and I used to play together when we were little. Then he was sent away to boarding school for six years, and when he came back he was different. Had this arrogant, fancy-school way about him. I stayed and worked real close with his dad before he died. His dad told me I could have some land, but when he died Will wouldn't allow it. Next thing I'm being thrown off the property.'

'What? How come?'

Luke shrugged. 'I think he was just a spoiled rich kid who didn't like how close I was to his dad. He was jealous. With his dad gone he was the boss, and getting rid of me was his first job. He's a dick.'

Lizzy cringed. Luke's words only seemed to make the picture of Will a bit clearer. Having his dad die couldn't have been easy, but to do what he did seemed a bit extreme to Lizzy.

'Anyway, I don't like to talk about it. Best left in the past.' He pointed to the event taking place in the arena. 'Let me tell you about roping,' he said and began to explain what each person was doing to capture the calf.

She spent the rest of the day watching Luke ride, and when he wasn't competing he sought her out to explain the rest of the events or tell her stories from other rodeos he'd competed in. Lottie hung out with them, hoping for a single-cowboy introduction but none came.

'Typical,' she said as the sky grew dark and the stalls had been packed away leaving only the beer tents and food vans. 'Trust you to find the only single bloke left here.'

'I'm sure there'll be a few around the drinking

tent, especially as the band gets going,' said Luke, throwing some hope Lottie's way.

At one point in the afternoon Lydia had spotted Lizzy with Luke and came running up to introduce herself, followed by Kitty.

'Wow, how many sisters do you have?' Luke asked.

'Four. Mary's away at uni.'

'So, five girls in the one family. Crikey!'

'You won the bull riding, didn't you? You're amazing,' said Lydia, fluttering her eyelashes as if someone had pointed a torch right in her eyes. 'You must be so strong to hang on for that long.' She reached across and felt his arm muscles, smiling.

Kitty reached up and plucked his hat from his head, putting it on hers. 'Wow, your hat is cool.'

He smiled and took it back. 'It's a favourite,' he said with a wink.

'Don't you two have better places to be?' Lizzy interjected.

'Nope,' replied Kitty. 'Besides, we've run out of money.'

Lizzy quickly reached into her little leather shoulder bag for her wallet. 'Here, take ten dollars each and go buy some dinner. And check in with Mum and Dad, they'll be wanting to head home by now,' she said putting the money into their grabby little hands.

'Can I buy you and Lottie a drink?' Luke asked when the girls had finally disappeared. 'And then maybe hit you up for a dance?'

He held out both elbows and they took one each. 'Wouldn't say no,' said Lizzy.

'Not to a winning cowboy,' added Lottie.

A big white marquee had been erected for the band. People milled in front of them, waiting and watching as the musicians did their sound checks. The beer tent next door was filled to overflowing, jeans and hats galore, mingling and laughing. There were wine barrels outside, used as tables along with log seats and plastic chairs. Other people stood about in clusters talking and drinking. Lizzy reached up to touch one of the hundreds of fairy lights that had been hung from the beer tent and in nearby trees, twinkling like diamonds on invisible strings. Lizzy, Lottie and Luke moved towards an old metal fire drum that was pouring out heat, glowing red inside and crackling as tiny red embers floated up and vanished in the night sky.

'It's so pretty,' said Lottie. 'We need more nights like these, hey Lizzy?'

She nodded. 'Not much beats camping by a bonfire on a clear-sky night.'

'How about you ladies grab a spot by that drum and I'll navigate the bar and bring us some drinks,' said Luke, dipping his hat as he disappeared into the congested tent.

By the time Luke came back Lizzy was alone.

'Where's your friend?' he asked.

'Whisked off to dance by some random guy.' She pointed her out to Luke. 'Dancing with the bloke who looks like he's doing the funky chicken,' she said with a giggle.

'Oh well, that won't do at all.'

Plonking their beers on a nearby table he took Lizzy's hand and swept her towards the grass that was now a dance floor. The band was playing Lee Kernaghan's 'Boys from the Bush' and coloured lights flashed through the gyrating crowd.

Luke pulled gently, bringing Lizzy up against his warm body and swinging her side to side, occasionally letting her go to fit in a twirl or two. Lizzy laughed, spinning around with her dress flaring out. The lights flashed around them as she leaned back into Luke. His heart was racing, pounding against her own beating chest. She smiled as he squeezed her closer.

Jane and Charlie flashed past, arms draped around each other, then disappeared behind dancing couples. Jane's face was glowing and Lizzy could see that they'd both been laughing. She didn't spot her sister again, until they stopped to finish their drinks. By then Lottie couldn't be seen either.

A whistling noise could suddenly be heard over the music and when the sky exploded with red sparks Lizzy jumped.

'Oh my gosh, I wasn't ready for that,' she said as another firework sailed into the air and blasted green sparks that lit up the night. 'Wow.'

The band stopped playing and everyone turned their heads skywards, mouths open, eyes wide and reflecting the colours of the fireworks.

Lizzy felt arms around her as Luke pulled her to him so her back pressed against his chest. As it was getting cooler, his body heat was welcome.

After the impressive display the sky grew dark and the crowd fell eerily quiet, a little delay before the noise started up again.

'That's the first time I've ever seen fireworks,' she admitted to Luke. She stepped out of his embrace and faced him.

'You're kidding?'

She smiled. 'No. Only what I've seen on TV from New Year's Eve. It was pretty cool.'

'You must get to see some in the city,' he said. 'They are cool. This was just a little taste.'

He licked his lips as he gazed at her.

'Lizzy,' said Jane, coming over to where they stood near a wine barrel. 'Finally I found you.'

They hugged each other. 'Luke, this is my sister Jane.'

Jane smiled at him. 'Hi Luke.'

'Nice to meet you, Jane. Would you like a drink? I'm off to grab another one.'

Both girls shook their heads. He dipped his hat and headed to the bar.

'Where's Charlie?' asked Lizzy, looking around. 'I saw you dancing before.'

'Yes, until the fireworks. How awesome were they? After that he left with Will and Caroline. They'd had enough,' she said.

The slight droop in her shoulders and press of her lips told Lizzy that Jane was upset he'd left.

'You really like him, don't you?' she said, leaning close so she could whisper it.

Jane smiled and nodded. 'I want to go back to the ute and sleep. Can I grab the keys, please?'

'Oh okay, I'll come with you.'

'I don't want to ruin your night.' Jane put up a hand to stop her. 'You stay.'

'It's been a great day and I don't want you to be alone. Besides, it's way past my bedtime.' And with that she yawned. 'I'll just wait to tell Luke.'

The firelight from the drums danced across his snowflake eyes as he returned ten minutes later.

'Hey Luke, we're going to head off now. I just wanted to say a big thank you for today. You made it the best rodeo I've ever been to.' Lizzy tucked her hair behind her ear and smiled at him.

'You sure you won't stay for another dance?'

He looked crestfallen and she almost reconsidered, but leaving Jane alone wasn't an option. 'I'm sorry. But I hope we run into each other, especially if you do decide to hang around. Can I get your number?'

'Sure,' he said slowly. 'I'm not that good with phones, so if you don't hear from me at some point just assume I've lost it, or broken it,' he said sheepishly. 'I'd hate you to think I was ignoring you.' He pulled out his phone, an old model Samsung. 'Can you put it in?'

'No worries,' she said entering her details. 'What's your number?'

'Um, it's written on the back of the phone.'

She flipped it over, saw the number written in white out and entered it into her phone.

'Thanks Luke. I had a great time. You'll have to come and visit us on our farm, we'll cook you up a feast.'

When Luke took her hand she thought he was going to kiss it again, but instead he tugged on it, pulling her closer to plant a kiss on her lips.

'That sounds like a plan. See you around, my lucky lady.'

'Bye Luke.'

Jane took her arm and they headed off into the darkness.

'Wow, he's a charmer,' said Jane. 'It's nice to see you happy.'

'I had fun. Have you seen Lottie? It's so busy, it's hard to find anyone.'

'Last I saw her she was talking with Ken Collins,' said Jane.

Lizzy frowned. 'Man, I'm a bad friend. I get side-tracked with Luke and she gets cornered by Ken. I must apologise later.'

They huddled closer together and took slower steps as the dark engulfed them. The band lights had faded away and now they relied on the stars and the shine of the moon off the vehicles to find their way to the ute.

'I'm glad I didn't let you go alone,' said Lizzy.

'So am I. We overheard an official talking to a police officer, saying that some things had been stolen from some cars and horse floats.'

Lizzy scoffed. 'No way! Out here? No one steals stuff out here. What is the world coming to? Maybe it's the druggies getting about.'

Jane shivered against her. 'Another reason not to be out here alone. Lizzy, can we just drive home instead? I haven't been drinking, I don't mind driving.'

Lizzy spotted her ute ten metres away and they suddenly increased their pace. The dark was cold and it felt like it had eyes. 'Don't have to ask me twice. Let's go home.'

9

His ears twitched, then he glanced left as if hearing something, but Lizzy remained quiet as she watched the joey kangaroo no more than fifteen metres away. Right near their shed was a small section of bush, and sometimes the kangaroos that lived nearby came in for a look. This cute little guy must be out exploring, she thought as she marvelled at him. She saw kangaroos all the time around the farm but it was still exciting to be so close to one. The afternoon sun was warm, only a smattering of white wispy clouds up above but a strong breeze gusted past, swirling up dust and loose leaves. The joey moved his head again and then took a few bounces closer to Lizzy as he heard the approaching vehicle. She could see him more clearly now, his brown fur and big blinking eyes with the longest eyelashes she'd seen. He rocked backwards, leaning his weight on his strong tail before Jane's car came into view and he took off with a jolt, his bounces erratic and new as he darted through the scrub.

Jane pulled up near Lizzy and leaned out the window.

'Hey, how's it going? You look busy,' she teased as she took in the sight of Lizzy crouched down on the gravel out the front of the shed.

'I was just watching the joey.'

'Oh, I missed him,' Jane replied as she stepped

out of the car. She was dressed in a pretty white top and stylish blue culottes that billowed out around her ankles.

'Anyway,' said Lizzy, 'I've just finished replacing a roller bearing on the comb. It wasn't good, fell to bits. Lucky we didn't end up with a header fire last year.'

Jane's hand went to her mouth. 'Oh no, that was a lucky escape.' She touched Lizzy's face and smiled. 'You have grease all over you.'

'What's new, hey?' Lizzy bent down to the comb front and put the lever back in its place then tightened the belt. 'So, how was your sleepover at Charlie's last night? I've been dying to ask,' she said as she dusted off her hands.

Jane's face flushed. 'It was lovely.'

'*Lovely?*' Her eyebrows shot up.

'Lizzy,' Jane said, glancing around, but no one was nearby. 'Well, it was nice being alone in the house with Will and Caroline gone.'

'Where were they?' Lizzy asked, slightly irritated by her own curiosity.

'Not sure, both had something on or somewhere to be. But I didn't have to tiptoe around, and I could relax with Charlie. We had a romantic dinner, watched a movie snuggled up on his couch and . . . ' She smiled, her eyes twinkling.

'I can guess,' she said. Her sister's face took on a wistful glow. 'Maybe I don't want to know,' she laughed.

'It was perfect, beautiful and sweet. It was hard to leave for work this morning.'

'I bet. Mum gave me twenty questions on

where you were. So, expect more when you walk in. Anyway, how were the kids today?' Lizzy had an image of Jane floating into the childcare centre, radiating smiles and sorting the kids without a care in the world. Lizzy wondered if she'd ever have that after-sex glow. She tried to tell herself that the farm was enough but every now and then she found herself thinking that it would be better with someone special to share it with.

Jane rolled her eyes. 'It was all going fine until I turned my back to take Max to the toilet, and within about ten seconds Zane had put glue and glitter all through his little sister's hair. I swear I need six eyes and ten hands to keep things kosher.'

'I think you are a wonder woman. I'd much rather play with machinery than a room full of snotty kids,' said Lizzy. 'You have the patience of a saint. Ready for a cuppa?'

'Actually, I can't stay. I just came to bring these.' Jane looked down at the cards in her hand before passing them to Lizzy. 'They're from Charlie.'

The top envelope was addressed to Jane and Lizzy. The invitation was fancy, handmade with care, but Lizzy couldn't imagine Charlie or Caroline making them. Probably paid someone to do them. Across the top it read *Bingley Barbecue*.

'He wants to celebrate buying Netherfield,' Jane said, 'make it feel like home, bring some of the locals together. He hopes they'll start to see him as part of the community.'

'Did he have to invite the rest of our family, though?' said Lizzy with a sigh. The other invitation was made out to *Mr and Mrs Bennet and family*. 'Lydia is going to love this.'

Jane's brow creased. 'I know.'

'Can't you pass on all the colds from the kids to her and Kitty, then they might be too sick to go,' said Lizzy with a laugh. Oh, if only it were that easy. 'I wish Luke was going. I'd be happier about turning up. I guess Will Darcy will be there?'

'I think he will be, yes.' Jane took the invitations back. 'I don't get it, though. If Will's such a horrible person how come he's Charlie's best friend? He can't be that bad, surely?'

Lizzy shrugged. 'Maybe Charlie gets the best of him because he fits Will's idea of an acceptable friend.'

'You think Will is that arrogant?'

'Oh Jane, you don't believe anyone's bad,' Lizzy said affectionately. 'But Will Darcy is yet to prove me wrong.'

'Will you still come with me, please? I don't want to go alone, especially if the rest of the family go.' She grimaced. 'Charlie wants me to meet his parents.'

Fear flitted across Jane's face and Lizzy felt the tug on her heart. There was no way she could disappoint her sister. 'Of course I will. Do we have to dress up?' she asked, pulling a face.

'Only a little, whatever you're comfortable in.' Jane smiled. 'Yes, your jeans will be fine.'

Lizzy did a little dance. 'Sweet. All right, I better keep going. I want to get the other bearings checked before dinner.'

'Got much to do before it's ready for harvest?'

'Lots. The tin on the auger has worn through, it leaked so much grain last year. The rest we can't afford to fix and just have to hope the belts and tyres last. We are getting there, Jane, we just need another good year and we'll start to climb out of the red.'

'Good. I hope it is. I know how much this place means to you. To all of us.'

As Lizzy watched Jane drive back to the house she felt the weight of the Bennets on her shoulders. She wasn't working so hard to keep the farm just for herself, but for her parents and her sisters. It was their home, had always been and none of them wanted to leave. During harvest Kitty and Lydia took turns driving the chaser bin. Margaret cooked and fed them all, delivering meals to the paddock and shifting field bins. When Jane wasn't at work she helped in so many ways to keep them all going: cleaning, checking on sheep and often sitting on the header with Lizzy to keep her company at the end of a long day. So, it wasn't just Lizzy who was passionate about the farm. As much as Lydia and Kitty were slackers in the sense of being normal teenagers, they did get off their butts to help more than most kids their age. Even if they moved away for work in later years the farm would still be home, and no one liked the thought of it not being there.

Her thoughts were interrupted by her phone beeping. Wiping her hand on her jeans she pulled it from her pocket.

Hey lucky charm, I got that harvest job. I'm driving for Jacob Elliot. Just having to upgrade my licence to drive the road train. In the meantime I'm doing some odd jobs about the place.

Lizzy smiled and sent one back.

That's cool, Luke. Jacob carts our grain, so that means you might be out our way a bit.

Luke wasn't on social media — Lydia had checked every Luke Wickham on every media platform — and he wasn't great on a phone either, much like herself, but they had managed to keep in sporadic touch. She smiled down at her phone. The idea of seeing Luke again made her belly flutter.

Lizzy finished checking the bearings and made it back to the house just on dark. The air was starting to be tinged with the coolness of night and the stars were starting to twinkle and yet there was enough light that she could still take in the landscape, which was like a sleeping giant. She knew every rise and fall of the terrain around her and felt the stars guide her home. Today the closer to home the stronger the scent grew of an Indian market with curry powder, turmeric, cumin and ginger.

'Oh that smells so good, Mum.'

Margaret, decked out in a frilly pink apron, was by the stove putting rice in a pot to boil. Kitty was setting the table, no doubt under protest judging by her dropped bottom lip and sloth-like movements.

'Chicken curry for dinner. Go and shower, you have time,' Margaret said, smiling back at Lizzy.

'Thanks, Mum.'

In her room she found Jane reading. 'Hey, did Lottie get an invite to the barbecue, do you know?'

Jane shrugged. 'I'm not sure. I think it was mainly neighbours and . . . ' Her cheeks tinged pink.

'And the more influential people in the community?'

'Umm, maybe. But I can ask him to send her an invite. Was she annoyed that we left her at the rodeo?'

'No, turns out she had a fab time without me. Her text the next day was a little cryptic — maybe she found a nice guy.'

'You haven't asked her?'

'Nah,' said Lizzy. 'I didn't want to pry. Lottie will tell me when she's ready.'

'So, do you want me to ask if Charlie can invite her if he hasn't already?'

'Please? I know she'd love to go. I'll owe you one,' said Lizzy.

Jane's laugh was soft like falling snow. 'No, dear sister, this is just an even-up. Who came to look after me when I was sick and stayed in hostile territory with Will Darcy?'

Lizzy grinned, her hands on her hips. 'Ha, true.'

Without another word Jane started texting Charlie, so Lizzy gathered her blue striped fleecy pyjamas and fluffy socks, and headed to the shower.

★ ★ ★

'Did you see, John? Did you see the invite to the Bingley property for a barbecue on the weekend? And Mary will be home for it. Oh, how wonderful!'

'Yes, dear,' he replied while scraping the enamel off his bowl in an attempt to get the final crumbs of his dessert. 'You showed it to me twice already. I don't think I have Alzheimer's yet.' John put down his spoon and squinted at Margaret. 'But remind me, who are you again?'

Jane and Lizzy stifled smiles as their mum rolled her eyes.

'Don't you mock, John,' Margaret replied with only feigned annoyance and she bustled back to the kitchen bench. 'Well, I'm very excited to be invited to the Bingleys'. The girls at the CWA are all very jealous, none of them got invites.'

Jane leaned over to Lizzy. 'At least the invitation got Mum off my back about staying with Charlie.'

'Twenty questions when you got in the door?'

'More like a hundred,' Jane said ruefully. She stood up and collected their plates. 'I'm going to do the dishes and then call Charlie.'

Lizzy nodded as she got up and pushed in her chair. Lydia and Kitty were already back by the TV watching some reality show and complaining loudly. 'She looks like a tart! That lipstick is *so* wrong for her. He should go with Sarah, she has *much* better taste in fashion,' said Lydia. Kitty mumbled an agreement.

'I'm off to do the BAS. Night, all.' Lizzy smiled at her dad.

'I'll bring you a coffee in a minute if you like?'

offered Jane, turning from the sink, a tea towel over her shoulder.

'Thanks, that would be great.'

Lizzy collected a few things from the makeshift office in the TV area and took them to the quiet of her room. Where Jane had a little make-up desk, Lizzy had one opposite for bookwork. She would move the whole office in here if it would fit but their room was cramped enough as it was.

Throwing the box on her desk she started to pull the bills out one by one and sort them along with bank statements and the cheque book.

'I think this headache calls for some tunes.'

KIAN's 'Waiting' was the first to play.

'Much better.'

She signed off the BAS form just as the last song on her playlist, Tom Walker's 'Leave a Light On', started. And she was the only one in the house with a light left on.

10

'Oh Mary is home! Mary is here!' shouted Margaret from the back door, flapping her hands as if she were trying to take flight.

It was Saturday morning, they had an hour before they were due at the Bingley barbecue and Mary had arrived just in time.

Jane and Lizzy headed outside, jumping off the back verandah as Mary climbed out of her little white hatchback.

'Hi sis,' said Lizzy.

Mary turned around at the open car door, tucking her fringe of soft dark hair behind her ear, the rest held up high on her head in a loose bun. She had Lizzy's brown eyes but Jane's sharper features except her style preference was secondhand vintage. Like today's outfit which was no doubt from her favourite recycling shop, a long-sleeved brown blouse with white dots matched with a corduroy green skirt that went to her knees.

'Hello Lizzy, hello Jane,' Mary said with a yawn. 'That drive doesn't get any shorter. But it's good to be back.'

She gave her sisters a quick hug, which was more a pat on the back.

'She's home, finally,' said John, coming to stand behind Lizzy. 'How's it all going?' He reached out to carry her small bag.

'Studies are good, Dad. I've started up piano

tutoring as well and it's going well.'

Margaret pulled Mary into a hug. 'So good to see you. And you're just in time to come with us to the Bingley barbecue.'

'We can't wait,' said Lydia, who had arrived with Kitty in tow. 'We spent all yesterday trying to decide what to wear.'

Mary's dark eyes glanced at Lizzy to interpret. 'The what?'

'You remember, dear, I rang and told you all about our new neighbours,' said Margaret.

Lizzy had to hide her amusement as Mary's lips pressed tightly and her gaze went to the ground.

'Um sorry, it must have slipped my mind,' Mary said. 'Can't I just stay here? I'm only here the one night. I have to be back tomorrow night ready for class on Monday.'

'Oh come on, it's just lunch. You'll be able to catch up with everyone all at once.'

Mary sighed. Out of them all, Mary handled public outings the worst. When she was little she'd often be found under a table reading a book. Later, when Lydia and Kitty started getting into trouble, it was Mary who would dob them in as if she were the law.

'Maybe you could play for us all?' said Margaret.

Jane and Lizzy exchanged a glance and only just managed to avoid a mutual eye roll at their mother's cunning.

'I *do* need to practise while I'm home,' said Mary, suddenly brighter.

Margaret clapped, much the way she did in

the sheep yards when penning up. 'Come along, all of you. We must get ready. I want you all in something nice, we can't look like the poor threadbare neighbours.'

Margaret pointed at the shirt Lizzy was wearing: it was covered in tiny grinding holes and was torn at the side where she'd caught it on a protruding bolt.

'But I love this shirt. I was going to wear this with my jeans,' said Lizzy, trying to be serious while she wanted to laugh.

Margaret wasn't fooled this time. Instead she pointed at John. 'She takes after you. See what you've created?' With a half-hearted huff she headed back inside the house.

'Not much has changed,' said Mary as she carefully stepped towards the house.

'I've got another holey shirt if you'd like to borrow it, Jane. We could be matching,' said Lizzy with a chuckle.

John reached over and put his arm around Lizzy's shoulders then dragged her against his warm, squishy body. The familiar scent of his aftershave wrapped around her like an extra arm.

'You'll get me into trouble,' he said.

'More trouble, you mean? You seem to find it quite easy without my help.'

He let her go, gently pushing her forward. 'Go on, get, you rascal. I need to go find my best suit to wear.'

★ ★ ★

'Are you nervous?'

Jane gave Lizzy a strained smile. 'Is it that obvious? I'm petrified. His parents are going to be there. What if the poor-neighbour-girl doesn't pass inspection?'

Lizzy understood now why Jane had gone with the floor-length cream dress with a long beaded blue necklace and blue shoes. Knowing Jane, she'd probably googled stylish outfits to make sure she was dressed appropriately. Even on a budget Jane could find something simple and make it more.

Jane let Lizzy wear her faded blue jeans but found a cream singlet and a soft khaki jacket to go over it. Teamed with sunglasses and tan ankle boots and a leather belt, Lizzy felt stylish and comfortable — a combination that didn't happen very often.

'Jane, you look amazing and Charlie adores you nearly as much as I do. His parents will love you. Just relax and be you,' said Lizzy with a smile.

'I hope Lydia and Kitty can behave.'

'Hopefully Mary can help keep a lid on their enthusiasm.'

Jane breathed out and adjusted her hands on the steering wheel. 'Yes, that's true.'

Lizzy tried to keep up some relaxed banter to keep Jane's mind busy but as they drove up to the Netherfield house she fell silent.

'Oh my god, is this even the same house we were at not that long ago?' Lizzy's mouth fell open. The big white homestead had been transformed. A fresh coat of paint made it pop out from a manicured garden.

'They must have had a whole army working on that garden. Look at the lawn, it's perfect.' Jane had slowed right down as they stared out the window.

Cars were parked near a new white picket fence as if directed into position. As Jane parked near the last car, Lizzy turned in her seat to look back at the house.

'Did you see the deck area off to the side?'

As they walked towards the house, where people were mingling on some of the lawn and the new deck area, Lizzy's eye was caught by the shed opposite the house.

'Oh wow. That looks like some shiny new harvest equipment. Do you think they'd mind if I snuck away from the party and went exploring?' Lizzy was now really envious.

'Sh. First we must greet and meet then eat.'

'Ha, I'm not one of your two year olds you can distract with a rhyme,' said Lizzy pouting.

Jane smiled, a brief relief from her nerves.

Lizzy saw Charlie darting across to them, his smile radiant and his eyes only for Jane.

'Finally you're here. You can help remind me who everyone is,' he said, reaching for her hand and giving her a quick kiss on the cheek. 'Hi Lizzy. Don't you two look gorgeous today?'

'Not as gorgeous as those shiny toys you have in your shed,' said Lizzy with a nod in their direction.

Charlie laughed. 'Trust you to spot them.'

'Any chance I could have a looksee at some point? I promise I won't drive off in one, but I can't promise there won't be drool left behind.' She smiled up at him as sweetly as she could.

'Yeah, sure. You have free rein to wander and look at anything you like.' He turned his attention back to Jane. 'Can I get you a drink first? There are some nibblies going around and the meat is nearly ready.'

They nodded and Lizzy followed Jane and Charlie over to a table set up on the verandah where a man was filling up wine glasses and handing out cold beers from huge ice-filled eskies behind him.

'Champagne, white or red?' Charlie asked.

'Beer for me, please,' said Lizzy while Jane took a glass of white wine.

'Now, best I introduce you to my parents.'

Lizzy had hoped he meant just Jane but he gave her a nod to follow, so she joined them as they made their way around the side of the house to the back lawn, where blue striped padded chairs and an outdoor couch were positioned for optimum conversation. Gorgeous lanterns were scattered around and bright flowers sat in jar glasses on tables and next to chairs to add pops of colour. Charlie stopped in front of a well-dressed man and woman, in their fifties Lizzy guessed, who were sitting in lush seats and chatting quietly.

'Mum and Dad,' he said, the slight quaver in his voice surprising Lizzy, 'I'd like you to meet Jane and Lizzy Bennet, our neighbours. Ladies, these are my parents, Collette and Tony Bingley.'

'Nice to meet you both,' said Lizzy locking her knees together so she didn't accidentally curtsy.

'So, this is Jane?' said Collette, not moving from her seat. 'The one you are supposedly dating?'

'Yes, Mum.'

'Nice to meet you, Mrs . . . um . . . Collette,' stuttered Jane, her cheeks staining red.

Collette hardly acknowledged Jane. 'I thought you and Alyssa were trying again?' she said, looking only at her son. 'When I saw her last week she seemed to think you were making progress.'

Charlie frowned. 'Mum, I told you we are over,' he said nervously, glancing to Jane.

'Lovely girl Alyssa, like my own daughter,' Collette said to no one in particular. 'Her mother and I have been best friends for years.'

Lizzy wanted to storm off with Jane, or tell this woman in no uncertain terms to get some manners, she couldn't decide. Jane had turned from red to white, making Lizzy's anger flare.

'Dad, you should talk to Lizzy, she's very clued up on farming,' said Charlie quickly. He kept shooting glances at Jane, his brow creasing more each time.

'Oh, I don't want to bore the girl with farm talk on a nice day like this,' said Tony. 'Caroline would be better suited. Where has she disappeared to?'

'She's checking on the caterer, dear. I'll go see if she needs help.'

Tony stood and helped Collette up from the chair. She smoothed out her dress and glanced at them. 'Lovely to meet you both.' Then she headed off into the house.

Tony remained standing for the moment then gestured to the chairs. 'Please take a seat. Relax. And tell me, Jane, what do you do?'

Charlie's mouth moved, wanting to answer for Jane but he remained silent. Jane took her time to answer. Lizzy could see her hands shaking and wanted so badly to hold her.

'I run the local childcare centre,' she said softly.

Tony nodded. 'Well, that would take courage, a room full of small children is no small feat. And you, Lizzy?'

Lizzy was surprised he'd remembered her name, but he looked like the kind of man who took pride in such things, if only to impress or for business interactions.

'I work at Longbourn.'

'Helping your father?' he queried.

Lizzy half-shrugged. 'We work together.'

Tony frowned as if not fully understanding what she meant. 'You do the bookwork?'

'Well, yes, but also the day-to-day running of the farm. Repairs, harvest, seeding.'

He looked surprised. 'Caroline does a few things, errands mainly or occasionally opening a gate, but she doesn't like to break her nails.'

Lizzy smiled and held out her hands. 'As you can see it doesn't worry me.' Her nails were short, her hands calloused and worn like old leather. They said more than words could.

He studied them, and this time he seemed to understand.

'How do you get around heavy issues?'

Charlie shuffled his feet and shot Lizzy an

apologetic smile. 'Dad is from the era where women make the best housewives and a man tends the fields,' he said.

'I'm not *that* old, Charlie. I'm just curious how Lizzy goes about the physical stuff.'

'And you're right, Tony. Women simply aren't built like men in terms of strength, but I have tricks to help me. I haven't encountered a problem I couldn't sort. Plus, Dad's there to lend extra muscle if I need it. But I prefer to tackle most issues on my own. I find great satisfaction from accomplishing jobs myself.'

Tony nodded in agreement but still seemed fascinated by the idea.

Lizzy took in the crowd, mainly the important people of the town, the Shire President and CEO, the local contracting boss and other neighbours plus the wealthier farmers from the area. Lizzy even spotted Ken Collins talking to Will. Now that was an unlikely matching and Lizzy had to stifle a smile. What would Will think of him?

Will stood taller than Ken. He wore black pants with a white dress shirt tucked in but two buttons were undone revealing a portion of caramel skin. Lizzy blinked the vision away and continued her inspection. Over his shirt he wore a grey suit jacket with a fine white pinstripe, and black leather shoes finished his ensemble. He didn't fit the traditional mould of a farmer. He seemed to speak like one at times, which to Lizzy just made him all the more confusing. When he looked over and saw her watching him his lips tugged at the side in almost a smile.

146

If he wanted saving from Ken, it wouldn't be from her.

Lizzy turned back to Tony and Charlie and tried to partake in small talk until there was a disturbance that started to catch people's attention.

Tony screwed up his face as he leaned forward to see what everyone else was looking at. 'What *is* that noise?' he asked.

Lizzy frowned and turned to Jane with a raised eyebrow. She couldn't hear anything . . . and then it sank in. Maybe over the years she'd tuned out, developing an immunity to the cries of her younger siblings.

Oh no, mouthed Jane.

Lizzy hunched over in the chair, too afraid to even look in the direction of Lydia and Kitty, who were squabbling with Margaret about why they couldn't have a glass of wine — especially because it was *free*.

'But Mum, I'm nearly eighteen! You can't stop me,' said Kitty.

Margaret sighed and glanced around before saying, 'Only one.'

'Aw, that's not fair! If Kitty can have one why can't I?' demanded Lydia.

Lizzy felt her stomach roll upon seeing Lydia in itty-bitty denim shorts, heels and a low-cut gold shimmery top.

'Please god, don't let her bend over,' whispered Lizzy only loudly enough for her sister to hear.

Jane spun around in the chair to see for herself. 'Oh *no*,' she groaned audibly this time.

There was nothing they could do except cringe. 'At least Dad didn't wear his suit.' Well, he'd worn the pants and shirt, leaving the suit jacket behind. Margaret, on the other hand, wore a feathered hat as if she were off to Oaks Day at Flemington.

'Jesus, who is *that*?' asked Tony.

Charlie took his arm. 'Come on, Dad, I'll introduce you.'

He glanced at Jane but she was too busy looking into her lap to notice. Lizzy gave him a smile of thanks.

'Hey, you two look as if someone died.'

Lizzy looked up to see her best friend standing before them. 'Oh, am I glad to see you.' She stood up and motioned for Lottie to take her place. 'Can you keep Jane company, please? I need to get some fresh air.'

'We're outside already.'

'Then somewhere far, far away from . . . this,' she said gesturing to the party. 'I need to cool off,' she said curtly. Her blood pressure was still sky high thanks to Collette.

Lottie nodded. 'You go. Jane and I can play spot-the-fashion-fraud,' she said with a smirk.

Jane sipped her wine as Lizzy left, picking up another beer on her way past the table. She would need another ten to make her feel better about being here. On the upside, the nice green-and-white header was very welcoming. She made her way to the shed, eyes drawn to the front wheels that resembled tracks on an army tank. It was a 780 model Claas Header, and on closer inspection she saw that it wasn't brand new. Still, she gauged this one to be worth half a million at least.

She whistled as she closed her hand around the step rail. 'Permission to board,' she said as she launched herself up the ladder, six steps to the top.

'Not planning on stealing it, are you?'

Lizzy swore and spun around, nearly dropping her beer. Quickly she placed it down on the platform. Will Darcy stood just below the ladder looking up at her with those dark unreadable eyes. 'You making sure I don't?'

He half-shrugged, his eyes never leaving her face.

'Charlie said I could take a look, and I'm going to do just that,' she said turning around and opening the door.

Inside it was like another world. A seat that was actually comfortable and strange buttons and bits. It was so different from Longbourn's old basic header with aircon that kept dying and rotors so out of balance she felt like she was sitting on a washing machine the whole day.

She put her hand on the controller, like a joystick. In theory they were all similar, this one probably came with a million more little adjustments to get a better crop sample.

'Do you want to start it up?'

Lizzy startled again. *Damn him.* 'I thought you'd gone back to the party?' she shot back accusingly, her teeth gnashing together slightly. He was ruining her magical moment.

'Seeing your face looking at this header is much more fun,' he said flatly.

She couldn't tell if he was serious or teasing.

The cab was suddenly filled with his leathery cologne. For a moment she lost all thought, made worse when his arm brushed across her to start the header.

All thoughts of Will, though, vanished as the Claas purred. 'Oh my god, it's so cool.'

Without being asked, Will took her through its running operations. She was glued to every word, fascinated by the technology. 'It's amazing. Not that I need to know any of it. My little New Holland is not far from retirement as paddock scraps.' She frowned, glancing at Will. 'You seem to know a lot about this one.'

'I was there when Charlie bought it. It's the 2013 model, but it'll serve him well here. I use the same on my properties.'

His properties. Plural. Suddenly the cab seemed too small. Lizzy turned off the header and shooed Will out of the seat.

'I want to get out.' *And drink my beer.*

When they both reached the ground Will's phone beeped.

'It's Caroline wondering where I am. She needs help with the meat.'

'Well, you best go,' said Lizzy. She tried waving him off again.

His hands flexed at his sides and his lips moved slightly in that quirky way of his, like he was going to say something but didn't. Finally he turned and took a step, but then he paused and glanced back at her. She frowned at him, which made him turn back and continue all the way to the house.

150

Lizzy skolled some of her beer and when he was finally from her view she sagged back against the header. 'Well, that was awkward.' With a shake of her head, and a weird goose-bump tingle over her body she pushed it all from her mind and walked over to the next shiny toy. A big green chaser bin.

11

Lizzy returned to the barbecue reluctantly and only because Jane had messaged saying lunch was ready and she didn't want to eat alone.

The food was served by staff in a buffet style on the verandah.

'Wow, the food is amazing,' said Jane as she glanced at Lizzy's plate of roast beef, potatoes and colourful salad creations.

'I know. Can't wait to eat it,' she replied. Already her mouth was watering, eager to dig in.

Lizzy turned to leave from the buffet and nearly ran into Will.

'Sorry, Lizzy,' he said steadying her with a warm hand on her shoulder.

She was surprised he'd spoken, more so at the apology. He glanced at her plate then back up to her face and then withdrew his hand awkwardly.

'No food dropped, all is okay,' she said with a half-hearted smile. 'So, I see you know Luke Wickham?' she blurted out suddenly. 'He's staying around here for a bit, did you know?'

The light that had been in his eyes was suddenly snuffed out. His neck muscles strained as he moved his head; it was like he'd just swallowed something awful.

'I wish I didn't know him,' he muttered.

'He had a bit to say about you,' she countered.

Will shoved his hands into his pants. 'That doesn't surprise me. He loves to talk. Could sell ice to eskimos. Makes friends as quickly as he loses them.'

She frowned. 'At least he can make friends,' she replied. *And isn't a snob.* 'He doesn't rub people up the wrong way either,' she added.

'You'd do best to stay away from him.'

Her mouth dropped open. Who did he think he was, warning her off Luke? 'You may think you control everything, but you don't control *me*,' she spat, then walked off muttering under her breath until she plonked down next to Jane at the long table set up on the lawn, complete with a white linen table cloth and blue napkins. It was so prettily decorated Lizzy felt like she was at a wedding. A shame Will had put her in a foul mood, yet again.

'How fancy are the plates,' whispered Jane.

The blue patterned plates and heavy silver cutlery were set off perfectly by the bouquets of blue flowers placed every so often along the table. Charlie sat near the end with his parents and Jane beside him. Opposite Lizzy was Caroline, who was taking photo after photo of the table set-up. 'It's for my Insta page. You should follow it; I have six thousand followers,' she said smugly.

'I wouldn't follow her to water in a dry desert,' Lizzy said quietly enough for just Jane to hear.

Much to her dislike, Will pulled out the chair beside Caroline.

Luckily Lydia and Kitty were down the end far from their ears.

Her dad was to her right and Margaret was on his right talking excitedly to her friend Mrs

Bowman, wife of the Shire President.

'Such a beautiful day, and this lunch is divine. How lucky are we,' Margaret said with a chuckle.

As Lizzy dug into her meal, intent on enjoying every bite, she was caught between two conversations: her mother's voice chattered on one side while Lizzy heard Collette speak to Jane.

'So Jane, what do you do? Do you live in town?' She was daintily sawing some of her meat into bite-sized pieces.

'I run the local childcare centre and I'm still at home,' said Jane quietly. 'It helps the family,' she added quickly.

John cleared his throat beside Lizzy but didn't say a word.

'We all pitch in to help keep the family farm going,' said Lizzy firmly when she caught Tony's frown.

'Have you thought of selling the farm?' Tony asked John. 'You only have daughters.'

Lizzy bit her tongue.

'It's not my farm to sell,' said John matter-of-factly, looking calmly at Tony as he continued. 'It belongs to my girls. It's up to them.'

Lizzy smiled, proud of her dad.

'Even if you're struggling?' replied Tony.

A red mist clouded her mind and it took all her effort not to jump down his throat. It was no secret they were struggling, but anyone who mattered also knew that they were working hard to rectify it and forge a future for Longbourn. Filled with sudden anger, Lizzy put her fork down with a clatter and leaned forward, eyeballing Tony.

'You know as well as most that farming isn't a sure bet. Mother Nature holds most of the power, and we were unlucky to have some bad years back to back: drought, floods, frosts, hail. But we haven't given up. We're working hard. Longbourn's our home, and I plan to see it come back to its full potential,' said Lizzy forcefully. 'Selling is not an option,' she added. 'We won't be pushed off our own land. Not by anyone.'

Tony raised his eyebrows but didn't reply. She glanced around the table and caught Will watching her with something in his eyes. Empathy? Support? Admiration even? She couldn't figure it out but whatever it was felt strange coming from him. But at that moment it was enough to make her feel a little calmer.

Lizzy picked her fork back up and stabbed at her meat, feeling less hungry now but she shoved some in her mouth anyway.

'Oh, didn't you know, Doris?' said Margaret, unaware of the stony silence that had taken over the end of the table. 'Yes, our Jane is with Charlie Bingley. Such a beautiful couple. They would make gorgeous babies,' she said, her voice beaming with pride.

Lizzy watched Will turn his head slightly, his attention caught on their conversation. It was hard not to; Margaret Bennet had an overpowering voice.

'How lucky we were to have a wealthy, handsome lad move next door. Finding husbands out here is hard. Lizzy is the one I worry the most about.'

Can I die now? Lizzy glanced at Jane. She had

laid her cutlery across her nearly empty plate and was staring at it. Charlie cleared his throat and began to tell Tony about his next plans for Netherfield.

'Last week Caroline attended a party in Melbourne and met Curtis Stone,' Collette said loudly to anyone who would listen. 'And then she was at Kate Ritchie's book launch.'

'Yes, it was a beautiful event. Kate wore a gorgeous white Lisa Ho dress. She looked stunning as always,' preened Caroline.

Lizzy tried not to roll her eyes, trying instead to feel grateful that the Bingley women were at least drowning out Margaret, but it did nothing to alleviate the irritation she felt.

'I was looking at the crops yesterday. Some of the leaves had chunks missing from the side and splits down the middle,' Charlie told his father.

'It might be boron,' said Lizzy, who couldn't help but overhear. Their conversation was much more interesting than Caroline rabbiting on about the pink Jimmy Choo shoes she'd picked up last time she was in the city.

Tony and Charlie glanced at her.

'Does it look like sawtooth notchings along the edge of the leaf?' she asked. Charlie nodded. 'And would it be in sandy, more acidic parts of the paddock?'

Tony glanced at Charlie, who nodded again.

'Sounds like boron to me. You could try a foliar but the timing of application needs to be right to avoid damage.'

Charlie was smiling ear to ear. 'I told you, Dad, Lizzy knows what she's talking about.'

Tony shook his head, clearly still coming to terms with the notion of a female farmer. 'I still put trust in our agronomist, he's the one with the qualifications. He's been with us for years.'

She nodded. 'If that's what works for you. Personally I love learning about how to read the plants. It's no different from Mum knowing which manures make her celery grow the best or when the nematodes have got her tomatoes.'

Everyone was now looking at her, and suddenly she felt like she was drowning under the weight of them. Pushing her chair back, she stood and collected plates from Jane and their father.

'Lizzy, leave that. The staff will be out shortly,' said Collette.

'It's okay, I know where the kitchen is,' she replied and headed inside to safety.

Lizzy introduced herself to the woman in the kitchen who seemed surprised when Lizzy started to help stack the dishwasher.

'Thanks Lizzy, I'm Clara, but you don't have to do that. I'm getting paid.'

Lizzy laughed. 'Well, you couldn't pay me to go back out there right now. It's much nicer in here.'

She reached for another plate to scrape just as Will stepped inside with more plates.

'Thank you, Clara.'

She smiled up at him, batting her eyelashes. 'No worries Mr Darcy.'

Will glanced to Lizzy, but she just stared back at him as she went about cleaning dishes. She raised her eyebrows, almost challenging him to say something.

'Will, there you are. Come on, come and help me set up the croquet,' said Caroline, leaning through the door, her milk-chocolate hair hanging down like a silk veil as she watched Will expectantly.

Lizzy watched him go, and again was mildly confused when he paused at the doorway to glance back at her before disappearing outside.

★ ★ ★

The verandah offered Lizzy the perfect place to survey the party scene. People mingled around the seats on the lawn. Will and Caroline pushed in the croquet hoops. And over by the far corner of the lawn Lottie stood chatting with Ken Collins. Ken was smiling and Lottie threw her head back and laughed. Whether she was laughing at Ken or with him Lizzy couldn't tell but she drew in a breath and prepared herself to face the man she had rejected. It wouldn't be fun, but she couldn't leave Lottie stranded. Before she could take a step, the tinkling of piano music reached her ears. Lizzy spun around to where Charlie and Jane sat further along the verandah.

She caught his eye with a wave of her hand. 'You have a piano?'

Charlie nodded as the music grew louder. Lizzy found herself drawn into the house, following the music to the sitting room. She paused by the door to watch Mary, as she had countless times over the years. Her sister played with such passion it was clear the world had faded away for her. It had started as Mary's way to escape her younger sisters, by drowning them out, but it had become the true love of her life.

Now, as Mary played this beautiful piano, Lizzy could truly appreciate her sister's talent. Her music was hypnotic and spinetinglingly good. She looked regal, her perfect straight-backed posture, her face glowing.

When Mary finished playing Lizzy clapped so loudly that she jumped.

'Lizzy, you frightened me,' said Mary clutching at her chest.

'That was beautiful, Mary. I'm so proud of you. That gave me tingles.'

Mary smiled, softening her hard features and serious nature.

'Please play more?'

'I intend to. This party is rather dull.'

With that she turned back to the piano and continued to play. Lizzy listened for a bit then remembered Lottie and turned to head back outside — but crashed straight into Will.

'Jesus, do you follow me everywhere?' she quipped, looking up at him.

'Sorry, I came for the music. Is that your sister? She's very good.'

'That she is. You sound surprised?' Her eyes narrowed.

'No. Maybe. Well . . . ' He sighed, realising he was making a hash of it.

Lizzy immediately felt another fight building, but her anger evaporated when she saw the glassy shine his eyes had taken on.

'It's just, my mum used to play,' he said with a sadness that Lizzy had never seen before. 'I haven't heard someone play in a long time. It's nice,' he said softly. 'Brings back memories.' He sat on the arm of a chair, settling in to hear more.

He closed his eyes as Mary began a new song. Lizzy watched him for a moment; he had become so still, as if lost in his memories as he absorbed the music. She screwed up her face, trying not to let it affect her as she quickly headed outside. But the image of his face remained with her and she couldn't figure out why it had disturbed her. Was it the rawness of his words about his mother? Something vulnerable she'd not seen in him before? Shaking her head she tried to focus on anything but Will.

Outside Lottie was nowhere in sight, so Lizzy went to join Jane who was sitting alone on a two-seater in the corner of the garden.

'How's it going with Charlie and his folks?'

Jane shrugged. 'I don't think they like me,' she said quietly. 'I don't think Tony really sees me as a person or his son's girlfriend and I'm not sure if his mum and sister will ever approve. Not when they try to pretend I don't exist in Charlie's life.'

Lizzy frowned. She'd overheard Collette talking to Caroline earlier about Alyssa again. Technically she'd been eavesdropping behind the lattice arbour covered in a thick creeping rose, but when it concerned Jane she'd been too engrossed in their conversation to move away.

'Charlie is lucky Alyssa's patient,' Caroline had said to Collette. 'He'll come around. She's perfect for him, a lawyer with influential parents.'

'I hope you're right. He just needs a little push in the right direction,' she'd replied.

They had moved away and Lizzy hadn't heard any more but that was enough for her to despise them even more.

'If he or they hurt you I'm going to put sugar in their fuel tanks and sprinkle caltrop over their land like everlasting seeds.'

Jane smiled. 'You wouldn't dare.'

'For you Jane, I would.' She kissed her sister's cheek. 'Do you want another wine? It can't make this party any worse,' she said with a grin.

'Sounds good. Red please.'

Lizzy went to the drinks table and while she was waiting for the waiter to pour the red she saw Charlie and Will talking inside through the window. Charlie had his hands on his hips and Will was doing a lot of talking. That was very unusual, she thought with a smirk. She watched a moment longer, suddenly noticing the hurt or maybe angry expression on Charlie's face. What were they talking about?

'There you go, one red and two beers.'

'Thank you, kind sir,' said Lizzy looking back to the waiter as she took the two beers in one hand and the red wine in the other.

'Will you be all right with that?'

'Yes, thank you,' she said, with a last glance at Charlie and Will, who were still in deep discussion. With a frown she headed tentatively towards Jane.

As she sat down the kitchen staff came pouring out with trays filled with bite-sized cheesecakes, mini mud cakes, baby lemon pies and chocolate-dipped strawberries.

'Now *this* is living,' said Lizzy as she took a napkin and as many desserts as she could get away with. 'It just made this party ten times better,' she said with a grin.

Jane chuckled, and for the moment that was enough to put Lizzy at ease.

12

Lizzy lay with her eyes closed, listening to the magpies' morning calls. Beyond them she could hear their rooster Ozzie crowing for all he was worth.

With a yawn she opened her eyes, only a pre-dawn glow filtered in through the gap in the curtains.

Across the room she saw Jane snuggled up with her doona almost around her head but her eyes were wide open.

'What are you doing awake at this hour?' whispered Lizzy.

'I couldn't sleep,' said Jane. She sighed heavily. 'I keep running yesterday over and over in my mind. I'm so sure his parents don't like me, and Caroline just ignores me.'

'Did you get any sleep?' The doona moved as Jane shrugged. 'Oh Jane. You really like Charlie, don't you?'

She nodded. 'Probably more than I should for the short time we've been together. He feels like the one, Lizzy.' She closed her eyes. 'And I probably blew it yesterday. I was so nervous I couldn't talk, couldn't do much of anything. My nerves were shot by the time we got home, and . . . ' She shuddered in a deep breath. 'I had an anxiety attack not long after.'

'Oh Jane, I'm sorry I wasn't here to help.' Lizzy had gone back to work on the farm after the barbecue and didn't get in until dinner time.

'It's okay. I put some music on and tried to sleep. I haven't had an attack since I was a kid when Tanya was bullying me every chance she got, but all this pressure from Charlie's family is stirring it up again. I haven't told Charlie about my attacks, I don't want him to know how weak I am.'

'You are *not* weak,' Lizzy growled. 'Never say that, Jane. Stress affects us all in different ways.' Lizzy propped herself up on her elbow. 'Tanya was just a jealous little girl, and Charlie's parents are behaving no better. I found Collette quite rude.' Lizzy had hoped to see Charlie stand up to his mum and defend his girlfriend, but instead he'd remained quiet and let her prattle on about his ex-girlfriend.

'Do you think Charlie feels the same way about you?' she asked carefully.

Jane rolled onto her back and stared up at the ceiling. 'I don't know. He says he likes me a lot, and he's been so caring and thoughtful. He's not someone who would lie, he has a soft and gentle heart. But I think he gets a lot of pressure from his parents.'

'Yeah, I think so too. I'm sure he'll be in contact soon enough. Anyway, it doesn't matter what his folks or his sister think. Only Charlie's opinion matters.'

★　★　★

It wasn't until later that morning as Lizzy was fixing a hole in one of the fences and Jane was keeping her company that Jane's phone buzzed with a message from Charlie.

Lizzy watched the anxious smile fade from Jane's lips as her face fell.

'What?' she said worriedly and went to Jane's side.

'It's from Charlie. He says he's heading back to his parents' farm to help out there for a while and that he won't be in contact much.' Jane's big blue eyes looked up at Lizzy, like big heavy raindrops. 'He's pulling away from me already,' she whispered as if short of breath.

'Try not to think the worst, Jane.' But her words felt forced; deep down Lizzy was doing the opposite.

'I knew they didn't like me. Do you think his parents have some sort of control over him? Maybe they concocted a story to make him go home, just to get him away from me? To separate us?'

'Who knows?' said Lizzy. But she wouldn't put it past them, especially Collette after what she'd overheard at the barbecue.

'He's never gone this long between texts before, and I don't want to be the needy girlfriend sending him millions. But it's killing me to wait for his replies.'

'Well, best I keep you busy, then. Pass me the wire cutters, please.' Lizzy didn't know what else to do. Talking about it was only agitating Jane more. 'Once we're done here would you mind watching me take Pippa through her paces with some sheep? I need to practise with her more before the sheep trials.'

'Sure,' she said a little distractedly.

Lizzy did the final trim on her fix-up job. 'There, that should do it, for a while at least.'

'Nice job.' Jane smiled but clearly her heart wasn't in it.

'Don't worry, Charlie will reply when he can, I'm sure.'

★　★　★

A week later — a week of restless, broken sleep for Jane and resultant dark circles beneath her eyes — Lizzy's words came back to bite her.

She was mucking out the chook yard with Lydia, who had gone for a drink and hadn't returned yet, when Jane came running towards her. She was on the verge of tears when she reached the door of the chook pen.

'What is it, Jane?' Lizzy dropped her rake.

Jane held out her phone, one hand over her mouth.

Lizzy read the message from Charlie. *Sorry, been busy and out of phone range a lot.*

'He doesn't say much,' she said, handing Jane's phone back.

'Do you think he's lying? Charlie loved to talk. This . . . this isn't the same guy,' said Jane with a sob.

A horrible uneasiness settled in Lizzy's belly. 'It's possible he could be out mustering or they really are in a crap mobile-signal area.' The words sounded unbelievable to her own ears, but for Jane's sake she had to try.

The chooks gathered around their feet, fluffing

their brown feathers and eyeing off Jane's painted toes. Jane bent down and picked one up, hugging the fluffy bantam to her chest.

'If he wanted to break up, wouldn't he just say so?' she wondered quietly while nuzzling her face into the bird's soft feathers.

Lizzy touched her shoulder. 'I would have thought so. Maybe he is just really busy. His parents are probably keeping him flat out.'

'Yeah, maybe you're right,' Jane said, but her weak smile didn't reach her eyes.

★ ★ ★

'I know it's you — no one else rings this early in the morning,' said Lottie by way of greeting.

Lizzy headed outside and sat on the chair by Pippa's bed, tucking her legs up, her flannel pyjamas keeping the morning chill away. 'Sorry, I just noticed your missed call from last night. I've been a bad friend. I haven't seen you in ages, not since the barbecue and even then we didn't get to talk much. But anyway, how are you? Same old, same old?' she asked, picturing Lottie spending her days at the pub.

'I've been great, actually. Best I've been in a long time. I think I'm ready to move on, Lizzy, ready to take the plunge. I just don't want to lose what we have when I go,' Lottie's voice took on an emotional tone.

'What? Hey, that will never happen. No matter where you end up, we'll still be tight. Friends for life, through thick and thin.'

'You promise?' There was a childlike concern in her voice.

'Pinky swear,' said Lizzy with a chuckle. 'I just want you to be happy, my friend. You sound happy.'

'I am. I've had the best month. We must catch up face to face for a proper chat. When are you free?'

There was an anxious edge to her voice that concerned Lizzy a little.

'Maybe in the next few days?'

'Cool, come see me the moment you have time. I miss you,' said Lottie.

'I miss you too.'

★　★　★

That night after dinner the family sat around in the lounge room watching TV. Lydia and Kitty sat in bean bags, glued to their phones with the odd camera flash illuminating the room for their Snapchat selfies. Halfway through *Australian Story* Margaret came rushing into the centre of the room, making sure she had all their attention. 'I just got off the phone from Patricia.'

'I wondered why it was so peaceful,' said John under his breath.

Margaret continued on quickly, her breath coming fast. 'You'll never guess what she just told me. I can't believe it.'

Lizzy wondered if she had time to make a cuppa before her mum got to the actual gossip.

'It's about Charlotte.'

Lizzy sat up, glancing at Jane. 'What about Lottie?'

She suddenly had a funny feeling that Lottie's phone call and need to see her had been about much more.

'It's horrible,' said Margaret clutching her hands together. 'Patricia said Charlotte's going out to live with Ken — your Ken, Lizzy.'

Margaret gurgled like she was drowning.

'What? Are you sure. Ken? Ken Collins? It's a joke,' said Lizzy. It had to be. Lottie wouldn't be that crazy. Would she?

'It should have been you, Lizzy.'

Margaret was close to wailing, as if she'd just lost a child not a marriage prospect for her daughter.

'I did see them together at the rodeo,' said Jane hesitantly looking to Lizzy, who frowned in response. This was all just too weird. Lizzy remembered seeing them together at the barbecue as well. *Surely not?*

'Patricia says it's true. Dave has a 'worker wanted' sign up at the pub as well,' added Margaret. 'Dave's telling everyone how his girl's got herself a Shire President. Oh Lizzy, why did you turn him down?'

Why did Charlotte not? Was Ken going around asking any woman now?

'Well,' said Lizzy, 'there's only one way to clear this up.'

★ ★ ★

169

'Is it true?' Lizzy demanded. 'Are you dating Ken?' She shut her bedroom door and leaned back against it before sagging to the floor.

'Damn it. You've heard.' Lottie let out a rush of air that whistled through the phone. 'I'm sorry you had to find out like this, Lizzy. I wanted to tell you in person. I know you don't like him. Maybe that's why I've been a bit slow in filling you in.'

Lizzy felt like she'd been stabbed in the heart. She also felt like a bitch. 'Wow. Lottie, I'm so sorry you felt you couldn't tell me. I don't hate the guy. He's really nice. He just wasn't for me. But I want you to be happy.'

Ken Collins!

'I *am* happy. For the first time in ages I feel free.'

Lizzy could hear it in her voice. A tone she hadn't heard in a while. 'Good. I'm so glad. When did all this happen? Are you really moving in with him?'

Lottie sighed. 'Thank you. I've been dying to talk to you about it but I was worried what you'd think.' She laughed. 'It all happened the night of the rodeo, would you believe? We got talking at the bar, and after a few drinks he really relaxed and I found another side of him. He really suffers from a lack of confidence and I think he overcompensates but that night we talked for hours. About his chooks, his farm, his dreams. We found we had so much in common. He's really quite funny when he's relaxed.'

'Wow.' She wanted her friend to be comfortable talking about Ken, even though she couldn't

170

get the image of him from her mind. 'I guess I was too quick to judge. I've never seen him after a few drinks. Didn't know he suffered from lack of confidence.' It explained a lot.

'Yeah, I'm so glad I got to see the real him. We started talking and texting a lot and got together at the Bingley barbecue. It's funny how you view people when you get to know them. I see Ken in a whole different light now. He's actually quite fit under those clothes.'

Lizzy quickly covered her mouth as she spluttered. 'Have you and he . . . What was it like?' During his advances Lizzy had tried not to imagine what any of that would be like with Ken.

'Really good. He's so attentive and just wants to make me happy. I haven't been with a bloke who hasn't thought about himself first ever. Makes a nice change.'

Lizzy tried very hard not to picture it. 'And so you're moving in with him?' It seemed like such a big step.

'Yeah, he offered me a job back at the rodeo. He's been looking for a live-in house cleaner, chook feeder et cetera and I'd been seriously thinking about it. I didn't want to rush it, even though I wanted to take the job. I just needed to be sure. But it feels right. I'm leaving at the end of this week. I'm going to have a party when I get there; please say you'll come?'

'Of course I will.'

'Oh Lizzy. You should see his chooks, he loves them and it shows. He's teaching me everything he knows. He's so patient, and he said I can do as much on the farm as I want. Finally I get everything I've ever wanted.'

'So, you've been to his place?' Lizzy's head was swimming. So much had happened to Charlotte that Lizzy felt like she'd been asleep.

'Yes, a few times. He has a beautiful home.'

'I wish I could have been there for you through all this, Lottie. I'm such a bad friend.'

'I was worse, not believing that you'd have my best interests at heart. I should've known better.'

'What matters now is that you're happy, and if you're happy then I'm happy. You'll always be my best friend.'

'I love you too,' said Lottie. 'I am going to miss you lots. Will you come and visit me when you can?'

Lizzy bit her lip as her nose prickled. 'As much as I can. Better come and visit me too.' They were silent for a moment. 'I'm going to miss you,' she said, her voice cracking. 'Let's have drinks at our spot soon to celebrate.'

They hung up with plans in place. It felt as if life was about to undergo a big change that Lizzy wasn't ready for. At least Lottie's dream to leave the pub was coming true.

After a few minutes to herself, Lizzy headed back out to the TV room to fill the rest of the Bennets in.

'Yep, Lottie is moving to live with Ken.'

'For real?' said Jane.

John looked up, unsurprised, while Margaret threw her sewing down onto her lap.

'How are we ever going to marry you off,' said Margaret.

'You don't need to, Mum. I'm married to the

172

farm,' said Lizzy with a grin. 'Lottie wants us to go to her house-warming party next week.' Lizzy glanced to Jane. 'We can go and visit Charlie's parents' farm — it's not far from Ken's.'

Jane's eyes widened and she smiled.

The first real smile since the Bingley barbecue.

13

Ken Collins' farm was the other side of Toongarrin, making the trip from the Bennets' farm about an hour's drive.

'I'm glad it's just us going. I need a break from the family,' said Jane as she rested her head against the door of Lizzy's ute.

'Me too.'

'I sent Charlie another text this morning. I couldn't help myself. It's been hard to hold back but I just want him to know I'm still here.'

Lizzy was sure Charlie knew exactly where her sister was.

'Do you think he'll reply?'

She shrugged. 'He only seems to reply to my general texts about what he's up to. He won't text anything personal anymore, no *I miss you* or *Morning, gorgeous*. It's like I'm talking to a friend. His last one was a condensed version of his day, as if he's trying to prove how busy he is.'

'Have you tried calling?'

'I gave up. He never answers. I don't think he wants to hear my voice.' She stared out the window, her shoulders sagging as if laden with bricks.

'Do you ask him why he never calls?'

'Sure, but he just says the same thing: he was in a meeting, he was out working, his phone was flat or signal not good enough for a call.' Jane sighed. 'I think he's just too scared to break up with me and he's hoping I'll get sick of waiting and do it for him.'

'That's pretty bad.'

'Lydia told me it's called ghosting,' said Jane. 'But surely Charlie's not like that? Surely he'd just tell me the truth?'

Lizzy sighed. 'The fact that he keeps sending the odd text . . . it makes me think he doesn't want to let you go yet, which means he still cares.'

Jane screwed up her face. 'So, what do you take from that?'

Lizzy shrugged. 'Maybe he's being influenced by his family? If he wanted to end it he could have by now. I didn't take Charlie for a gutless person. But sometimes it's hard to judge people.' Look at Ken, she thought.

'Well, going to see him should shed some light on things,' added Jane. She wrung her hands together on her lap. 'I'm freaking out a little at that thought. Excited to see him but scared it could be the last time.'

Lizzy didn't know how to reply, so she just reached over and covered her sister's hand with hers.

'Have you heard from Luke lately?' Jane asked.

Lizzy shrugged. 'A few times, just a quick hello or asking me to a party he's at but I'm always too busy.'

'You could make the effort,' Jane said.

'You know I'm not much of a party person,' she replied. 'We'll cross paths when the time's right.'

'We're here.'

The tree-lined driveway opened to reveal a large home with verandahs all around and a well-tended garden. Off to the side was a large vegie garden and beyond that chook yards galore.

Under the white arbour stood Lottie and Ken, both waving like they were on an Outback Experience advert. Lottie ran to them squealing when they stopped out the front.

Lizzy jumped out just as her friend threw herself into her arms, nearly bowling her over.

'I can't believe you're here!'

Lottie and Ken looked like a matching couple, both in jeans and blue checked shirts. Ken had dirt down his jeans and his shirt had little holes all over it, probably from the grinder or welding. To Lizzy he looked nicer when in his farming gear. More approachable.

'Hey Lizzy. Hey Jane,' he said with a warm smile.

'Hi Ken. You two look so good together,' she said, meaning every word.

They glanced at each other with genuine affection.

'Come on, let's have a cuppa and then we'll show you around. You have to see the chooks and what we've done to the vegie patch,' said Lottie, leading the way into the house.

'Wow, your home is beautiful, Ken,' said Jane as she glanced into the rooms they passed. 'It has so much character. Modern but with history.'

She bent over to touch a collection of wooden animals, next to an old framed black-and-white photo of a young man.

'Thank you, Jane. That's my great-grandfather. He made all those by hand. This place was just a little shack once, but it's been renovated over the years.' Ken walked into the kitchen area and turned on the kettle.

Lizzy had always known Ken to be well presented, always freshly shaved and nicely dressed, but his home wasn't just clean, it was perfect, magazine perfect. The kitchen was a mix of white and black with stainless-steel appliances made warmer by the jarrah floorboards and little touches around the place, like a large wooden chopping board, and pictures in rustic frames. 'It has such a homely feel. It's gorgeous, Ken.'

Lottie beamed at Lizzy's praise. As they sat around chatting over cuppas Lizzy realised how easily the conversation flowed. It was weird seeing Ken in a different light. She watched him as he spoke, and the way he watched Lottie when he thought no one was looking. It was hard not to feel bad at judging Ken so harshly. He made Lottie happy and in turn Lizzy was seeing a better Ken for it. He still looked like he'd melt near a flame but she no longer had the heart to even joke about it.

As they went outside to see the prized hen she watched Ken hold every door open for Lottie, even for the chook pen. Lizzy glanced at Jane, who was watching Lottie and Ken laugh together; she was smiling but her eyes were sad. Jane had experienced this magic and lost it.

177

Lizzy was still hoping to find it one day. Watching Jane, Lizzy couldn't help but wonder if it was better to stay single and just concentrate on the farm. She didn't have time or room for heartache.

Before lunch Lizzy went out in the paddocks with Ken while Lottie and Jane set up for the party.

Sitting beside Ken in the ute Lizzy felt relaxed and comfortable. Maybe it was knowing Ken didn't want to date her?

'Your crops are looking great, Ken. Heads are nice and full.'

'We've been lucky with no frosts, but I'm not counting my chickens yet, still could be a few late ones.'

She nodded, and then the cab fell silent for a moment. 'I'm very happy for you both, you know that? I've never seen Lottie so contented,' she said turning to him. 'And I've been worried about her lately.'

Ken closed his eyes and nodded. 'Yes, she told me about her personal struggles.'

Lizzy flinched, surprised that Lottie had shared something like that with him already.

'She said only you and her dad knew about it. I'll call you if I feel she's ever heading that way again.'

He smiled, and she warmed to him instantly. This Ken was someone she could be friends with. Someone she was happy to see her best friend with.

'Thanks Ken, I'd appreciate that very much. But I don't think we have to worry. You've given her more than just a relationship. You've given her freedom, compassion and a confidant.'

'You think so? I can't believe how lucky I am to have found her, or that she gave me the time of day.'

Lizzy felt a little stab, sure some of his words were directed her way.

'It all worked out for the best, didn't it?' she added.

He nodded and grinned ear to ear. 'Yeah, it sure did. You mean a lot to Charlotte, I'm glad you're here. Truly.'

'Aw, thanks Ken. I'm glad I am too. It's great to see you both in your element here on the farm. It really suits you.' His face turned a little red. 'Can you show me your sheep? I'd love to see your stud rams too, if that's okay?'

'It would be my honour, Elizabeth.'

It was another hour before they made it back to the house and in that time Lottie and Jane had transformed it with decorations, balloons and a table set up for twenty.

'We made all the salads and marinated the meat. And Jane whipped up her famous pavlova,' said Lottie. 'I guess you two talked non-stop farming?'

Lizzy beamed. 'Of course. It's my favourite subject,' she said laughing. 'It was great. I expect regular updates now. You'll be a full bottle farmer before too long. Oh, which reminds me . . . ' Lizzy ducked off to the spare room where they'd put their bags and dug out her gift for her friend.

'Here, this is for you, from us.' Lizzy handed

over the small wrapped box and stood by Jane. 'A little going-away-cum-house-warming present.'

Lottie shook it. 'What is it?'

'Open it. Hurry up.'

She ripped off the paper and lifted the lid on the box then gasped. 'Oh wow!'

Lottie lifted out a silver bracelet, complete with charms.

'It's so you don't forget us. See, there's a B, for the Bennets. A bottle for the pub. A chook because they've always been your favourite and now you have lots. That one is a mountain to remind you of the hill.'

'The love heart?' she said, glancing up.

'That's because I love you lots. And there's a star on there to remind you that we'll always look at the same ones.'

Lottie's bottom lip quivered. Her eyes welled up and she sniffed. 'It's the most amazing gift I've ever received. I love it.' She threw her arms around Lizzy and laughed, with tears in between. 'Thanks Jane,' she said, eventually peeling herself out of Lizzy's embrace to hug her too.

Ken stepped forward to admire it then took it from Lottie so he could put it on her wrist.

'Thanks,' she said as he reached up and brushed a tear from her face. 'God, I probably look a mess. We better go get cleaned up before everyone starts to arrive.'

'It's okay, we have time,' said Ken calming her as she started to fidget. 'It's only some neighbours and close friends, a way of us celebrating with the special people in our lives. It won't be an interrogation, I promise,' he said before kissing her forehead. 'Just relax and be yourself.'

★ ★ ★

'Caroline said to arrive at ten for morning tea. She said there would be scones,' said Jane after they'd helped Lottie clean up the next morning. Jane had made the arrangements with Caroline the previous afternoon while Lizzy had been out with Ken. Lizzy was feeling a little apprehensive about it now, even though she was the one to mention a visit in the first place.

'Oh, sounds like she's making an effort,' said Lottie.

'Or got the help to make them,' said Lizzy under her breath.

'Thank you so much for coming,' said Lottie as she walked Lizzy and Jane to the ute.

Ken had said his goodbyes after breakfast, and it had been nice to have a couple of hours on their own with Lottie. Girl time before they headed home via the Bingley farm.

'Call me when you get home. I want to hear all about it. I haven't been there yet but Ken assures me it's fancy,' said Lottie giving them both a hug.

'Will do.'

As they drove away Lottie waved frantically, her new bracelet jingling in the sun.

'I'm so glad I came,' Lizzy said to Jane.

Jane nodded but remained silent, her eyes on the road. The road that would take her to Charlie.

It was a half-hour drive from Ken's farm to the Bingley estate, making the trip home longer again but for Lizzy it would be worth it just to see Jane get some answers and hopefully smile again.

Jane sat forward as they turned onto Bingley Road and drove past the biggest farm sign she'd ever seen. Lizzy smiled as they made their way along the wide, even gravel road.

'I bet they have their own grader,' she mused. She hadn't seen one pothole yet, and that was saying something.

Lizzy followed the road around to the left, where they came up to a homestead with history. Stone walls and old bricks around the windows, bullnose verandahs and a sprawling well-kept garden that made it very welcoming. Dotted around the home were big shady lilac trees creating shade and cosy areas, adding to the aged feel of the place, as if the homestead had been there for hundreds of years.

There were two utes and a car parked next to the house in a large shed. 'Maybe they're all here for morning tea,' she said to Jane.

'Gosh, I'm so nervous. Do I look okay?' asked Jane softly as she adjusted her lemon dress.

'You're gorgeous. Let's go say hi.'

Their house was grand, old but restored and well maintained. There was a pool and a big patio area with an outside kitchen. Lizzy had only seen things like this in city homes, not in the bush.

Caroline met them at the door in a black pencil skirt and white silk ruffled blouse. She wore black high heels and makeup. 'Hello ladies, welcome to the Bingley Estate.'

There were no hugs, just air kisses that were half-hearted at best.

'Won't you come inside and I'll show you around.'

'Thanks Caroline. Beautiful house,' said Lizzy. Jane had her hands clasped together and was in no fit state for small talk, so Lizzy took the lead. But Caroline didn't need much encouragement, she rattled off details of artwork on the walls, collectable hat boxes from her great-great-grandmother and the designer tiles in the kitchen. No family photos, though, no personal touches at all.

'Please take a seat and I'll have coffee made.'

Caroline gestured to the plush high-backed chairs that sat in a room filled with windows. The purpose of this room, it seemed, was simply for sitting and looking outside or reading, as suggested by the wall of floor-to-ceiling book-shelves.

A woman, maybe ten years older than Caroline, came into the room bearing a tray of coffee.

'Ah, Justine. Can we have the scones now too please,' said Caroline.

Justine smiled and left. At least she wasn't in a maid's uniform, thought Lizzy. But her black T-shirt and black leggings might go close to one.

'Justine has been with us for ages. Collette hired her when I was about ten.'

Lizzy had never heard anyone call their mother by their first name in conversation before. What felt even weirder was sitting in a room with only three of these chairs and one little glass table set up with jam and cream plus three side plates with knives. Only three.

Justine brought in the fresh scones.

'Thanks Justine, they look amazing,' said Lizzy.

'Don't let them get cold,' she said, her smile a little forced.

As she reached for a warm scone Jane shot Caroline a frown. 'Won't Charlie be joining us?'

She saw the flutter of her eyelashes and the tightening of her jaw as if she'd been waiting for this moment.

'Oh, didn't I mention that he's not here?' she replied flippantly. 'Yes, he went with Tony to the city for a while to look at some investments. Collette will want to show him off to all her friends while he's there too,' she said smugly.

There was a long silence.

'No, you didn't mention that,' whispered Jane as she sat there with her hands in her lap staring blankly at Caroline.

Caroline smiled. 'He's in such demand, my brother. I think Collette has quite a few parties lined up for him. I think Alyssa will be there at her parents' place, they hold wonderful parties by their large pool. It's always on the social calendar,' she added.

Lizzy opened her mouth. She'd had it with this woman and was going to let her know how awful she'd been but at the last minute she caught Jane's shake of her head. Lizzy closed her mouth, jamming her teeth together, and closed

184

her eyes so she didn't have to look at Caroline. At least until she could get herself under control. When she opened them again Jane had taken a tiny bite of a scone while plastering a small smile on her face.

'It's a shame Will isn't here,' Jane said clearly. 'He would have loved to have seen Lizzy again.'

Lizzy's eyes bulged, probably just as much as Caroline's. But then she saw the spark in her sister's eyes. *Oh, well played, Jane.*

The silence lasted for long seconds before Lizzy's phone chimed and she glanced at it. A message from Luke: *Hello my lucky clover.*

Lizzy stood up. 'I'm sorry, Caroline, but we have to leave. There's a problem back on the farm and I'm needed. Please thank Justine for us.'

Jane stood, following Lizzy's lead.

'I hope it's nothing too serious,' said Caroline unconvincingly.

'No one hurt, but I'm needed there as soon as possible.'

'Not a problem. Thanks for stopping in.' Caroline stood as they headed for the door.

★   ★   ★

'What's wrong at home?' asked Jane as they climbed into the ute.

'Nothing,' she said as she revved the engine into life. 'I just didn't want to stay one second longer with that horrible woman.'

'Then who texted?' Jane asked, still confused.

'It was Luke. Perfect timing, I'll have to thank

him. Caroline is awful.'

'I know. How could she do that?' said Jane, her face pale. 'How can people be so cruel? She knew I wanted to see him.'

'Who knows, but she's not worth our time. I liked what you did there with Will,' she added.

'Well, I've seen the way he listens when you talk and she's noticed too, that's what made it work so perfectly.' Jane slouched in the passenger seat. 'I'm so tired, Lizzy. Tired of Caroline, tired of thinking about Charlie, tired of not knowing. I just want to be back home.'

'That I can help with,' said Lizzy as she pointed the ute in the direction of Longbourn.

Neither Bennet sister looked in the rear-view mirror as they left.

14

'Oh, I'm glad you're home,' said Margaret as they walked inside. Her face was eager and her hands rested on her wide hips over her pink frilly apron, which was her favourite and so well worn it had been repaired many times. 'How did things go? Did you see Charlie?'

Lizzy put her hand up. 'Mum, not now, please,' she said softly. 'Any chance of a couple of hot chocolates?'

Jane continued on to their bedroom, head down, small steps as Margaret watched her carefully. 'Oh my. Poor Jane. I take it things didn't go well.'

'No, Mum. He wasn't there.' Lizzy didn't want to go into the horrible details. 'She just needs some space.'

'You go to her. I'll make up two mugs, and I think I have some Tim Tams hidden from the girls that I can dig out.'

Lizzy hugged her mum. 'Thank you.'

Jane was on her bed curled up with tears streaming down her face. 'Janey!' Lizzy rushed to her side, kneeled beside the bed and brushed back her hair. 'Don't waste your tears on Caroline,' she whispered.

Jane raked her fingers over her eyes, dragging tears across her cheeks and hiccupped as she tried to speak. 'It's . . . it's not . . . her,' she sobbed between words.

She pushed her phone towards her and Lizzy took it, frowning as she read what was on the screen.

I'm sorry. I just can't fit in a relationship at the moment. I'm so sorry, Jane. I won't forget the time we had together.

'What!' She glanced at her sister, trying to comprehend. 'No phone call, no face to face. By text message!' Gutless. Coward. Idiot. Lizzy had many names for him but kept them to herself. It wouldn't help Jane for her to vent her anger. And to think she'd thought he was a good guy. 'I can't believe he would do this,' she muttered. Maybe he was more like his sister than they had realised.

Jane just sobbed harder. Lizzy reached for the tissue box on the bedside table and handed her a few. 'I'm so sorry, Janey.' Tears welled in her own eyes and her nose prickled so badly she had to rub it. Lizzy wrapped her arms around Jane and held her tightly while her sister cried her heart out. A small tear leaked from Lizzy's eye and she let it fall down her face. 'Sh,' she whispered over and over, unsure of what else to say.

A few minutes later there was a knock at the door. 'It's only me,' said Margaret softly and entered with a tray filled with steaming cups and chocolate biscuits. 'I know it won't fix anything but it might help a little,' she said placing the tray down beside them on the table. 'My poor baby. Come here.'

Lizzy moved back so Margaret could get in and scoop Jane up into her plump arms and ample bosom. Just like when they were little

Margaret rocked her gently and rubbed her back. 'I love you, my sweet, gentle child. We all love you so much,' she whispered.

★ ★ ★

Jane tried to put on a brave face but Lizzy heard her crying during the night for that whole first week. Sometimes she'd crawl into her bed and hold her because there was nothing else she could do to help her.

As time went by Jane's night cries subsided and she soldiered on like a strong Bennet woman. Lizzy busied herself with farm work and watched the crops put up big full heads and held her breath as the last of the frosts came through.

Lizzy had spotted Will, at least she thought it was him, in town and sometimes on the boundary fence at Netherfield. Each time she'd seen red and had to stop herself from charging over to give him a piece of her mind about his friend and his horrible ghosting. But the moment always passed too quickly, and she deemed that a good thing. No point stirring up trouble. It wasn't going to help Jane.

'Lizzy, have you seen your father?' called out Margaret from the kitchen window one Monday morning.

'Yeah, he's in the yard with the mob. We have the truck arriving any minute to take them to the sale,' she said while Pippa waited for her next command. Lizzy was trying to fit in some more practice for the sheep trials, but it was probably time to give the sheep a break from being

189

rounded up and moved. 'That's enough for now, Pip.' She called her back to her side.

The back door slammed as Margaret came out towards her. 'Here's a flask of coffee for him.'

'Thanks, Mum.' She took the silver flask.

'There's enough there for you too,' she said with a smile as Lizzy headed for her ute with Pippa on her heels.

She threw the flask onto the passenger seat and started her ute just as she caught movement in her rear-view mirror: a big green Western Star truck hurtling across their farm, sheep crate in tow.

'Nice, right on time,' she said checking her watch and then giving chase.

The truck pulled up by the sheds next to the sheep yards where her dad had them all penned up. Pippa jumped off the ute and straight into the yards to help her dad get them into the race.

The truckie climbed down and turned around, making Lizzy skid to a halt in surprise. 'Luke! Luke cowboy Wickham?'

'Hiya, lucky charm. Bloody nice to see you again.' He stepped forward and picked her up in a big bear hug. He smelled of wool, sweat and cigarette smoke. His blue singlet showed off his lean tanned arms. He was a wiry bloke, like a nimble rock climber.

He put her down, snuck a kiss on her cheek and held her at arm's length. 'You're still gorgeous. So, these your ewes I'm picking up? I wasn't sure, but when they said Bennet, well, I had my fingers crossed I was headed to your place.'

'This is a brilliant surprise. You should have messaged.'

He rolled his eyes. 'I would have but I lost my phone. The boss gave me his spare one.' He pulled it from his back pocket. 'Would you mind putting your number back in?'

'Sure,' she said with a smile and entered it. 'Do you have to head off once you're loaded up or can you stay for a bit?' she asked as her dad made his way over to them.

'I got to head off, get this lot to the sale yards in time,' he said sadly.

'Oh, Dad, this is Luke Wickham, I met him at the rodeo. Luke, this is my dad, John, and my dog, Pippa.'

Luke stretched his hand out and John shook it. 'Nice to meet you, sir,' he said before dropping to the ground to pat Pippa. 'You're a pretty girl,' he said scratching her ears.

'Now you know your way out here you'll have to come out for dinner. When are you free next?' she asked him as he stood back up.

He gave her that cheeky smile. 'I'll be back tomorrow.'

'Good, you'll have to come for dinner tomorrow night,' said John. 'I'll let Margaret know.'

Lizzy almost jiggled on the spot in excitement.

'Well, thank you, sir, I'd be honoured. Now shall we get these pretty ladies aboard too?'

With a big grin Lizzy nodded and headed for the sheep yards, whistling for Pip as she went.

Luke climbed back into his truck and reversed it up to the ramp with Lizzy's help. She opened up the back and Luke climbed in to open the gates to load up top first. Then they began the sometimes difficult task of getting the ewes on board. Sometimes they were happy to run, other times they were practically carried up the race and ramp. By the time they had all eighty loaded Lizzy's fingers and back ached. When she walked she felt like a gorilla with heavy arms at her side.

'You work bloody hard. I'm impressed. Got a good dog there too. Teach her yourself?' he asked.

'Sure did,' said Lizzy beaming. 'Still needs more work but she's got the smarts.'

'So do you,' he said stepping closer and reaching up to caress her chin. 'See you tomorrow, lucky charm.' He gazed at her for a long moment before he swung himself up into the truck like a monkey.

'He seems like a nice bloke,' said her dad, coming to stand beside her as they watched the truck leave.

'Yeah. He's good fun. Thanks for letting him come for dinner, Dad.'

He shrugged. 'I think we could all use some new company.'

Lizzy's mum was not as happy about the arrangement when John broke the news to her over dinner. 'Who is this man? Where does he come from? What does he do?' she demanded.

'Mum, he'll be here tomorrow, ask him yourself,' Lizzy said.

'Oh, is he the cute cowboy from the rodeo?' asked Lydia.

When Lizzy nodded Lydia's face lit up. 'Ye-es!

Tomorrow is going to be *ah-mazing*. Mum, can I borrow some money? I need to find a new top.'

'Lydia, you have lots of tops. Pick one of them,' said Margaret as she sipped her soup.

Lydia shot daggers across the table, while Lizzy watched Jane carefully.

'Don't worry,' Jane reassured her in their room later that night, 'it will be nice.'

'But I do worry. I know you're still hurting,' said Lizzy softly.

Jane pressed her lips together before trying to smile. 'Yeah, I am. I'm not sure if it will ever stop hurting.' Then she sagged, shoulders drooping. 'Oh Lizzy, I do try but I gave him all my heart. I'm not sure I'll ever get it back.' Her eyelashes fluttered as she blinked rapidly to clear her eyes. 'I should be angry but mainly I'm just sad because I miss him like crazy.'

Lizzy could only hope that Charlie was regretting his decision right now.

'Just take one day at a time, sis. One day at a time.'

★   ★   ★

The following day, as the dinner drew closer Lizzy started to feel a belly full of butterflies take hold. In the end she quit working and went home for a long hot shower. It took forever to decide what to wear. Dress up and look nice and feel as if she was trying too hard, or dress casually and maybe seem uninterested? In the end she went with jeans and a grey T-shirt with an Aztec pattern, a Christmas gift from Jane. As she met Lydia in the hallway, dressed up in her best skinny jeans and a tight black tank top with a sparkly pair of lips on the front, she frowned.

'Lydia? Are you off to a party?'

Lydia frowned in return. 'No, just dinner.' She strutted off towards the dining room.

When Lizzy heard her ask John what time Luke was due to arrive, she had a feeling that tonight might not be as fun as she'd originally thought.

'He's here, I see some lights. Kitty, quick!' shouted Lydia from the lounge room.

'Ready for the circus?' asked Jane coming out of their room and slipping her arm around Lizzy. 'Big, deep breath.'

'I'm trying. If I keep it up I might hyperventilate,' Lizzy replied with a grimace.

'It'll be okay. As long as Lydia doesn't decide to serenade him with her amazing voice.'

Lizzy snorted. 'Oh, I hope not. That karaoke machine was the worst thing Mum ever got her.'

'He's turned off his lights, he's getting out,' said Kitty with her head pressed up against the window.

Lydia practically pushed her aside to have a gawk out the window before turning to straighten her top and wait by the door.

John sighed and dropped his *Farm Weekly* on the side table before climbing out of his chair. 'Let the poor bloke be, okay girls,' he said. 'It's not nice being outnumbered.'

Margaret's sigh from the kitchen was audible. 'Your father always invites people over when we have nothing in the freezer,' she moaned to Lizzy and Jane. 'Again I've had to create something out of nothing, and I had no ingredients for a decent dessert,' she huffed.

'The apple pie looks amazing, Mum,' said Jane.

'Oh, it will have to do, won't it,' she snapped, pushing her hair back from her sweaty forehead. 'Girls, please set the table and use the good napkins.'

So much for not wanting Luke here, thought Lizzy with a slight smile.

'Hey Mr Bennet, nice place you have here.'

Luke's voice floated through their house causing the hair to stand up on the back of her neck. Just be casual, she warned herself.

Her dad was introducing Luke to Lydia and Kitty and then brought him into the dining room as Lizzy headed out with the spoons. 'Hey Luke. Glad you could make it.'

She liked the way his face lit up when he saw her, those eyes of his drinking her in as if he hadn't seen water in a month. Up and down her body they went.

'Hey, lucky charm,' he said giving her his trademark wink.

He was in worn jeans with one of his big shiny-buckled belts. His black T-shirt read *Save a Horse, Ride a Cowboy.*

Margaret 'humphed' as she joined them, placing a large bowl of braised shanks in the middle of the table.

'Mum, this is Luke. Luke, my mum, Margaret.' Lizzy watched to see if her mum would get his T-shirt. But she didn't seem to notice as he walked over to her and took her hand. 'Lovely to meet you, Mrs Bennet. I see where your daughters get their good looks from,' he said with a big smile.

'Oh.' Margaret blushed, looking pleased.

Lizzy heard her dad chuckle-snort, which turned into a cough. He cleared his throat and told Luke to grab a seat.

Lydia and Kitty sat either side of him, Lizzy opposite. At least this way she could watch those pale blue snowflakes dance all night.

They all sat while Margaret brought out a large dish of mashed potato and then steamed vegetables.

'Don't let it get cold, dig in,' she told them.

'How long have you been a cowboy?' asked Lydia. 'Do you have a girlfriend?'

'Are you staying around here long?' added Kitty.

The poor bloke was peppered with their questions but he seemed unfazed by their attention. Lizzy was about to speak when she felt something brush her leg, and they didn't have a cat. It wasn't until she caught Luke staring at her with a cheeky smirk that she realised he was running his foot up and down her leg while continuing on as if nothing was happening.

'Girls, let him eat,' scolded Margaret.

John smiled apologetically at him.

'It's okay,' Luke said licking the sauce from his lips. 'I'll be around for a little bit,' he said. 'I'm single, for now,' he added and glanced back at Lizzy.

She nearly dropped her fork as her heart thudded beneath the heat of his gaze.

'And I've been riding bulls for about five years now.'

He continued as if he hadn't just implied he was on the verge of getting himself a girlfriend while feeling up Lizzy's leg. Meanwhile Lydia was beside him preening as if she were in the running.

'I grew up on a station. Spent my whole life around cattle and on horseback. It's home.'

Lizzy tried to keep her face neutral as thoughts suddenly raced in her mind. Was he was talking about Will Darcy's property? Where they grew up together? She couldn't imagine Will on horseback.

'And now driving trucks?' John asked.

'Ah, this is just an in-between job. I'd love to get an overseer's position on a farm, like my dad was. But all this is helping to build up my resume.'

'You like driving trucks?' asked Lydia.

Finally a decent question from her, one Lizzy was half-interested in.

'Yeah, they're fun, but not the idiots I share the road with. Out here is all right, but when I have to drive in the city . . . geez, they have no idea. I've rammed a few that have darted into my stopping space.'

'I've done a bit of truck driving,' said John. 'Understand exactly where you're coming from.'

By dessert she could tell he'd won their mum over. Everyone was laughing at his stories, even Jane. Luke's foot made its way up Lizzy's leg a few more times, and by the third time she tried hard to ignore him but when she finally glanced at him he just smiled his cheeky smile to show he knew he'd outwitted her. At which point Lydia noticed and grabbed his hand so she could have his attention.

'Tell us another story, Luke,' Lydia begged.

'This one time I was camping out with the lads during the muster and I'd set my swag up with my mate Paul and then we had to go check the horses. When we came back, we ate and crawled into our swags then Paul started screaming, and I mean screaming like a girl. He had a snake in his swag.'

'Oh my god,' said Margaret.

'No way, did it bite him?' said Lydia.

Luke shook his head. 'Nope. Bloody snake was dead. Pissy Pete had whacked it earlier as it slid through camp and thought it would be a laugh to stick it in Paul's swag as a kind of initiation on his first muster. Hell, it was the funniest thing I'd ever seen.'

'Poor snake,' said Jane, cringeing. 'I think I would have died of fright.'

'Paul laughs about it now but he admits that was the worst moment of his life. He's afraid of snakes. Had many snakes in your swag, Lizzy?' he asked with a raised eyebrow.

Lizzy shook her head, too embarrassed to reply. Luckily no one picked up on his double meaning.

They were clearing the table with Luke still telling yarns, mainly from his days mustering or at rodeos, and often laced with innuendo that

— much to Lizzy's relief — slipped right by her mother. Lizzy didn't understand how she could miss it when Lydia and Kitty would snigger. Luke, as he told it, had led a very exciting life. Not one mention of Will Darcy the entire time, though, which made Lizzy wonder even more about their estrangement and past.

As the evening wore on, Margaret tried to give him the hint to leave and also to send Lydia and Kitty off to bed because they had school in the morning, but they wouldn't budge for anyone. It wasn't until ten o'clock that Luke eventually worked it out and said his goodbyes.

'Thanks for a fabulous meal Mrs B, and for the port Mr B. Lovely to meet you both,' he said, glancing around the house again. 'Such a nice warm home you have.'

'I'll walk you out,' said Lizzy quietly, and Jane stood by the door, preventing their younger sisters from following.

It was dark outside, not much moon to see, so Lizzy took Luke's hand. 'Just stay behind me.'

'Know your way blindfolded, hey?' he said, tightening his grip on her hand.

When they got to his ute he didn't move to let her hand go, instead he turned to face her. He reached out, finding her shoulder and then her face. 'Thanks for a great night.'

'You managed well with my crazy family,' she said, trembling from the cold or his warm hand that now cupped her face.

'Goodnight, lucky charm.'

She could sense he'd moved, that he'd entered her space, but even knowing it didn't stop the jolt when his lips pressed against hers. He pulled her in against his lean body and kissed her firmly.

Before she could think about how he tasted and the kiss, his hands moved her around and pressed her against the door of his ute. Then he nuzzled his body against hers.

'Mm,' he groaned against her lips. 'You smell so good.' He began to kiss down her neck, fingering her hair before his hands found her breasts. He groaned again. 'Such a good handful,' he murmured.

Lizzy was having trouble keeping up with him. A goodnight kiss she'd half-expected but this was the next step up. Just as she was about to say something his lips found hers again as he pushed himself between her legs. His tongue was busy, along with his hands that had somehow weaved their way under her shirt.

She leaned back and sucked in the cool night air. Her head was spinning and a little foggy.

Luke breathed heavily against her face. 'Wow, these feel so good. Any chance we can sneak away?' he asked against her ear.

Lizzy was already shaking her head. 'I have to get back or Mum will be out,' she said.

'Bugger,' he said leaning back.

Lizzy was glad for the space. He'd surprised her with his intensity. 'Now *that's* the way to finish a night. See ya later, lucky clover.' He reached back, found the door of his ute and opened it as Lizzy stepped aside.

Light spilled out from the interior light. It was so bright she felt like a police officer had shone a torch on them, and she had a guilty feeling along with it.

'Hope to see you around, Lizzy. Real soon.'

With that cheeky grin of his he climbed into his ute and drove off. Lizzy didn't head straight inside. Instead she was rooted to the spot as she tried to process what had happened. He was a fast mover and a decent kisser, if a little wet. But it had been a while.

Lizzy righted her T-shirt and wiped her mouth. Before she reached the door she'd decided not to tell Jane about what had just happened. Not yet, not until she could work out how she felt about it. Sure, it had been nice and exciting, but the speed of things edged it into almost an awkward feeling. Maybe he was just really that into her. Lizzy wasn't sure what to think. Her phone beeped and she read the message before she opened the door.

Love your hot lips, lucky charm.

15

'Damn.'

They were definitely white dots. And they were moving in her crop. Eating it, flattening it. And they didn't look like Bennet sheep. No, they looked too good to be hers. They had to be Bingleys.

'They must have got through the fence,' she grumbled. It didn't take a rocket scientist to figure out how, considering their border fences were only just hanging by rotten old posts. 'Pippa, bring them in,' she said, pointing to the sheep.

Lizzy opened the corner gate before driving back and climbing over the fence. She walked through the barley to help aid Pippa as she pushed the sheep into the corner of the paddock to the open gate. Lizzy shook her head in despair as she passed a section of fence that was stretched and broken at the bottom near a busted post that had likely been in the ground since her grandfather's day. The hole in the fence looked like Highway One for all the local animals — she saw kangaroo, fox and now sheep prints all around it — and went out onto the road that headed to the creek crossing. The fences were bad along this stretch and the sheep could have got out anywhere on the Bingley side. She didn't know how far she'd have to take the sheep to put them back where they came from, so she left the ute behind and walked with Pippa, moving the twenty-odd mob back through the muddy creek. The paddock on the other side wasn't in crop, just a pasture paddock — and a very green one at that — so she figured that was the one the sheep had been grazing. 'You girls are fat enough without needing my crop.'

Soon her legs felt weary, especially with the mud stacked under them from the crossing. After twenty minutes something caught her eye and she glanced to the left to see a ute driving through the paddock. As the new-looking white Land Cruiser drew up close and parked, Lizzy stopped and stared.

'What are *you* doing here?' she said, a little too shocked to be polite as Will Darcy stepped towards her and gripped one of the steel pickets just the other side of her. He wore stained jeans with a tear just above the knee, and his work shirt was rolled up to his elbows.

'I came here to check over everything for Charlie.' Will's words were slow and measured. He cleared his throat. 'He's been quite busy, so I said I'd come and see how Peter, his manager, was going,' he said as he frowned at the sheep. 'I heard a dog barking and came to check it out.'

Lizzy nodded but remained silent. She was still taking in this vision of Will. A worn, grubby cap on his head, buttons undone on his shirt revealing his golden chest and the same golden skin on his lean, muscled arms. Dirt under his fingernails. Struggling, to take her eyes off him, she frowned.

'Were these girls on your place?' he asked.

Lizzy blinked, trying to focus. 'Um, yeah. They thought my barley looked good.'

'Ah, sorry about that. Charlie has Peter on fencing duty too. I've been helping him with a few. We haven't got to this one yet, obviously.'

Lizzy shrugged. 'If my fence wasn't stuffed, they wouldn't have got in either. I'll try to fix it, but those roos don't help.'

He nodded. 'I'll go open the gate and stop them from heading into the bush at the end.'

Lizzy made the mistake of looking up into his dark eyes. They caused her skin to pimple and the hairs on her arms to stand up as if she were in the middle of a massive electrical storm. His eyes were like two twirling tornados coming right at her. Then he did the darndest thing: he smiled before turning back to his ute. Lizzy gulped in air as if she could finally breathe through the storm.

With a shake of her head she moved Pippa on as she watched Will drive down and open a gate, then he walked through to stop the sheep from running straight past.

Pippa moved the sheep through the gate, except for one ewe that darted for the bush. More often than not there seemed to be one who thought they could make a great escape, and usually Lizzy would just leave it and wait for it to realise it was all alone and come running back to the pack, but Will thought otherwise. On instinct he threw himself at the ewe, his big arms wrapping around the escapee, bringing it to a halt.

Lizzy watched as he climbed off the ground

without letting go, and plucked up the big ewe as if it were a baby lamb then carried it towards the gate. He didn't grunt or show signs of strain under the weight of the ewe that would have been around eighty kilograms; too heavy to get a good price at the sale yard.

He put her down, and she immediately darted off to the rest of the mob. Will stepped towards Lizzy, more dirt down his shirt and pants. Her fingers twitched as she resisted the urge to reach across and brush it off.

'I've got fencing gear on the back of the ute. Want a hand fixing it?'

Lizzy frowned. 'That seems like an offer too good to be true. Is there a catch?'

He smiled again, causing her to take a step back as if needing a buffer zone from its power.

'You help me fix this one first? Can't have them getting back out, and they will. Clever bloody things remember how they got out and they'll remember how to find your crop again.'

She nodded, agreeing with him. Which hadn't happened often since they'd met. 'Sure, that would be great. All my gear is back at the sheds.'

As Will went to get the ute Lizzy took charge of the gate, waiting for him to drive through before closing it. Instead of getting in she climbed up the side near his door and hung on.

'It's just up here, near that big thistle weed,' she said pointing the way until he pulled up.

'Did you notice any more along here?'

'Nah,' she said, getting down as he climbed out. 'This was the only hole, but I came out just before the corner up there.' She pointed about three hundred metres up.

Will didn't waste any time. He reached over the tray and gathered his red wire strainer, some pliers and some extra wire.

'Bugger it. We used up all the Gripple joiners.'

Lizzy raised an eyebrow. 'You'll just have to slum it the old-fashioned way. Luckily you're with a pro. I'm good at anything that's the hard way or the old way.'

He almost smirked with a hint of a laugh, his eyes smiling at least.

Without speaking they went to work. Will attached the wire strainer to one end while Lizzy attached the other end on the broken strand of wire. There were four lines still intact, so only four to repair at the bottom. They made fast work of each one, fixing the best they could with pliers and some extra wire to reinforce some of the stretched wire. Lizzy caught Will watching her tie the last one off, an unreadable expression on his face.

'What?' she said as she finished and stood up.

His lips pressed together and his head moved in a minute shake. 'It's better than it was,' he said finally as they put the tools on the ute. 'Will we get to your fence in the ute?' he asked.

'Maybe, if you're keen enough to drive through the creek. Otherwise you could park just down there and we can walk.'

His hands gripped the steering wheel. 'I'm always up for a challenge.'

She couldn't help but stare at the expression on his face: it was delight mixed with daredevil. Suddenly she had a moment of panic. What if he got them bogged? Did he know what he was doing? Sure, he'd shown he knew a thing or two about fencing, but how much of a real farmer was he?

Will put the ute in four-wheel drive, and she breathed a bit easier. The creek bed drew closer and Lizzy found her hands — along with other parts of her body — clenching as she waited for the slippery slide and wheel spin.

'Hang on,' he said and the ute dipped over the edge and down to the creek.

She gripped the handle next to her head and hoped Pippa had all four paws firmly planted on the back tray. With a quick glance she noted she was still there, tongue hanging out the side and a grin that revealed all her teeth.

They slid sideways to the sound of the engine revving and mud splattering. It flicked everywhere, even up near her window and as they slid the other way before climbing the bank on the other side Lizzy found herself smiling and enjoying the wild ride.

Will glanced at her, clearly reading her mind. 'We get to do it again on the way back.'

She couldn't help but return his smile and felt a strange electricity fill the cab. Who *was* this bloke? This Will was actually having fun and he wasn't so bad to be around. And they weren't even fighting! Her lips curled slightly.

'Left or right?' he asked.

She blinked, trying to process his words.

'To the hole in your fence?' he clarified.

'Oh, right.' She pointed just up the track. 'Near my ute.'

He pulled up alongside it and they got to work on the fence in comfortable silence, just them and the breeze making the crop roll like gentle waves along a shoreline. Galahs squawked nearby but overall it was peaceful, just the two of them working on the land, miles from anyone, with views and fresh air.

When they were done Will wandered into her crop and had a closer look. Automatically she followed, curious about his thoughts. She waited quietly beside him, as they crouched down.

'Is this Trojan wheat?' he asked as he held one of the heads in his fingers.

'Yeah, how did you know that?'

He pointed to the spikelets at the bottom. 'I've been told that Trojan is one of the varieties that can fill all of the bottom spikelets.'

'That's assuming it's happy and has no issues with the soil,' she said.

'True,' he agreed and stood up. 'Would you like to come on a crop tour with me? I know Charlie asked you to go with him one day, but seeing as he isn't here and I do have to have a look . . . well, I'd like your opinion.'

Her mouth fell open. 'Oh.'

'You're probably too busy,' he added, his hands clenching at his sides as he turned to leave, his head down.

She automatically reached out, latching onto his bare arm to stop him. Why she stopped him she wasn't sure. Maybe it was the disappointment in the sag of his shoulders that made her rethink. 'I can spare some time.'

He looked up as if to see if she was sure.

'I'd really like to take a look and meet Peter so I know who to talk to if we have any more neighbour issues,' she said.

Will nodded and glanced at where she held his arm. She let go immediately and set off for his ute. Lizzy faltered mid-stride halfway back, suddenly wondering if this was a good idea; after all, she was still angry with Will and Charlie. Especially because deep down she had a niggling feeling that Will had had some part to play in Charlie's decision to leave Jane.

He caught her up, interrupting her thoughts, and as they swung their legs over the fence she asked, 'Do you mind if Pippa comes along?'

'Not at all. She's a great sheep dog. I have three at home.'

Lizzy smiled as she climbed in the ute. 'Three? All working dogs?'

'Yes. We also have a little Jack Russell cross with a beagle, a Jackabee called Mickey. He's my little sister's dog. Georgie loves him and he loves her. Sleeps on the end of her bed,' he said shaking his head.

'You have a sister?'

'Hang on,' he said as they entered the creek again.

'You're having fun,' she shot across the cab as he dithered in the creek instead of taking the easy exit. Mud and slop was flying everywhere. He probably wouldn't even be the one left to wash it. Poor Peter.

'Just a little,' he said.

His teeth were straight and white and took all her focus with those perfect lips of his.

'Yes, Georgie is my sister. She's the love of my life.'

The pride that radiated from him was immense, and she saw that it was the way she felt about Jane. Her heart softened towards him then, just a little. Will Darcy did have a heart, and it seemed it belonged to his sister.

'Does she travel with you much?'

'No, she's still at school and stays on the farm with Jess, her mum.'

Her mum. A half-sister? But Will continued on before she could ask any more.

'I'll show you the barley first; it's on our way. Mick seemed to know what he was doing. He'd already finished seeding when Charlie bought the place.'

'I know. And he sold off his sheep six months before that. He was a good farmer. I loved chatting with him about all things farming. Charlie should get a good crop.'

They looked at the barley, then the wheat and lastly the canola, which was all flowering, offering an amazing sea of bright yellow against the green. Then they found Peter at the sheds putting more fencing gear on the back of the ute.

Will made the introductions, and Lizzy was surprised to find Peter's face lined with years in the sun and grey in his stubble and hair. She wasn't sure what she'd expected, maybe a manager closer to Charlie's age.

'I'm just here until Charlie comes back. I think he really wants to run this place on his own but I think his family has other ideas,' said Peter, his voice raspy like a smoker's.

Will and Peter shared a nod as if both understood something she didn't.

'Righto, well if there are any problems don't hesitate to call me.'

Peter smiled, one tooth chipped. 'No worries, young Miss.' Then he gave Will a nod and moved to his ute. 'I best get back to it.'

'Cheers Peter. I'll be there when I can,' replied Will. He turned to Lizzy as Peter backed out of the shed. 'Feel like a quick cuppa before you go?' he asked.

Without thinking she found herself saying, 'Yes, why not.'

Will drove past the sheds, and as they got closer to the house Lizzy's jaw dropped.

'Oh my god. Is that . . . is that . . . '

She stared at the black machine before them. Massive blades hung above it, shining in the sun like a lethal weapon.

'A helicopter, yes it is,' he said with a hint of amusement in his voice.

'Wow, I've never seen one before. Well, not this close.' She looked at him. 'Is the power mob checking poles out this way?' she asked.

There was a pause before he finally spoke. 'Ah, no. It's mine.'

'Pardon?' She stared at him, mouth open again. 'Did you say this helicopter is *yours*?'

He had the good grace to look a little sheepish as he nodded. 'Would you like a ride?'

Would she ever.

16

'Can I have a closer look at it?' Lizzy asked as Will stopped the ute nearby. 'I can't *believe* you own a chopper.'

'Sure, have a look. I'll go make coffee,' he said.

Lizzy didn't even know he'd left; she was too focused on the machine that looked like something from a spy movie, nothing like the ones stations used up north for mustering. She stepped closer and looked up at the two big blades that seemed to sag just slightly. Lizzy put her hand on the black metal body and leaned forward to look inside, wondering how often Will was chauffeured around, from the farm to the city to events. It would certainly save hours of driving time, especially considering the spread of his properties. Time was precious, and in his case money was no object.

Lizzy glanced around, saw no one was about and quickly pulled out her phone for some sneaky shots of the helicopter, putting her phone away just in time to see Will appear from around the corner of the house with two steaming cups in his hand. He walked slowly and paused by a garden seat.

Lizzy walked over to him and took the one he offered, joining him on the chair in the shade of a lilac tree. The tree was just starting to bud up with tiny white and purple flowers, its leaves not far behind after being naked through winter.

'Thank you.' The coffee warmed her belly nicely and she sighed. 'Have you had that long?' she asked.

'My dad bought me the Jet Ranger as a gift for getting into uni, but it was a gift he used a lot to get between our properties.'

'That's some gift.'

He shrugged. 'It was more for the business. It's not the best thing I got from Dad,' he said with a sad smile.

'Oh?' What could top a helicopter? 'What was? If you don't mind me asking.'

He looked a little out of his comfort zone suddenly as his fingers drummed against his cup. He cleared his throat. 'Best thing Dad gave me was his old Akubra hat that I'd grown up seeing him wear.' His voice wavered a bit. 'I was twelve. I'd just broken in my first horse, with Dad's guidance. He'd smiled down at me, I could see how proud he was.'

Will's hands settled and his body relaxed as if caught up in the memory.

'And then he lifted that hat from his head and stuck it on mine. Said I was a real man and a real man deserves a real hat.' He smiled and let out a shaky sigh. 'It was light brown felt with a plaited leather bit around it, and a feather I'd once found for him stuck into it.'

Will turned his head, his dark eyes wide and more open than she had ever imagined seeing.

'That's so beautiful, Will. I'm sorry, I heard your dad passed away.'

He nodded slowly, still watching her.

'Nearly three years ago. I was away at uni. One

of those one-in-a-million accidents. A tyre blows on a rough track, he crashes and isn't found until the next day. It wasn't instant. He died from his wounds.' His lips pressed together hard before he looked away. 'It haunts me, wondering how long he was out there, dying slowly. They say it was quick, but people like to tell you things that they think will make you feel better. I believe the truth is always the only option.' He lifted a shoulder in a half-hearted shrug. 'But no one really knows what happened that day, except my dad.'

'I'm sorry,' she said again. 'I've never lost anyone except grandparents. I can't imagine how you feel.'

'I lost my mum when I was five. I don't really remember her, so it was just Dad and me for years.'

'Oh wow, Will. I don't know what to say.' Lizzy's hand moved towards him but she pulled it back and focused on her coffee cup. She remembered being moved by him watching Mary play the piano, it all fell into place. His emotion in that moment had felt so personal.

'There's nothing to say.' He turned back to face her. 'Thanks for listening, though. I usually can't get a word in with other girls.'

Lizzy almost laughed but he was actually serious. 'Not even Caroline?' she asked.

He sighed and shook his head, his lip curling slightly as if he found her comment amusing. 'Caroline's different. She already knows me, we've been family friends for a long time. Most girls I meet don't take the time to know the real me. They're too preoccupied with fashion, parties and social media or the money.'

Lizzy smiled.

Will's eyes narrowed. 'It's true. I can see the dollar signs glistening in their eyes. They pretend to want to listen to what I'm saying but I can see it floating in one ear and out the other.'

'Ah Will, sounds awful,' she said. 'All that attention. Well, you won't have to worry about that with me. I'm not big on clothes unless it's hard-wearing and durable; I love my food but I prefer to eat it than take a photo of it; and, parties?' Lizzy laughed. 'We don't see too many of those around here unless it's a few coldies around the bonfire for someone's birthday.'

'That sounds like my cup of tea.'

'Really? I didn't take you as a bonfire kind of bloke. Might get ash on your designer shirt or melt the end of your fancy shoes,' she said with a smirk.

He was good-natured enough to take her jibes with just a roll of his eyes. 'I think I've been around Caroline for too long. Charlie's parents kind of took me in over the years. They like to keep up appearances.'

So do you. No one was forcing him to dress in the finest clothes. Yet the Will beside her in worn work clothes was different. More down to earth.

It was confusing, trying to marry the two Will Darcys. They didn't seem to fit, just like her conflicting feelings. She wasn't sure what to feel, but it was actually nice sitting here with him, talking rather than sparring.

'Finished?' he asked.

She frowned.

Will nodded to her cup.

'Oh yes, thanks.'

He took her cup and put it on the ground by the chair.

'Still want to take that flight?' he asked, standing.

Eagerly she stood up. 'For sure. That would be amazing. But I can't promise you how I'll react. I've never even been in a plane.'

'Well, I hope you enjoy this, then. Come on.' He walked her over to the helicopter and opened the front passenger door.

She glanced around. 'When will the pilot be here?' she asked, feeling her nerves go crazy as she climbed up onto the small leather seat.

Will gave her a headset to put on.

'Shortly,' he said with a smile before shutting the door.

He headed around to the other side while Lizzy stared at all the gauges, not understanding any of them.

'Buckle up,' said Will as he climbed in next to her.

She gaped at him. 'What are you doing?' He put on his own headset and pressed some buttons. 'Oh my god, you're the pilot.'

He went about his pre-flight check. 'No one else is here,' he said smugly, clearly enjoying her reaction.

She crossed her arms and tried to relax as the helicopter came to life, focusing on the whirr of the blades as they began to spin dizzily above.

'How long have you been flying?' she asked as

she gripped her seat, suddenly not feeling so keen about this joy flight.

'Relax.' He reached over and touched her shoulder then withdrew it just as quickly. 'I've been flying planes since I was sixteen and helicopters not long after that. You're safe. I fly all the time.'

His words didn't stop her heart from racing. It was all suddenly happening too fast as the helicopter was ready for take-off. Will shot her a smile as they lifted off. She felt her stomach roll and held in a squeal. He was waiting for a big reaction but she refused to give him one.

She looked out the window as the ground fell away and the homestead grew smaller. The utes and tractors started to look like Matchbox cars.

'Would you like to see your place from the air?' Will's voice came through her headset.

Lizzy's mouth was too dry to reply, so she nodded eagerly. As Will watched her for a moment she wanted to yell at him 'Watch the road!' but in the air there was no other traffic. No trees to hit, either. It still didn't stop her from panicking just a bit.

Her eyes, which may have looked like dish plates, roamed to the front window as she tried to get her bearings. 'This is so cool.'

Pulling out her phone she took photos of Longbourn. She thought about sending her dad a text saying 'Look up, it's me in a helicopter!' but John was probably in the shed tinkering and wouldn't even notice the big black metal bird in the sky.

'Sheep are all where they're supposed to be,'

she said with a smile.

'Anywhere else you'd like to go?' he asked.

'Can we go to town? I'll show you our hill.'

After a buzz over the town she pointed him to the hill. 'We have bonfires up there all the time. Oh, well, Lottie and I used to.' Her chest suddenly ached for her friend.

'Looks like a nice view from up there,' he said.

'It's beautiful when the sun sets as you're sitting in front of a crackling fire.'

'I'd love to experience that one time I'm back here.'

Lizzy frowned slightly, wondering if he was for real. If Jane and Charlie were still together it might have happened, but not now.

'Hey, why has Charlie dumped Jane? Do you know what's up with him?' she blurted suddenly.

Will's shoulders stiffened and he seemed very interested in his gauges. His words came through the headset, soft and a little strained. 'He has a lot of pressure on him from his parents and the farm. It's not easy on him either.'

Lizzy sucked in her bottom lip as she pondered his words. Knowing what Charlie's parents were like, Will's statement was valid. She hadn't really given much thought to the pressures Charlie might be up against. 'But still, there was no need to hurt Jane like he did. I thought he was more of a man than that,' she added.

Will stared at her and frowned. He looked like he was about to defend Charlie but when he finally spoke, it was an apology.

'I'm sorry for that. I'm not sure what

happened but I'm sorry Jane got hurt.'

Her breath hitched momentarily.

He cleared his throat and then turned the helicopter so sharply Lizzy flung out her hands to find something to cling to as she finally squealed. 'Ahhhhh! Is this what a rollercoaster feels like?'

'I haven't even started,' he said and then did a few more sharp turns and drops.

Her stomach was in her mouth then on the floor then trying to squish out her ear. This was utter madness — and so much fun.

'You're lucky I haven't eaten much all day,' she said feeling the blood drain from her face and then rush back with force.

He settled the helicopter into a smooth flight path and watched her carefully for a moment. 'I have sick bags somewhere if you need one. I'll take you back now.'

Lizzy smiled. She wouldn't dare mess up his expensive machine. Then again, the look on his face might be worth it. They flew in silence all the way back, Lizzy busy watching the helicopter shadow move across the land like an ant scurrying home.

Pippa was waiting on the back of the ute when Will landed the helicopter back at the homestead. The touchdown was smooth and Lizzy had to concede that he really did know what he was doing.

Will came around, hunched over beneath the blades, and opened her door. Lizzy got out, her legs a bit wobbly but Will reached out a large, warm, steadying hand. She gripped it, staring at their hands as she waited for her legs to regain some blood. Her mouth felt dry as she glanced up at him.

'Thanks Will. That is something I'll never forget.' Nor something she'd ever get to experience again, no doubt. 'I can't thank you enough.'

His eyes were so alive with power. It made her skin tingle and her head a little fuzzy. Lizzy squeezed her eyes shut, scratching at her neck as her opposing emotions raged a war.

'My pleasure. I get a kick out of taking newbies up in the air. Makes me appreciate the whole experience again, you know?'

'Makes you stop and smell the roses?' Her belly flipped with unease; it was too weird that they were almost getting on.

'Something like that,' he said with a grin.

Lizzy realised he was still holding her hand and slowly withdrew it, feeling her face burn with heat. She suddenly felt like running away, a huge desire to be alone.

'Ready for home?' he asked.

'Please. Thank you. Dad might be worried.'

Will drove her back to her ute. They were both quiet but an unspoken energy filled the air. Lizzy spent the whole trip fidgeting and biting at her lips while she stared out the window, feeling a little claustrophobic.

'See you later, Lizzy,' he said as he pulled up by her ute and she opened the door and got out.

Pippa got off the back and stood by her side.

'Bye.'

He nodded and drove off in his mud-covered ute.

17

'These are amazing! I wish I could have gone too, though I'm not sure I would have kept my lunch down,' said Jane as she flicked through the photos on Lizzy's phone.

'It was so surreal. He really knows how to fly. Crazy.'

'So, have you changed your mind about him?' said Jane, handing her phone back as they sat on her bed in their pyjamas.

'No. He's still . . . him. Rich, snobby. But I did kind of see another side of him. Maybe a person I would have liked if he wasn't born with a silver spoon in his mouth.' She sighed at the memory of his words at the cabaret, and of what he'd done to Luke Wickham. 'I don't think I could ever trust a guy like him.'

'It's a shame. He's so wealthy,' Jane said with a smirk.

Lizzy wanted to ask Jane if Charlie's wealth had ever crossed her mind when they were dating, but she couldn't. Mentioning Charlie always made Jane flinch, and besides, Lizzy knew that Jane wasn't one to care about money. Charlie could have been as poor as Luke and she still would have fallen for him. He was the yin to her yang.

'Is Luke still coming for dinner on Saturday?' asked Jane.

'Yeah. I told him I wouldn't be here but he's

keen to come anyway. Reckons Mum's cooking is worth it even if I'm not here.'

Jane laughed. 'He has Mum wrapped around his little finger.'

'And Lydia and Kitty. I don't know how he handles their carry on.' Lizzy sighed.

'But the sheep show's too good to miss, Lizzy. You've been working towards this for years with Pippa. I know you'll both be brilliant. And the prize money could be so good for you. You're going to get the chance to breed your working dogs, I just know it. This is just the start. I wish I could be there too.'

Lizzy sighed. If Jane was right, then all the reading and watching training videos would have been worth it. Lizzy loved working with Pippa, and starting a stud for working dogs could be a great side earner. She just needed somewhere to start.

'I'll send you constant updates. And I'm sure Aunty Joy will film some of it too.'

It was Wayne who'd found Pippa for Lizzy. He loved his dogs, and over the years he'd taught her everything he knew about training them, which had whet her appetite for more. It had been a year since she'd visited her aunt and uncle in Wundella, and the town's sheep show was renowned as one of the best, so this trip was long overdue. Pippa would love the journey. She did her best work with an audience, whether it was John and Luke or Jane and Lottie.

'I'm trying not to set my expectations too high. There'll be some amazing dogs there that have been trained by the best.'

'Don't sell yourself short,' said Jane as she climbed into bed. 'Go in believing you're just as good. Pippa is amazing. She'll show them all.'

'I hope you're right,' Lizzy replied with a smile. Her plan was to keep an eye out for the perfect mate for Pippa, one that could add to her abilities. Butterflies started to dance in her belly with the thought, but she forced her nerves away. It was a long time until Saturday.

★ ★ ★

It turned out that Saturday was coming around before she knew it. With sheep to shift and machinery to put back together, plus the usual bookwork, Lizzy was in a mad panic early Friday morning, packing like her life depended on it.

'Thanks, Mum,' she said as Margaret passed her a container of food for the trip.

'Dress well, dear. Appearances do count. If you were looking for a person to do business with would you have more faith in a well-dressed man or one who looks like he's just staggered out of a pub?'

Lizzy rolled her eyes. 'It's okay, I've packed my best jeans and my blue R.M. Williams shirt.'

'Your boots are on the verandah. I got Kitty to polish them up last night.'

'Aw, thanks Mum.' Lizzy gave her a hug and headed to the door with her bag over her shoulder.

Her dad followed her and picked up her polished boots. 'I'll bring them. I filled up your ute and checked your tyres,' he said. 'And I put in an extra bottle with water for the radiator if she gets too hot or gets low. Must swap that one out one day,' he said frowning with frustration. 'You call if you run into trouble. I'll come from this way or if you're closer to Wayne, you know he'll come too.'

'Thanks Dad. Call me if anything happens around here,' she said, throwing her bag onto the passenger seat. She whistled for Pippa, who came promptly and jumped up on the ute. Lizzy clipped her onto the short chain and then patted her head. 'I hope you weren't off rolling in anything gross. I washed you so you'd dazzle them with your shiny coat,' she said leaning closer and risking a sniff of her fur. It was a dangerous exercise; sometimes the smell of rotting animal stink could burn your nostrils like caustic soda.

Pippa looked at her with irritation. She hated being clean and, like most dogs, much preferred her dead-animal perfume.

'Right, best hit the road.'

'Take it easy and let us know when you arrive,' said John.

The eight-hour drive was nothing compared to her usual sixteen-hour stints in the tractor at seeding or the header at harvest. But she nodded her head like a good girl.

'Bye Dad.'

⋆ ⋆ ⋆

The dark bitumen took her past endless paddocks filled with green pasture, some with

224

cereal crops, others bright yellow with canola, past salt lakes and bush reserves and little towns that city people wouldn't have heard of. Lizzy didn't mind taking short cuts on gravel roads — she was raised on them, plus her ute didn't get much over a hundred anyway. The container of goodies Margaret had packed her was open on the passenger seat, and Lizzy lasted three hours before pulling the lid off to attack the slices and cakes.

She stopped every hour or so for a break and to let Pippa off for a run. It added time to a long trip, but they both needed it. Lizzy needed to rest her mind; the drive gave her too much time to think about Jane and Charlie, about the unfairness of the situation and the appalling behaviour of people like Caroline and her parents. Lizzy also thought of Will and Luke, their shared past and completely different futures. She'd sent Luke a message before she'd left, letting him know she'd be at the trials, but she hadn't heard from him yet.

It was getting dark as she pulled into Wayne and Joy's driveway. Their house came into view, the sun setting behind it, causing the house to look like it was encased in a golden orb. The outside lights were on, ready for her arrival. Lizzy pulled up alongside Wayne's red Nissan ute, turned off her engine and then let out a sigh.

'Finally!' She heard Wayne's booming voice as she sent a text to Jane and her father confirming her arrival. 'Doesn't that ute go above eighty?'

She climbed out of the ute just in time to be wrapped up in his beefy arms and crushed against his beer belly.

'Hiya Lizzy Loo. I missed you,' he said kissing the top of her head.

Leaning back she took in his bearded face, slightly ginger and very much bushman length, and smiled. 'It's great to see you too, Uncle Wayne.'

'Best you take your bag and get inside before Joy goes crook that I've kept you from her,' he said with a chuckle. 'She's been in a tizz all day. You head in and I'll go put Pippa in her pen.'

'Cool, thanks.'

He then began to lavish attention on Pippa, whose tail was wagging so quickly it resembled Will's helicopter blades.

Lizzy walked along the familiar old brick pathway to the back door. 'Aunty Joy, I'm here,' she called out as she opened the door, slipping off her shoes as she had on every visit since she was twelve.

Again she was pounced on without warning the moment she entered.

'I can't believe it, you're here!'

Joy was as soft and cuddly as her husband. *Never trust a skinny cook*, was one of his favourite sayings and Joy's cooking was bloody amazing. Lizzy went to pull back but Joy wouldn't let her.

'Stay a little longer, honey,' she said holding her firmly.

Joy smelled like apple, cinnamon and flour. Her hair was cropped short, to save time she'd said, and her smile could rival Julia Roberts'. Her green eyes sparkled like emeralds at the bottom of a lake, her face so warm and soft. Everyone loved Joy; she oozed love and openness.

'I bet you're tired and hungry?' she asked, finally moving Lizzy out to arm's reach. 'Dinner's just about ready. Chuck your bag in your room then come and sit and we can chat while I serve up.'

'Sounds perfect. I'll be right back.'

When she opened the door to the spare room — which had always been known as 'Jane and Lizzy's room' — warmth wrapped around her. Joy had the oil heater going. Fresh sheets were on the bed and a fluffy towel was rolled up on the end of the grey quilt. It felt like arriving at her second home. Memories of her youth flooded back. Playing Monopoly on the floor during a hail storm. Swimming in the thick muddy dams. Getting towed behind the quad bike on a knee board through endless puddles. Leaving their younger sisters at home to visit for school holidays had always felt like going away to camp.

Dropping her bag into the room, she closed the door and returned to the kitchen to find Wayne sitting at the breakfast bar telling Joy how excited he was to see Pippa perform.

'I hope she can live up to your expectations,' said Lizzy.

'Don't be like that, lass. It's all experience. Drink it in and learn. Then come back next year and knock their socks off.'

'You must come back next year!' said Joy, blinking her long eyelashes hopefully.

'It's already in my calendar.'

Joy served them up steaming shepherd's pie with a side of vegetables before joining them at the breakfast bar. With just the two of them they never used their dining table. Instead it was home to mountains of washing, lambs' bottles and teats, mail and egg cartons.

Lizzy told them everything that had happened at Longbourn over the past few months since their last phone call. About Jane and Charlie, about Luke and even about Will and his helicopter.

Over apple pie and ice-cream she showed them her photos.

'Did you know that Will Darcy lives not far from us?' said Wayne.

'Really?'

'Yep. Pemberley is amazing. I'll have to take you over there after the trials. You have to see the old homestead and the horses.'

'Will they mind us popping over?'

'Nah, I know Paddy, he's the head overseer there. Young Will hasn't been home all week and isn't due back for a while, so Paddy said yesterday at the pub.'

'What were you doing at the pub?' accused Joy.

'What do you think, woman? Buying your port,' he said with a wink as he reached across and kissed her cheek.

'Oh, you sly dog. Don't think you can butter me up that easy.'

While they bantered on, Lizzy couldn't help but wonder what Will was doing. Still at

Charlie's working with Peter? Or maybe he'd flown to the city for one of Caroline's fancy events? Then she grew annoyed with herself for caring; it was none of her business what he got up to. On the plus side, at least she didn't have to worry about running into him out here.

'You look beat, love,' Joy said, interrupting her thoughts. 'How about you go and have a hot shower and crawl into bed?'

Lizzy looked up to find Joy and Wayne watching her with caring eyes.

'I'll help you with the dishes first,' she said, standing up and trying to collect the plates, but Joy slapped her hand away.

'You'll do no such thing. You're our guest. Besides, we have a new addition in the kitchen now. Wayne got me a dishwasher for my birthday,' she said with a grin. 'Although I think it was more for him because he was sick of helping me with the dishes.'

'Too right I was,' he said with a chuckle.

Later, showered and resting in bed, Lizzy flicked through her photos again. In one of the helicopter shots she had accidentally caught Will in her selfie. He was looking ahead as he flew, his face relaxed and happy. Her mind went back to the moment he'd helped her from the helicopter and taken her hand. Just her hand. Yet somehow it seemed so much more personal than the intense kisses Luke had given her after dinner at Longbourn. Was it because she didn't like Will? Or that the story about his dad and the flying experience had heightened her own emotions?

With a curse she almost threw her phone on

the floor by the bed. 'Be gone, Will Darcy,' she muttered before rolling over.

Tomorrow was an important day and she didn't need him invading her thoughts.

18

The house was buzzing when she woke at six. The smell of bacon wafted through the place as Lizzy listened to Joy hum some old song. Outside Wayne was unlocking gates and talking to the dogs. No doubt a pep talk before today's events.

With a smile she got out of bed, eager to join them. Wayne had entered the trials with Raff, his tan Kelpie. Last night they'd made their own personal wager that the one with the lower score over the two-day event would buy the other one a beer.

'Good morning, pet. Eat up. Big couple of days ahead.' Joy stopped and frowned at Lizzy. 'Are you nervous? You look nervous. Wayne, does she look nervous?' asked Joy as he entered the kitchen.

Wayne pinched her cheek gently. 'Yeah, she'll be a little nervous, I'd say, but a big feed will fix that. Eat up, Lizzy, and then we'll head off.'

Her stomach was so churned up she only just managed to eat her egg and one rasher of bacon. 'I'm scared I'll hurl if I eat any more,' she told them by way of apology.

Wayne patted her arm. 'It's okay, Lizzy. Nerves are good. That's why they start with Novice Day — throw you straight in so you don't have to wait, and leave the experienced ones for the Open event on Sunday. Once we get there you'll relax a bit. Come on, we better head off.'

He stood and kissed Joy. 'Thanks for brekkie, love. Ready to go in five?' he asked her.

Joy pulled off her apron and smiled at him. 'Thanks to that dishwasher I'll be ready in three.'

With the dogs on the back of Wayne's ute they headed into town. Lizzy squished in between them in the front seat and was in control of the music. But it was just background music as her mind was going flat out on what was about to happen. Joy and Wayne spoke on occasion, about the locals and who had dogs entered, but Lizzy just nodded.

They pulled up in the parking area, then checked the dogs were okay and headed to the trial area — a cricket oval enclosed by a white picket fence. Inside the fence on the grass the obstacle course was set out. Seeing it set out made Lizzy's mouth go dry.

'Might be coffee time,' muttered Joy, as if reading Lizzy's mind.

Two teenage boys walked past — jeans, boots and cowboy hats were the order of the day — eating hot doughnuts, the cinnamon sugar covering their fingers.

'And some of them, Wayne, lots of them,' added Joy as she watched the boys pass, her mouth open.

Wayne chuckled as they headed off past a row of stalls set up for the event.

'Could I interest you in some bark collars? Or we have some new leather collars?' spruiked a man in a tent full of canine wares. The collars were displayed on a white table and some hung

232

from a rod in every colour with different styles of name plates.

Wayne shook his head as they continued. The next tent was stocked with shirts for sale: good farming ones with collars and long sleeves in vibrant pinks, greens and blues for the ladies and prints or patterns for the blokes. Joy shot Lizzy a look that said, *We must stop there.*

'I'd like to have a good look after my event,' Lizzy said. 'First I'd like to watch some of the other competitors and get a feel.'

'Good plan, Lizzy,' said Wayne. 'Try to get comfortable.' He nodded in agreement.

'Oh look, that's Bruce Holland.' He pointed to an old man standing out in the arena with a white felt Akubra hat, a red Kelpie alongside him. 'That's his bitch Kellymare Sue,' said Wayne as they sat on a bench seat near the oval. 'I don't like the look of those young Dohnes, though. They're making it challenging,' he added. 'But I'll nick off and fetch us those doughnuts.'

Lizzy gripped her knees as she watched the sheep, knowing her time to compete was getting closer. Wayne was right about the sheep: they weren't making it easy. She watched Bruce, who had fifteen minutes to complete the course. He wasn't allowed to assist the dog; he could only direct by signal, whistle or voice. Bruce was doing well with signals and had Sue casting out beautifully, his red dog taking her time as she assessed the sheep.

Lizzy had tried to memorise the regulations and rules so she knew what not to do, but it was easier said than done. She and Pippa would start with a hundred points and would have points deducted for all sorts of things — sheep going off course, Pippa losing control of the sheep. They could also be disqualified if Pippa bit a sheep or crossed between Lizzy and the sheep. It was pretty full on, and watching the display in front of her wasn't helping calm her nerves.

'Well done, Bruce and Sue,' said Joy, clapping as he finished his trial.

'Not bad. Seen Sue do a better run,' said Wayne as he returned with coffee and a white paper bag of steaming sugariness and offered its contents to the women. 'Again that's more to do with the sheep, but everyone'll be in the same boat.'

'No thanks. Stomach's too tight,' said Lizzy. That was a first, her knocking back a sweet treat.

'How do you think Pippa's feeling?' asked Joy.

Lizzy glanced down at Pippa sitting beside her on her lead. Her muscles were quivering on and off in anticipation, like they did when she knew she was about to go bring in the sheep, and her ears were pointed up like satellite dishes tracking sounds from space. 'She's excited. She knows something's about to happen.'

'Go get 'em, girls,' said Wayne, clapping his big hand on her shoulder.

'Good luck, love,' said Joy.

Lizzy nodded, unable to open her mouth, for it was drier than a water trough in a drought.

She released Pippa upon entering the arena. While Lizzy felt a little sick she could tell that Pippa was excited by the sound and smell of the

234

sheep and other dogs. Pippa always got excited about sheep work. All the dogs here were the same.

Lizzy glanced at the watching crowd, then forced her focus back to the task at hand. She stood at the peg, waiting for the sheep to be released down the other end of the oval. Pippa was close by, still but her eyes watched Lizzy eagerly, knowing a command would come soon. And then the bell went. Fifteen minutes started. With a whistle she cast Pippa out to the right, and in that moment Lizzy forgot the churning in her stomach as Pippa and the sheep became her whole focus.

Pippa moved behind the sheep and then gently corralled the sheep in a straight line to Lizzy; the rules stated she had to keep them moving within an eight-metre corridor, and Pippa took her time, Lizzy making her pause often, which allowed the sheep to move steadily together. So far it was working well.

They had three obstacles: the race, bridge and pen. Lizzy had to walk on a set path marked out on the ground. The bridge she found the hardest, because the sheep didn't like the surface of the bridge and it was higher than Pippa. The pen was the last one and sometimes the most difficult because sheep were hard to move into a small space when they had a whole oval to roam around. Lizzy had to guess the way the sheep would move, watching their bodies and their eyes and then keep one eye on Pippa to pass on her commands and keep her where she needed her.

With a few swift commands Pippa stepped

then stopped, and the sheep moved. Another step closer she went, then Lizzy got her to stop. The front ewe stepped into the small pen and the other two followed. Pippa sat by the entry on command while Lizzy moved over to shut the gate. Only once the gate was closed did Lizzy take a deep breath and let it out in a rushed sigh.

Finally they'd finished the course and the bell sounded again.

She gave Pippa a pat. 'Well done, Pip. Good job.' As she headed back to the seat they announced her score.

'You did amazingly, Lizzy. There's a trainer in you, that's for sure,' said Wayne pulling her in for a bear hug.

Joy was right behind him, lined up to do the same. 'Congratulations, Lizzy. Brilliant run. I filmed the whole lot.'

They had a little bit of time before Wayne's trial. Music wafted through the white and blue pop-up tents, mixed with dogs barking, sheep baaing and handpieces humming from the shearing shed. The smell of sheep poo and lanolin was strong, mixed with coffee and roast meat from the Lamb Van parked down near a tree at the end of a row of stalls.

Wayne stood in front of them, his belly stretching his long-sleeved green shirt. 'Righto, I best get Raff and see if I can't beat your score.'

'Better do your best, dear. Lizzy got eighty-nine, that's the best so far,' teased Joy.

He scratched at his beard. 'It's going to be hard, those sheep are runny and unpredictable as the day goes on. It could be all the distractions from the shearing and field day,' he said glancing towards the more populated part of the show.

'Here we go, here come the excuses,' laughed Joy, giving Lizzy a wink.

Lizzy stood up and held Wayne's arm. 'I'll go and put Pippa back by the ute, but I'll be right back. Good luck, Uncle Wayne. Go get 'em, Rafferty Raff.'

Raff started well and the three sheep kept to the corridor as he moved them towards Wayne. But things went downhill from there.

'They won't look down the obstacles,' mumbled Lizzy.

'Oh, damn sheep. They're making Wayne and Raff work for it. Oh, that's better, there they go,' said Joy.

She gave a running commentary as the sheep went through the gates, over the bridge and into the pen. Then she turned to Lizzy. 'You won the bet, Lizzy. No one will beat your score today. I'll eat my hat if I'm wrong.'

'Lucky you're not wearing a hat, Aunty Joy.' Lizzy smiled at her.

Wayne arrived back not long after with Raff, whose tongue was hanging out the side of his mouth as he stood obediently by Wayne's legs.

'Ah well, I tried my best and so did Raff. Sixty-three isn't bad.'

'You did amazingly considering they were so flighty, Uncle Wayne. Shall we go find the beer tent?' she asked with a grin, throwing her hands on her hips.

'Bloody ratbag. All right, I'll buy you a beer seeing as you beat me. Still feel like I should be buying you a soft drink instead.'

'Ha ha, I've been able to drink for years now. I hope they sell Coronas,' she said.

'Shit, you're going to send me broke just like Joy.' He laughed as Joy elbowed him. 'I'll buy you both a drink.'

The beer tent was elbow-to-elbow with chatty, denim-clad men and women. They found a spot to stand near a tall table and waited.

'See, I'm a man of my word,' said Wayne, plonking two beers on the table and a Coke for Joy. 'There you go, my gorgeous designated driver,' he said pressing a kiss to her cheek.

Lizzy listened to the conversations around her; talk of dogs, trials and sheep. She sighed contentedly and sipped her beer.

At the end of the day they announced the Novice placings. A table had been set up by the beer tent and the officials stood by to hand out the awards while the announcer held the microphone.

'And first place in the Novice event is Elizabeth Bennet with Longbourn Pippa with a fabulous score of eighty-nine. Congratulations. We'll be keeping an eye on your progress,' said the announcer.

Lizzy walked up in front of the gathered crowd, feeling heat prickle at the back of her neck and butterflies in her stomach. One official handed her an envelope and another a twenty-kilogram bag of dog kibbles.

'Bad luck on missing out on third place, Uncle Wayne,' she said, dropping the dog food at their feet.

Wayne waved her off, his face glowing. 'I'm so bloody proud of you, Lizzy. My own little protégé.'

Joy scoffed. 'Yes, Wayne, because her first place is all *your* doing,' she said with an exaggerated eye roll.

'Too bloody right. I set the seed and found the perfect working dog for her. Ain't that right, love?'

Wayne threw an arm around Lizzy and beamed down at her. His smile was so wide it looked like a fox tail was spread across his face as his beard twinkled in the sunlight.

Lizzy couldn't wipe the smile off her own face. Pippa had done it. She'd shown off for the crowd and proved she could win. She was so proud of her girl. 'Yes, Uncle Wayne, I do owe you for finding Pip and giving me the bug. Bloody amazing feeling.'

Joy elbowed Wayne in the ribs. 'It's not all you gave her. Now she has your potty mouth!'

They all burst out laughing and headed for the ute, the bag of kibbles on Wayne's shoulder and the envelope in Lizzy's pocket.

Once the dogs were settled on the back they piled in and Lizzy finally opened her envelope.

'Holy crap.' A pile of green notes fell into her hand. 'There's . . . there's like — ' She counted them. 'Bloody hell, there's a thousand dollars in here!'

'Well, I'll be,' said Joy, her head bent over the money.

Wayne chuckled. 'That's a huge prize. I heard today from one of the fellas that they got a great sponsor for the event at the last minute.'

'Geez, they were generous. Wonder what the Open winner will get?'

Lizzy re-counted the notes, suddenly feeling rich and at a bit of a loss as to what to spend it on. New ute tyres, a stud ram, new roof for the old shed that had been damaged in the last storm, or maybe a sheep feeder, or to keep the bank off her back.

'Who was it, love?' asked Joy. 'The last-minute sponsor?'

The sun was dipping towards the land, the sky growing darker as Joy turned on the ute lights.

'Will Darcy.'

Lizzy's head jolted up. 'Will Darcy?'

'Yep. Jim said they nearly fell over when he handed over the cash. They normally just have dog food and bits.'

'That's wonderful. How nice of him,' said Joy.

Lizzy swallowed, her heart racing as she shoved the money back into the envelope at a rate of knots.

'I wonder what made him want to sponsor the dog trials?' said Joy.

Rolling the envelope through her fingers, Lizzy found herself asking the same question.

19

'Morning, Jane.'

Lizzy pressed her phone to her ear and held it there with her shoulder while she stacked up pancakes on her plate. Last night she'd called her sister straightaway to tell her the good news. Then Jane made her recount the whole day in detail. Which made her wonder why she was calling this morning.

'Hey Lizzy, be glad you're not in this house this morning. Lydia has somehow managed to talk our parents into letting her stay with Carol and Neil in Toongarrin for a few days. I told them it was a bad idea.'

'Oh no. Carol and Neil are too old for a crazy teenager. She'll run amok. They're worse than our parents on the discipline. God, I can see her walking the streets already, sneaking off to parties. How did she wrangle that?'

'I don't know. There must be someone there she wants to catch up with, maybe kids that she's met through school. Probably one is having a party. She's going to end up in trouble, I just know it.' Jane's voice was low and full of worry.

'I'll call Dad and tell him not to let her go if you think it'll help?'

'Please? Mum won't listen to anything I've said.'

'Righto. I'll try Dad. Talk to you later.'

They hung up and she promptly called John,

241

but the call went to voicemail. 'Dad, please don't let Lydia go to Toongarrin. There's no one there to watch out for her. She's too young.' Then she called Margaret, but the house phone rang out, so she tried her mobile and left a similar message.

'Best I can do,' she said with a sigh.

'Lydia?' said Joy.

Lizzy nodded.

'Always been a handful. There's a reason we only ever had you two older girls here,' she said with a chuckle.

'Yeah, we're not that silly,' added Wayne as he came into the kitchen. 'Hey, I was just speaking with Paddy and he said we should come over after lunch and he'll show us around Pemberley. That'll work in nicely. That way we can see half the Open trials.'

Lizzy frowned. 'We don't have to go there, Uncle Wayne.' She was starting to have a weird reaction just thinking about anything to do with Will Darcy: her gut would churn, her skin would tingle and her tiny arm hairs would stand on end as if she'd rubbed against a balloon.

'It's all right. I told you no one will be home. Well, maybe young Georgie, but she's a lovely girl.'

It was settled regardless of what Lizzy thought. But she had to admit she was a bit curious to see the Darcy empire and maybe even Georgie.

At the trials the weather was a little cooler but the sheep just as difficult. Lizzy watched in awe as the handlers worked their dogs. Some entered three times with different dogs. It was fascinating to see how each dog worked with the same handler. It became more about the dog's personality.

'I'm glad I stayed to watch the Open event,' she said as they left the arena. 'Those dogs were amazing and the trainers.'

'Make you excited to come back?' Wayne asked eagerly.

Lizzy nodded. 'For sure.'

On the drive to Pemberley, Wayne gave Lizzy a rundown on the homestead and property, but nothing could have prepared her for the reality. It wasn't just the ridiculously huge sheds or near-new farm machinery, it was the amazing gravel roads that were like highways. At home on Longbourn, Lizzy felt like she bruised her kidneys just getting from the house to the shed; it was impossible to dodge all the potholes in her ute. Will must have a full-time grader driver here, which was an extravagant thought for a farm. She spotted the belly dumper, which would cart around the gravel. He's probably got his own bulldozer for pushing up the gravel too, she thought as she stared in wonder.

'It's like being at a Machinery Field Day,' Lizzy spluttered as they drove past open sheds. 'He has every machine imaginable.'

'And there are probably lots you can't see,' said Wayne. 'Paddy said he'd be at the workshop today, so we'll go there first.'

The 'workshop' made her burst out laughing, maybe a little hysterically. 'It's massive!'

Wayne parked off to the side and they walked into yet another huge shed. It was split into two sections, each with side pits and hoists: one for servicing trucks and bigger machinery, and the other for the farm utes. Three workers wearing blue KingGee shirts and pants with the Pemberley name in white on the breast pocket were busy replacing tyres.

'All these guys are qualified diesel and auto mechanics. Their sole job is to do the upkeep on all the vehicles,' said Wayne.

They turned to the right into an office; on one wall hung belts of every kind, spare filters and parts on shelves, and against the opposite wall were stacks of new tyres. It was a buffet of parts.

'This is unbelievable,' mumbled Lizzy. Then she saw all the motorbikes. 'I'm so jealous I must be as green as a pea.'

'Nah, more a sage colour,' teased Wayne. 'I knew you'd like it. Ah, here's Paddy,' he added and stepped towards a tall man who came out of a small room in the back corner.

'G'day, Paddy. Thanks for letting us have a look around. This is my niece, Elizabeth Bennet.'

She held out her hand. 'Lizzy. Nice to meet you, Paddy.'

'Likewise, Lizzy.' His grip was strong and she instantly liked him. 'Let me take you up to the homestead, I'm sure you wouldn't mind a quick drink before we head around outside.' He motioned towards the dual-cab Land Cruiser in the shed and they all climbed in. 'The homestead was built in the 1860s by Andrew Darcy. He had Edmund Wright to design the stone homestead, coach house and stables, all of which have heritage listing.'

'Sounds like you know a fair bit,' said Lizzy.

Paddy nodded. 'My father worked for Mr Darcy, I grew up on this place and now I work for Will. My father retired ten years ago and I stepped into his role. Couldn't find a better boss than Will. He has his old man's work ethic and loyalty, yet he has compassion, which he must have picked up from Jess over the years.'

'Is that it?' said Lizzy pointing to a cream stone building that came into view. It had a simple but elegant garden around it that was obviously tended to regularly.

Paddy laughed. 'No, that's my place. Many years back when I was just a little fella Mr Darcy renovated the old coach house for my father. Dad's in a nursing home now, but I live in there with my wife and our kids. Mel, my wife, works at the main house on occasion too. Mr Darcy offered us another homestead but my father wanted to remain closer to Mr Darcy's side. They were great mates.'

This wasn't the main house!

'Darcys have been here a long time,' she said more to herself.

Paddy smiled proudly. 'Sure have.'

Lizzy wondered where Luke and even his dad fitted into this picture. It seemed they didn't. A prickling sensation niggled at the back of her neck but she tried to ignore it as she drank in the amazing surroundings. Further ahead loomed big gum trees, pine trees and smaller trees encasing an area that all looked green and well tended. They drove up the maintained road and suddenly the trees opened up to reveal a sprawling lawn and a cream stone two-storey homestead. It was very much a Victorian English country house. A sweeping verandah like a tent with lattice corners went the whole way round, and the second-storey windows were enshrouded by ornate white shutters. Black coach lights adorned the walls near the main door, and wicker chairs sat perfectly placed along the stone-floor verandah.

Lizzy felt as if she were in another world, following Paddy on a cloud as she took in the breathtaking home. Even Joy was silent despite the occasional looks they shared. Wayne had been here a few times before and yet he still had a big smile on his face.

Inside didn't disappoint, either. High ceilings with intricate cornices and detailed ceiling roses and arches. Chandeliers and oak floorboards, passageways wide enough to drive a ute down, and thick doorways that led into seemingly endless no-expense-spared rooms.

'Will hasn't changed a thing from when he was a kid. I think it makes him feel closer to his mum. She did the original redesign of the house before he was born.'

'Oh, that's sad. It's not right growing up without your mum,' said Joy quietly.

'I'll take you to the sitting room and see if Jess can bring us some refreshments,' said Paddy leading them through the house.

Lizzy was already in a blur trying to figure out which way they'd come in. She assumed the bedrooms were all on the top level, because the bottom floor seemed to be made up of various entertaining areas: dining rooms — one formal and one casual — a TV room that resembled a movie theatre, a study lined with books upon books and populated by single leather high-backed chairs that looked perfect for reading in. This was by far her favourite room. Lizzy stopped in front of a floor-to-ceiling bookshelf and browsed the spines. A vast array of fiction, educational books, history books and even record-keeping books from the Darcy family.

'Oh, hello?'

Lizzy drew her finger away from the book she was about to pull out and spun around at the sound of the soft voice.

'Ah, hi. Sorry.' She glanced around the room and realised the others had moved on. She was all alone with a pretty young woman watching her curiously. She looked to be about Kitty's age with long brown hair, luminous eyes and freckles. She was barefoot and wore old jeans with a white singlet.

'Can I help you?' she asked enquiringly.

'Um, I'm Elizabeth Bennet, I'm here with my uncle. Paddy was showing us around.'

No sooner had she finished than the girl's eyes grew wide and she stepped closer.

'Oh my god. Elizabeth Bennet? Lizzy? My brother has told me all about you! Wow, it's so nice to meet you. I'm Georgie, his sister.'

She stuck out her hand to Lizzy and shook with gusto. Lizzy liked her there and then. She had Will's smile, though in Georgie it seemed more effusive and more frequent.

'Hi Georgie, so nice to meet you too.'

'This is Will's favourite room. He's usually working over there all hours of the night,' she said, pointing to a huge jarrah desk in the corner.

'I think it's my favourite too. I love books. I just want to stay here and read them all.'

Georgie rolled her eyes. 'Urgh, now you sound like Will. I'd rather be outside riding my horse or helping the boys with the sheep. I have to make the most of being home from boarding school,' she said sadly.

'You should take time to read too, I guarantee you when you get lost in a book you'll be hooked.'

'Maybe. Do you have any recommendations?'

Lizzy smiled. 'I could think of a few. I could email you a list.'

'Could I have your number too?'

'Sure.'

They swapped numbers and email addresses then, glancing towards the door, Lizzy nodded. 'I better catch up with the others before they send out a search party.'

'I'll come with you,' said Georgie setting off after her.

Lizzy stepped through the doorway and ran smack bang into a firm chest. Her face, ever so briefly, was pressed up against warmth, and a leathery lavender scent filled her senses, making her feel slightly concussed.

'*Will!*' scolded Georgie. 'You just about crushed poor Lizzy to death.'

Georgie's words brought realisation. Quickly Lizzy pushed back against his chest and found herself firmly in his gaze.

'Sorry, Will. I didn't see you there. I'm just trying to find my uncle,' she stammered.

He seemed to take delight in her fluster, for his lips curved ever so slightly as if he was trying not to openly smile.

'They're in the sitting room. I'll take you,' he said turning. 'I see you've met Georgie?'

Will opened his arm and Georgie stepped into it, hugging him tightly. It was a cosy, warm hug that made Will's eyes sparkle with so much love Lizzy had to look away. She was not used to the rawness of his emotions. Clearly Georgie turned him to putty.

'Yes, she's lovely. I'm sorry, I was told you weren't here and yet here you are finding people traipsing through your home.' She felt her face redden at the complete invasion of privacy. Lizzy knew she would die if Will was ever shown through her house unannounced.

'It's okay. We're used to it. All our private stuff is mainly upstairs,' said Georgie.

'And Paddy's here. This is his home too,' said Will. 'I'm glad you're here.'

His words were so sincere she gaped up at him blankly. He did look relaxed today. He was in light-wash jeans and a U2 T-shirt. 'Nice shirt,' she said without thinking.

His eyebrows shot up. 'You like? Georgie bought it for me.'

'Yeah, 'cause he's always playing them. He has old taste in music,' she scoffed and put her finger in her mouth as she led the way. 'I told him he should try Amy Shark.'

'Oh, I love her,' said Lizzy. Georgie beamed.

'Hey, there you are. Thought you'd got lost,' said Wayne as they walked into the sitting room.

The table was laid out with biscuits and cake. Joy was already halfway through a chocolate slice, and Paddy was sprawled back in a chair as if he really did live here. Lizzy almost laughed as she suddenly thought of the difference between this house and the Bingley home — she wasn't at all sure Caroline's family would be as relaxed about their workers in their home.

'All right, cuppa time!'

A woman bustled in with a tray filled with cups, a teapot and a milk jug. She was a bit younger than Joy, and she had Georgie's freckles. Her hair was up in a loose bun and she wore jeans and a floral top.

'Lizzy, this is Jess, Georgie's mum.'

Jess's mouth dropped open a fraction as she turned her eyes to Lizzy.

'And the housekeeper,' she said with a grin. 'So nice to meet you, Lizzy.' Jess put down her tray and pulled Lizzy into a hug, enveloping her in lavender. 'Grab a seat. I'll get you a drink and then we'll talk.'

Will and Georgie shared a two-seater chair while Lizzy sat in another. It was a bright room in soft mint with wooden floors and wooden furnishings. The chairs were a mixture of brown leather but were worn and cosy.

Georgie tucked her legs up under her and rested against Will.

Everyone seemed to know who Lizzy was, which made her wonder exactly what Will had been telling them. The crazy bush woman from next door to Charlie Bingley's new farm? Had he amused them with anecdotes of their strained meetings?

When she glanced their way, Will and Georgie were watching her.

20

'So, what brings you up our way, Lizzy?' asked Jess as she sat on the armrest of the couch next to Will and Georgie.

Seeing Jess so relaxed put Lizzy at ease despite the grand surroundings.

'I came to visit these guys,' she said gesturing to Joy and Wayne. 'And I entered the dog trials yesterday.'

'Oh, I heard you were great. I'd like to meet Pippa,' said Georgie.

Lizzy stared.

Georgie sat back. 'Will told me. He watched your event,' she added softly.

'I didn't see him there.' Will was watching her and remained silent. For a moment she couldn't think of what to say. 'Pippa would love to meet you too. She loves people nearly as much as she loves sheep,' she ended up blurting.

It was heating up in this room, not helped when she took another sip of her hot coffee and felt her hot flush intensify.

Georgie grinned and started telling her about how she had convinced Will to let her have a sheep dog to train. Lizzy nodded and listened but her thoughts were slow as if trudging through mud. Will had been at the trial. He'd seen her but hadn't said hello, and today she was seeing the warm, happy, adoring brother. It was all just too surprising and strange. When would she figure out which was the real Will Darcy?

'Can I show you my puppy?' asked Georgie, interrupting her thoughts. 'His name's Dudley.'

'I'd love to meet him.' Lizzy shot up quickly, eager to leave this room and be back outside.

Georgie jumped up and led her through the house out the back.

'Will wouldn't let me have a dog for years because I was away at boarding school and he said it wouldn't be fair on the dog. But I'm in my last year now and I plan to come home and work here.'

'And your brother's happy with that?' Another flash of memory hit Lizzy: Will not believing she was a proper farmer capable of making Longbourn a success. How would this attitude bode for Georgie?

Georgie frowned. 'At first he wasn't. Said he wanted me to finish school. Education's important. The world's my oyster. All that stuff.'

'But?'

'Well, I told him that this place was my oyster. I love it here, I'm happiest here and I don't see why I shouldn't be doing what I love.' Georgie smiled. 'Will had no comeback for that. I said that if he wants me to be happy, then he needs to let me help out here with him.'

'So, you wore him down?'

Georgie shrugged as they headed down a well-used path, chicken pens off to one side. 'No, I wouldn't say I wore him down. He just saw that what I said was the truth, and he wants me to be happy. He's down to earth, my big brother, even though he has this massive task that keeps him so busy. I want to help ease that pressure, and I don't see why in this day and age I can't help my brother run the family business.'

Some family business, thought Lizzy. If she was Georgie she'd have wanted the same thing, so she understood exactly where Will's sister was coming from. Sometimes the land seeped into your blood and became a passion, regardless of whether you were a man or a woman.

'This is Dudley. Still a terror and loves to chew everything.'

Georgie opened the door to a large wire pen and a chocolate ball of cuteness was in and out of their legs and jumping around. Lizzy bent over and picked up the squirming puppy.

'Hello Dudley,' she said. The pup paused as he studied her while she spoke to him. 'Are you a good boy?'

He leaned forward and licked her face. Lizzy laughed and put him down.

'Do you think he'll make a good sheep dog?' asked Georgie as she tried to pat him.

'He will if you train him. I read a lot of books and watched a lot of YouTube clips. It helps to go in with as much knowledge as you can.'

'Oh, I will. It'll give me something to do back at school,' she said with an exaggerated sigh. 'I hate it there. I miss home too much.'

'You sound just like me.'

Georgie tilted her head as she spoke. 'You're nothing like the girls Will normally hangs out with.'

Lizzy laughed. 'I'm a bit different to Caroline Bingley,' she said wryly.

Georgie laughed. 'Caroline is hard work. She's too focused on what people think and her social standing. It annoys me that she tries to be friendly with me to get closer to Will.'

Ah. Well, that just confirmed a feeling Lizzy had always had about Caroline. Her eyes definitely were on Will, but was it because of his wealth or the man he was?

'I noticed she liked your brother. What does Charlie think about that?'

Georgie screwed up her face as she glanced up at the sun. 'I don't know. Will and Charlie haven't been speaking lately.' She glanced around before continuing. 'I saw Charlie once in town and he was coming to say hello but then he saw Will and walked off. I could feel the tension. Something's happened, but I'm not sure what.'

'Oh, they seemed okay last time I saw them,' said Lizzy, but the fine hairs on the back of her neck rose as something niggled.

'Yeah, they'll sort it out. They've been best friends forever.'

Georgie put Dudley back with promises to play with him again soon and then they headed back to the house.

'You should stay for dinner. We could talk dog trials and all sorts of cool stuff. My mum makes the best chicken pie.'

Lizzy put her hand up before Georgie got a head of steam up with this idea. 'I'd love to but I have to leave tomorrow and I'd like to spend some time with my aunt and uncle. I don't see them very often.'

'Oh, I understand. But please come back and

visit again. Or could I come visit you on your farm?'

Lizzy smiled. 'I'd love that. But it's nothing like this place. We're just a little farm.'

'I know. Will told me about how bad your potholes are,' she said with a chuckle. 'He was tempted to send his road crew down there to fix them for you but was scared you'd kill him for it. He said he's never met a girl so proud and determined to do everything on her own.'

Lizzy couldn't reply straightaway. 'Oh, I see,' she said eventually, a little stunned.

When they got back inside everyone was standing and Jess was clearing up.

'Ready for a tour?' asked Paddy as he moved to the door.

They followed him outside to the Land Cruiser, Lizzy happy to get a little space to think and breathe. But as they got into the ute Will climbed into the front with Paddy.

She leaned forward. 'We don't want to keep you from any important business.'

Will turned to face her, a smile on his face. 'This is important,' he said with a grin.

She flopped back into her seat.

'Oh, this is so wonderful. Thank you, Will. You're so lovely,' said Joy, who was clearly enjoying herself and maybe just a bit smitten with Will.

If Lizzy thought Will was going to play guide and spruik about all the grand machinery and toys he owned, well, she would be wrong. For most of the tour of the farm he remained quiet, letting Paddy speak about the daily ins and outs of running the Darcy empire. At one point they all got out to walk up a steep hill — their local farm lookout and, as Paddy told them, a place they loved to come as kids.

Lizzy got to a steep point and as she leaned forward to climb onto a large rock her hand was held, pulling her gently up. When she stood straight, after getting her footing, she realised it was Will who'd helped her.

'Thank you,' she said awkwardly and withdrew her hand slowly before continuing up behind Joy. She glanced down at her hand, still tingling with warmth, as if she expected to find it marked.

She glanced back at Will, who hadn't moved, his hands together as he looked out over his land. The gentle roll of earth, the clusters of trees that were filled with noisy birds and the way the scattered clouds in the wide open sky covered the ground with shade, darkening areas so the land looked spotty like a leopard. Sheep and cattle could be seen in various paddocks along with their paths that marked the earth like age lines on a face. Lizzy paused to study the look of peace on Will's face. She knew that look; it was the same one she knew showed on her face when she watched the sunrays spread across Long-bourn in the morning. It was knowing the land she stood on belonged to her, not by deed but by blood, sweat and tears. So much so that it felt a part of her soul. She'd never thought that many others felt that way, but watching Will now she recognised something they shared. And Georgie would be no different; Lizzy could see the connection in her already. It felt strange to share something so personal with Will, even though he didn't know it. He loved his land, and as the afternoon light kissed his face she thought it loved him back.

Will turned, looking to Lizzy. He smiled, his face relaxed. 'It's beautiful, is it not?' He watched her while he waited for her reply.

'Breathtaking,' she said softly and offered him a genuine smile in return. It was impossible not to.

'Are you two coming?' Wayne called from further up the hill.

Lizzy turned around quickly and power walked up the rest of the way, feeling like she'd been caught flirting. She hadn't, but she'd been swept with a desire to reach out and touch Will's face where the sunlight made him glow, so she could touch the vulnerability she saw there.

She shook her head as she reached the top. *Silly, silly Lizzy!*

'You all right, love?' asked Joy.

Lizzy pushed away her sudden feelings of affection and fascination; they put her on edge. 'Yep. It's just so stunning, this view,' she said, looking around again for good measure.

'Hm, yes. The *view*,' replied Joy softly.

Lizzy didn't like her tone but let it pass. Being at the top of the hill reminded her of their special one back home and she suddenly missed Lottie. It was sad when life moved on and all those moments became fond memories. Did Will feel the same when he came here, she wondered, trying not to look back at him. Did being here make him think of being a kid again and the fun he had before his dad died and he had to become the busy boss? Had he ever come up here with Luke as kids? Did they make cubbies together in the scrub bush that covered the hill? She risked another glance at him, wondering if she would see some sort of reminiscing in his eyes, but he was deep in conversation with Wayne.

When the tour was over Paddy drove them back to the workshop where Wayne's ute was parked. Beside it sat Georgie on a beautiful brown horse. No saddle, still barefoot with her arms draped around the horse as if she'd been chatting to him.

'Gorgeous horse, Georgie,' said Lizzy, walking over to pat him.

'This is Sir Lancelot. Lancy. He's a Morgan horse Will got from Challa Station. He's so easygoing, and just loves me.'

'Everyone loves you,' said Will.

'It was nice meeting you, Georgie.' Lizzy wanted to get this show on the road and Wayne had already thanked Paddy and Will.

'So lovely to meet you both.' Joy stepped to Will and pulled him into an awkward hug.

Lizzy took the moment to quickly climb into the ute. As the others got in Will waved goodbye and then swung himself up onto Sir Lancelot behind Georgie in an effortless motion. He reached around Georgie for the reins and nudged Lancy into a trot. Their movements without a saddle were relaxed, like they were born on the back of a horse. Will didn't turn around but Georgie waved madly from over his shoulder.

'Well, wasn't that just dandy,' said Joy as they drove back to the main road. 'Just not what you would expect.'

'I told you, Joy, never believe all that blather online and in the media. Will's a good bloke, you can tell by the way his workers speak about him. Paddy respects him and is loyal. That says a lot about a bloke.'

'Yes, and Jess must give Will some grounding too. Such a lovely woman, and that Georgie is just delightful. She was very taken with you, Lizzy.'

Lizzy just nodded. It had been an unexpected day all round. On the drive home she pretended to fall asleep but her mind flashed up images: Will in his study with all those magnificent books; Will on the hill with the sunlight; Will with Georgie on the horse.

'Paddy told me, love, that Will had just recently stopped his best mate from making a huge mistake. Apparently he was dating this woman who was just a gold digger.'

Lizzy's eyes flew open as she registered what Wayne was saying.

'A gold digger?' said Joy.

'Yep. The woman's family's doing it tough, and they were after his farm and money. Nothing worse than a woman who'll marry you and then leave with half your farm. It could have ruined him, so Will put a stop to it before it began.'

'Sad what some women do, and they're the ones who aren't even interested in the farming life,' said Joy. 'Sounds like Will did him a favour.'

Lizzy was shaking.

'Lizzy, are you okay, love? Do you feel sick?'

She shook her head fiercely. 'No. Well, yes I do feel a little sick and angry and pissed off and ready to murder Will bloody Darcy. I knew he had something to do with it,' she seethed.

'Honey, what's going on?' asked Wayne as he slowed down to watch her.

'Will's best mate is Charlie Bingley. Remember I told you about Charlie who was going out with Jane until recently when he just up and vanished. I knew something was up. Poor Jane. She's devastated. She truly cares about Charlie.'

Joy inhaled noisily. 'Oh my god. Poor Jane. She would never be that kind of woman. Never. She couldn't hurt a fly.' Her hand came up to her mouth as wide eyes stared at Lizzy.

'I'm so angry. He's read Jane all wrong. She wouldn't want his bloody money anyway.'

'Let me get this straight,' said Wayne scrunching his face. 'Jane is the woman Will stopped his mate from dating?'

'Yes!' said Joy and Lizzy loudly in unison.

'Jesus Christ. If I'd have known I would have knocked his block off. No one hurts my little Janey. No one. I have a mind to turn around and drive back and set him straight!'

'Wayne, honey, let's just get home,' said Joy quietly.

'Yes, please Uncle Wayne. I just want us to get as far away from Will Darcy as I can.'

'But they need to be set right about Jane. It's such an injustice,' he grumbled.

'The whole world is full of injustice,' said Joy with a sigh. 'It's not our place to interfere when we don't know the whole story.'

Lizzy swallowed hard. She wasn't as forgiving as Joy. Every bone in her body wanted to give Will Darcy a black eye. How could he be so two-faced? So nice and hospitable to them and yet do what he'd done to Jane? Lizzy felt betrayed and a little humiliated; she had actually started to let herself like the guy. Her jaw ached from the pressure of her clamped teeth, which was starting to cause a headache.

That night she tossed and turned and dreamed of slithering, striking snakes from which she couldn't escape. At one point she woke with a start and lay panting, sweat on her forehead as she stared into the dark. All she could think of was her sister and the heartache she now endured because of Will Darcy.

Oh, how she hated him.

21

White cockatoos squawked loudly as they flew overhead in the drizzly morning sky. Sheep baaed and dogs barked. Lizzy was staring up at the rain drops as they fell towards her face. The moving sheep had stirred up the muddy pens, the smell of sheep poo in the air along with the damp wool. It was a unique scent that felt familiar, like home. The drops were cool on her skin, refreshing.

'Oi, daydreamer. Going to help by opening the gate or are you just going to mimic a fence post?' shouted Wayne, followed by one of his big belly laughs.

Lizzy glanced down and quickly opened the pen gate, water dripping from her fingers, and stepped back so the dogs could move them forward. She shot Wayne a big smile as Raffy and Jimbo, the Border Collie, brought the last of the sheep through. Quickly she shut the gate. Pippa barked from where she was tied up on the verandah, unimpressed she was missing out but Lizzy didn't want a wet dog for the long drive home.

'Well, that didn't take too long,' said Joy as she wiped her dirty wet hands on her old jeans. No one was concerned about the light rain. They'd be done before they got soaked through and the rain would pass.

'Thanks for your help, love.'

'Least I could do.'

'Next time you come you must bring Jane. It might do her good to have a break.'

'I will, I promise. Now shall we get these sheep finished? I can hear Uncle Wayne's belly rumbling from here.'

Wayne opened his mouth to reply but paused, turning at the sound of an approaching vehicle. Lizzy watched the white ute for a moment before patting Jimbo, who'd headbutted her legs demanding her attention. He was still young and craved any love he could get.

'Jimbo, what are you going to do when I'm not here to spoil you,' she said, scratching his ears.

'Oh my!' Joy touched Lizzy's arm. 'What is *he* doing here?' she whispered.

Lizzy had thought it must be a neighbour dropping around for a chat, but seeing Joy now she realised she was way off. Her belly churned and she was almost too afraid to turn around.

'Don't worry, Lizzy, I'll clear him off,' said Wayne.

Lizzy turned. Will was out of the ute and heading their way. He was in jeans and a military-style khaki shirt that enhanced his tan. Suddenly she was bolting across the pen, scaling a fence in one bound and heading for the large machinery shed at a brisk pace as fury and nerves battled within her. Seeing him again also brought back her humiliation; she felt like a fool, and she just couldn't deal with him right now.

She raced into the shed and pressed up against the corrugated tin. With her eyes shut she sucked in air trying to slow her racing heart. She could only hope that Wayne was sending him packing, maybe with a threatening fist or strong word. Joy would be right by his side backing him up.

'Lizzy?'

Her heart smashed against her ribs as her eyes flew open at the sound of Will's voice.

He stood a metre from her. How had she not heard him? Was her blood pounding that hard?

Lizzy looked around the side, but there was no sign of Joy or Wayne.

'Look, I've asked your family to give us a moment. I needed to see you before you left.' He frowned and pushed his fingers through his hair. 'I know we're from different circles and we got off on the wrong foot, but these past weeks have been hard for me. Really hard. After seeing you yesterday I realised I can't bear it any longer.' His jaw was tensed as he swallowed. 'I've tried hard to forget you, Lizzy. To not think about you.'

She frowned. 'What? I don't understand.'

He stepped closer, too close. She wanted to move away but the tin pressed firmly against her back. She focused on the water droplets that clung to his hair.

He reached out and brushed a wet strand from her face, his fingers warm on her skin.

'I want to be with you, Lizzy.' He said the words slowly, measured.

Too late, her eyes had found his lips, uncertain of what she heard them utter. Now she was transfixed as he formed his next words.

'I want to be with you,' he repeated, his voice

rasping a little. 'I've never felt this way about anyone.'

Will reached for her hand, caressing it and was bringing it to his lips when she pulled it out of his grasp. The water on her skin made her slippery escape easy.

'I'm sorry you feel that way,' she spluttered. Was this really happening? Will Darcy was asking her out? How was that even possible? 'I've never led you on and if you think I have, then I'm sorry because I never meant to.'

He grimaced. 'So, there's no chance?'

Lizzy threw her hands on her hips. 'No, none.'

He stood up straighter as if strengthening his core ready for a gale.

'Can I ask why?' His words were softly spoken.

'*Why?*' she scoffed, glaring up at him through her wet eyelashes. 'How could I be with a man who thinks I'm some *pretend* farmer? Who has ruined my sister's happiness? Tell me, Will, do you deny that you broke up Charlie and Jane?'

He squirmed uncomfortably but his eyes never left her face. 'No, I won't deny it,' he said firmly.

'How could you!' she spluttered.

He raised his hands in surrender. 'I was looking out for Charlie. He wears his heart on his sleeve, and it's been up to me to watch out for the undesirables. I won't have him taken for a ride, he gets hurt too easily. I watched them together and saw that he cared more than she did. At the barbecue Jane didn't even look interested.'

'You have no clue,' Lizzy said angrily. 'Jane is

shy and gentle. She was so bloody sick with nerves and anxiety that day having to meet his fancy family, who did nothing to put her at ease. It was like a lamb to a pack of hungry wolves. They made Jane feel inadequate and unworthy, completely ignoring her relationship with Charlie and talking about his ex-girlfriend as if they were getting back together. All she wanted was to please them and for Charlie to love her as much as she loves him, but you stole that from them.' Lizzy wiped at her face hoping her stray tear wouldn't be noticeable with the water dripping down her face from her hair. 'I've watched my sister's heart break. Her sleepless nights, her anxiety attacks — and it's all thanks to you.' She stuck out her finger and poked him in the chest hard.

Will was stony-faced but his eyes portrayed shock.

'You probably thought our poor financial state was cause for concern,' she said, vexed.

'No. Never.' He went to reach out to her but paused. His hand hung in the air halfway to her, as if frozen in time. 'Although it was mentioned . . . '

'What? *What* was mentioned?' she snapped.

Will had the decency to look uncomfortable as he scratched the back of his neck and glanced to the rain, which was now getting heavier.

'Well, your mum was overheard raving about how their marriage would save your farm from the bank. It does make one think.'

Her eyes narrowed and her muscles tensed so badly her jaw began to ache. She breathed out through her nose and felt like a dragon gearing up to spit fire. 'I know my family can seem a little uncouth and crazy at times.' Lizzy pushed images of Lydia's performance from her mind. 'But their hearts are in the right place, and they *are* my family. They would do anything for anyone. And they don't want handouts, nor saving by a rich man. As for you?' she hurled. 'What about Luke Wickham!'

Will's brow creased, his eyes darkened. 'What about Wickham.' His voice was so low it was almost a growl.

Lizzy ignored it and continued with renewed energy. 'Your behaviour towards him. How do you excuse that? He told me how you treated him.'

He threw his head back. 'Ha, I bet he did.'

'You laugh it off, even now. You grew up with him, and still you could treat him so badly,' she said, perplexed. 'When I first met you I thought you were rude, arrogant and you didn't care about anyone's feelings,' she said bitterly.

He looked down at her hand, brushing her fingers with his shaking ones.

'Yesterday I thought that maybe I was wrong,' her voice dropped, soft and slow. 'I saw another side of you. The son and the brother and the respected boss.' She gazed up at him, her heart pounding and her skin electrified. 'But then I learned about what you did to Jane and I knew I was right all along.' Her voice crept up, louder and shakier as she tried to contain the building rage. 'Self-centred and conceited. I could *never* date a man like you.' She slid sideways out of his reach and saw a flash of pain across his face.

They watched each other, chests rising as they breathed heavily. The air around them sizzled as the sound of rain on the tin roof echoed like distant gun fire. They were in their own war zone. Lizzy felt so confused, distrustful and yet there was a sense of loss but she wasn't sure what she'd lost. This man tore her emotions in so many directions.

Will closed his eyes and released a long slow breath as if he was gathering his thoughts. When he opened his eyes Lizzy saw he had his walls back in place. The cold hard face of the Will Darcy she first met.

'I'm sorry you feel that way,' he said sombrely.

The silence stretched between them.

'I'm sorry to have interrupted your morning. Goodbye Lizzy.'

Will turned and walked out into the rain, not even hunching to shield himself from its force. Lizzy sagged against the tin wall and watched him until he was out of sight.

It seemed like hours later when Joy came running into the shed, but it was mere moments. 'Lizzy, what happened? Are you okay? Will just left. What did he say?'

Lizzy didn't know if she could explain any of it. 'He came to say goodbye but I told him what I thought of him and what he did to Jane,' she said, suddenly exhausted.

Joy handed her a towel and wiped her face with another. 'He did leave rather quickly. Are you okay?' she asked again.

'Yeah. Nothing a cuppa and one of your

blueberry muffins won't fix,' she said forcing a smile.

Joy's shoulders dropped as she relaxed. 'Oh good. You had us worried for a minute. I had to stop Wayne from coming. I told him we shouldn't interfere.'

'Thanks.'

'Come on. Let's go dry off inside.'

Lizzy followed her to the house where they found Wayne already halfway through a muffin.

'I'm stress eating,' he said by way of apology. 'All good, Lizzy? I was going to give him a piece of my mind but he shot through like a skinned rabbit. You get stuck into him, love?'

She nodded and reached for a muffin while Joy put the kettle on. It was hard not to run it all back over in her mind. Will's face, their heated words. Him asking her out! How was that even possible after everything he'd said about her, and they always bickered? He was so hard to read — right now Lizzy couldn't even get a fix on her thoughts, as a million bits flew around in her head like an upended jigsaw.

'Lizzy?'

She looked up to see Joy and Wayne watching her closely. 'Sorry?'

'I asked if you'd like a few muffins for your trip home?'

'Oh, I'd love some please.'

Concern shone from Joy's eyes. 'Are you sure you're okay to drive home? You look beat.'

'I'm fine. Quarrelling with Will was exhausting but I'll be good when I hit the road. Thanks for letting me stay and for spoiling me as usual.'

'It's our pleasure.' Wayne threw an arm around her shoulders. 'We'd do it more often if you'd let us.'

'Call us when you get halfway and when you're home,' said Joy handing over a container with the still-warm muffins.

'I always do.'

Lizzy was relieved to be alone in her ute travelling home. Pippa lay with her head on her lap, her big brown eyes glancing up to watch her as if she knew something was up. It was a comfort, patting her soft head and ears. Dogs were easy to understand, unlike men.

Eight hours later when she finally drove down the driveway to home she was none the wiser. The only thing she'd decided was not to tell Jane about what she'd found out. No good would come of bringing up Charlie when Jane was trying so hard to move on.

Pippa sat up on the seat and peered out the window. She knew exactly where they were.

'Finally we're home, Pip. Can't wait to tell Dad about how awesome you were,' she said reaching across to rub her neck. Pippa acknowledged her for two seconds before watching out the window again, her front paws jiggling on the spot itching to get out.

Lizzy smiled and followed the lights from her family home. The sun had gone and left the moon watching over the land.

Already she felt better, just for being back where she belonged.

22

'Have you thought about what you'll do with all the money you won?' Margaret asked as she served up a plate of French toast the next morning.

'Probably give it to the bank,' said Lizzy with a sigh.

Last night over dinner John had asked a thousand questions about the trials and then for a description of Pemberley and the whole Darcy operation. Lizzy had happily chatted about Pippa's performance but she'd stuck to the basics about Pemberley, the house design and farming layout, plus all the machinery, leaving out Georgie and Will.

'Don't give it to the bank, love, you'll never see it again. May as well use it for something we don't normally have money for. Like new tyres,' John said with a smile, but Lizzy could see the sadness behind his façade.

'Yeah, maybe you're right,' she said, reaching across and holding his hand.

'Lizzy, are you going to eat?' asked Kitty as she was about to take the last bit of French toast.

'No, you take it. This coffee will do me fine. I think I ate enough at Aunty Joy's to sustain me until next week,' she said with a smirk.

'Gosh, they love their food,' said Jane. 'They always tell me I'm too skinny.'

'You are,' said Margaret as she finally sat to eat.

'I wish I could have seen you in action, and your win. I'm so proud, Lizzy,' said Jane.

'All that reading and training paid off. See, there's a lesson in there, Kitty,' Lizzy said, glancing at her younger sister who was on her phone while trying to eat. Lizzy looked closer when she didn't reply or roll her eyes and saw that Kitty had her earphones in and was probably listening to music. She lived with the blasted things in her ears.

'Waste of good advice,' she mumbled. 'When's Lydia due back?' she said suddenly.

Margaret sighed. 'Tomorrow. I've tried to call her but she never answers. I have to go through Kitty most of the time. How did I end up with such a difficult child? It's like my children got harder the more I had.'

'She's too spoiled, Mum,' said Lizzy. 'Jane and I never got away with half the stuff Lydia does.'

Jane pushed her chair out and stood. 'I better be getting to work. I'll see you this afternoon.'

'Bye Jane, don't let the ankle-biters get to you,' said John cheerily.

Lizzy got up with her and followed her out to the car as her phone vibrated.

'Hey, Lottie said she's coming down today for a visit.' She typed out a quick reply as she walked. 'I could do with some cheering up,' she said without thinking.

Jane turned around, her patterned skirt swishing around her ankles. With her blonde hair cascading over her shoulders and white blouse she looked more like a fashion editor than a day-care boss. How she didn't come home covered in texta, glue and glitter was remarkable.

'Lizzy, what aren't you telling me?' she asked, looking her square in the eyes.

Sucking in her bottom lip, Lizzy deliberated for a few seconds. 'I ran into Will at Pemberley.'

Jane touched her arm and her face filled with concern. 'Why didn't you tell me?'

'I . . . well, I didn't want to worry you with my small problems.'

'Lizzy,' she said like only a woman who worked with small sensitive children could. 'It's never a problem, you know that. Was it hard? Was he rude?'

'Well, that's the weird thing. He was nice, human almost,' she said with a shrug. 'But then he can be an arse in two seconds flat. He just drives me nuts. He's so conceited.'

'He sure knows how to push your buttons. You must tell me all about it when I get home, promise?' Jane took Lizzy's shoulders and shook them. She was quite strong for a slight woman.

'Okay, I promise. Thanks Jane. See you soon.'

Jane blew her a kiss as she drove off. Lizzy glanced back at her phone. Lottie was turning up at four. That would give her plenty of time to see what needed doing this week on the farm and catch up on anything she'd missed while she'd been away. Lizzy noticed she had a new email. Opening up her mailbox on her phone she saw the sender's name. Will Darcy. How had he got her address?

Georgie!

Lizzy clicked her phone shut, not wanting to read anything he had to say.

She stormed off. Pippa barked from her pen, not even giving Lizzy a chance to forget her.

'As if I would,' she said to her while unlatching the gate. Pippa did her usual mad dash across the yard, around the chook pen and over the old bathtub that had once been a home for ducks but now was upturned and had become Pip's favourite launching spot. She did this every time she was let out, unless there were visitors to upset her routine. Once she'd finished she would end up back at Lizzy's feet, waiting to see what was next.

'Got to wait for Dad. See what needs doing,' she informed her.

As if on cue, John stepped outside and pulled on his work boots. 'Lovely day. Shall we go see if the sheep are still where I left them?' he said as he made his way to Lizzy's side.

Pippa's ears twitched at her favourite word.

'Sounds like a plan, Dad.'

The day passed quickly with catching up and fixing another fence and a quick crop inspection.

'Lottie's going to meet me in town, Dad. She wants to go up the hill for old time's sake. While I'm in there I'll get those camlock fittings for the water truck. Anything else we need?'

John scratched his stubbly chin. 'Nah, think that's all, love. Maybe a cask of port if you go past the pub,' he said with a grin. 'One for the shed.'

Lizzy nodded as she headed for her ute. One for the shed meant one that Margaret didn't get to find out about — hidden in an old fridge that didn't work. 'No worries. Pip, stay with Dad.'

Pippa stopped following her and sat. She didn't move even after Lizzy couldn't see her in the rear-view mirror anymore.

* * *

'Is that for me?' Lottie said, eyeing off the coffee and caramel slice Lizzy had rested on the roof of her car as she stepped out in front of the pub. 'You're a superstar.'

Lizzy barely had time to turn before she was being hugged. 'Oh man, it's so good to see you!' Lottie planted a kiss on her cheek and then held out her hands. 'What can I take?'

The Charlotte before her was her best friend and yet she was different. She was in black tights, a blue hoodie and running shoes, but it was her face that looked different. Radiant.

'Here, take both and I'll drive,' said Lizzy. 'Nice tights, by the way.'

Lottie smirked. 'I'm getting quite fond of them. Ken and I do yoga together. It helps his back, and we've been doing some core work too.'

They discussed Lottie's newfound passion for fitness as they drove, and when they reached the bottom of the hill the caramel slice was almost gone.

'Oh, I miss Mrs Smith's cakes,' Lottie almost drooled as she finished off the final crumbs and climbed out of the ute.

'Not against your fitness policy or anything?' Lizzy asked.

'Oh gosh, no. I like being fit but it doesn't stop me eating everything in sight,' she said with a laugh. 'Probably a good thing we're so far from town otherwise I'd be in the bakery as much as I was the coffee shop.'

They stopped talking towards the end of the climb, pausing to settle their heart rates and take in the view.

'I've missed this. I thought I could remember it so well when I tried to picture it, but nothing compares to the real thing.'

'Yep. It's so good to see you.' Lizzy was busy watching her friend. 'How are things? What's brought on this sudden visit?'

Grabbing her hand Lizzy led her to the seat so they could sit.

'It's not sudden. And what makes you think something's up? I wanted to see my dad and you. Turns out the new girl at the pub is going okay, although not as good as me with the ordering and office work,' she said with a smile.

Lizzy nodded slowly. 'I know you, Miss. And I know when you're avoiding telling me something. What's up? Is it Ken?'

Straightaway she knew it wasn't, because Lottie's face beamed with love. Real love.

Lottie sighed. 'Well, there's no keeping anything from you, is there? I guess I better spill.'

'Oh-my-god-are-you-pregnant?' Lizzy shouted out as she stood up.

'Oh ha ha, settle down, will you.' Lottie pulled her back onto the seat. 'I'm not pregnant, not yet anyway,' she said with a grin. 'But Ken has asked me to marry him, and I said yes.'

Lottie reached into her pocket, pulled out something shiny and slid it onto her finger. Then she splayed her hand out for Lizzy to see it properly.

'For real? Well, of course, that ring is *incredible*.' Lizzy looked from the ring to her friend's face. There were happy tears in her eyes when she threw her arms around her.

'Now, I know what you're thinking, Lizzy: it's too soon for this. But Ken said he's not getting any younger and that he loves me and he wants to make a life with me. At first I thought I better take my time and think it through . . . but I kept coming to the same conclusion: I love him and I'm happy. What more is there to consider?'

Lizzy smiled. 'I wasn't thinking that. I was actually thinking how good you look, full of spirit and energy. And light. You are just beaming, and I'm so bloody happy for you.'

'Thanks Lizzy. That means so much to me. Will you be my bridesmaid?'

'Of course!' Lizzy sat back and snatched up Lottie's hand to closely inspect the ring. 'He went all out, hey?'

'Yep. I came home from delivering eggs to find piles of roses, the table set and dinner in the oven. It was perfect. I never thought I'd ever get this chance, Lizzy. I thought I'd end up in the pub forever.'

As the sun warmed them against the fresh breeze and the gum leaves flittered in the wind, they spoke about Ken and his proposal and possible wedding dates and plans. For Lizzy, being back here with Lottie was just what she needed to rest her mind from Will. Yet still as she listened to Lottie talk she pictured the way Will's lips moved as he'd spoken even when her mind had been in a tizz.

'Lizzy, what's going on with you?' Lottie's hand pressed against her arm, drawing her back to reality.

'Huh, what do you mean?'

'I mean this funny look you keep getting. And you're not yourself. Well, you are but I can still see something's bothering you. Now it's your turn to tell. Is it the farm, or something to do with me?'

Lizzy grimaced. 'Will Darcy asked me out,' she said suddenly. She was going to start from the beginning but the thing pressing most on her mind came out first.

'What? *Will?* When did this happen? Did you kiss him?'

'No,' said Lizzy scrunching her face. 'I told him he was the last man I'd ever date.'

'Oh, you should have at least kissed him first. Seen what all the fuss was about.' Lottie grinned and Lizzy slapped her arm.

'Be serious. It was awful.' Then she started from the beginning and managed to work herself into a bit of a state by the end. 'I was so furious with him, and . . . ' She paused, and forced herself to go on. 'And I was disappointed in myself for starting to actually like him,' she said truthfully.

'Hard not to like him, he's gorgeous.'

Lizzy frowned.

'But an arsehole, yes I have been paying attention. What happened next?' Lottie demanded.

'He said sorry and left.'

'Just like that?'

'Well, I didn't really hold back. I'm surprised he stayed as long as he did.'

'He must have really fallen for you.'

Lizzy let out another sigh. What if she'd been starting to fall for him? 'Oh Lottie, what am I going to do? It's all just so bloody annoying and confusing.'

'You know, you two might actually be perfect for each other. You butt heads, but maybe that will keep things hot? And you might be really happy with his big . . . bank balance.'

'Don't even joke about that.' Lizzy picked at a loose thread on her shirt. It was already torn, and the thread came away easily. 'I mean, what if — '

Her phone rang, causing them both to jump and then laugh.

'Hey Mum, what's up?' Lizzy said, but almost immediately the smile fell from her face.

'Far out. I knew this would be trouble,' she said after hanging up. 'I have to go. Lydia's gone missing.' She jumped up and headed down the hill, not checking to see if Lottie was hot on her heels.

'Missing? From where?'

Lottie had caught her and was keeping up with her rapid descent.

'She's been staying with friends in Toongarrin. Apparently she was last seen yesterday and never came back. Apparently she was off to see a man.'

'What? Which man? Do they know?'

Lizzy let the momentum make her take the last few paces at a sprint, almost running into her ute. Her lungs were burning but it still wasn't enough to shake the news she'd just heard. Nothing made sense. Nothing at all.

As she opened the door she looked at Lottie, no doubt displaying all the hurt, betrayal and confusion she felt.

'Kitty said she was meeting Luke Wickham.'

23

'Luke Wickham, cowboy Luke who was smitten with you?' Lottie asked as they got in the ute.

Lizzy had it in gear before her door was closed.

'Apparently not *my* Luke,' she said quietly.

'I thought you said he'd kissed you?'

'I did.' Her mind was spinning as she raced towards town. 'I have Luke's number,' she said, as much to herself as to Lottie. 'I'll call him and see what's going on. I'm sure we're just thinking the worst. Maybe Lydia went to have a cuppa with him before taking off somewhere with friends. She might have got lost, gone to a party and lost her phone. Got drunk and slept it off. Luke might be able to give us a heads up.' Lizzy nodded to herself, hopefully there was a simple explanation. 'Mum does like to blow things out of proportion.'

'Well, that's true. You call him and I'll run in and see Jane.'

'Thanks. Mum said she wasn't answering her phone but she's probably outside with the kids.'

Lizzy parked outside the old white church building with its big bright sign out the front 'Coodardy Day Care' with coloured handprints along it. Jane's car was parked under a shady tree off to the side.

She pulled her phone from her pocket as she watched Lottie jog up to the entrace. With a

282

wavering finger she found Luke's contact and pressed call while her heart pounded.

As the phone rang she tapped her fingers rhythmically against her leg. It rang out.

By the time Lottie came back Lizzy had called three more times, left two messages and texted another two.

'How did it go? All sorted?'

Lizzy frowned. 'No. He didn't answer. I've left messages.'

'He could be busy? At work? Didn't you say he was driving trucks? He could be on a long haul, hopefully not with Lydia in the truck. She wouldn't be silly enough to go for a ride and not tell anyone, would she?' Lottie leaned against the open window on the ute.

'I have no idea what Lydia is capable of these days. If she wants something badly enough she could do anything, and she'd been all over Luke on his visits.'

'Well, hopefully she uses her brain and calls home soon. Jane said she'll be home in half an hour and will try calling Lydia in the meantime. I'll head off to the pub and see what Dad's up to. I'll probably get shoved in the office to update his bookwork,' she said rolling her eyes.

Lizzy put her hand on top of Lottie's arm and smiled sadly. 'I'm sorry, Lottie. It's not the best end to a great catch-up.'

'That's okay. Keep me informed on Lydia, please. We can celebrate when you come to our engagement party next week.'

'I wouldn't miss it.'

Lottie kissed her cheek then stood back and watched her go.

At home Lizzy went straight to the house, where she found her dad trying to console his wife.

'Oh, thank god you're here!' said Margaret, who was sitting back on the couch while John stood nearby with a glass of iced water in one hand and his scotch decanter in the other. Margaret was pale and sweaty and fanning herself with a copy of the *Farm Weekly* newspaper.

'You're getting yourself too worked up, Mum,' said Lizzy in a calming voice as she felt her phone vibrate. She did a double take when she saw it was another email from Will Darcy. Subject line read: *Please read*.

No *I'm sorry*, just a demand for her attention. Everything he did just rubbed her up the wrong way. Well, there was no way she was reading anything from him right now, she thought, shoving her phone back deep in her pocket.

'I'm waiting for the 'I told you so' about Lydia going off to Toongarrin,' Margaret said angrily and then sobbed out, 'Where could she be? John, do you think she's been kidnapped? My baby girl!'

John put the glassware on the table and spoke to Lizzy. 'I was waiting for you to come home to stay with your mum. Mary's on her way. I'm going to head off to Toongarrin and see Carol and Neil and try to talk to the kids Lydia was hanging out with. And then drag her home when I find her,' he said sternly.

'Good idea, Dad. I've tried calling Luke but

284

he's not answering. We'll let you know if we hear anything. Mum will be fine. We'll be right.'

He nodded and moved about the house collecting his wallet and phone. The fact that he had already packed an overnight bag showed Lizzy how worried they really were.

Lizzy got a wet flannel and placed it across Margaret's forehead, covering her eyes. 'Just sit back and rest for a bit, Mum. Put your feet up on this,' she said sliding the coffee table across to her feet.

When her mum was settled Lizzy went in search of Kitty, and found her in her room, wrapped up in her fluffy aqua rug on her bed against the wall. She had her phone in her hands and was staring blankly at it.

'Has she replied?' Lizzy asked as she entered.

Kitty startled a little before turning to watch Lizzy sit beside her on the bed. Next to Kitty was Lydia's favourite star-shaped pillow that was covered in shiny yellow tassels. Lizzy picked it up, running her hands through the plush material.

'That's the one present I've got her that she's loved to bits,' mumbled Kitty. Her big eyes turned up to Lizzy, hopeful.

Lizzy's heart sank. 'So, you haven't heard from her, then?'

Kitty shook her head slowly. 'I wish I had. Normally I wouldn't be worried. But Lydia's never kept me out of any of her mischief before, she knows I can keep a secret. This is so unlike her. I was worried before Mum got the call to say she was missing.'

She looked at her phone.

'I've sent so many messages and rang, but nothing. I'd say she doesn't have her phone on her and that is soooo not like Lydia. Lizzy, do you think she's okay?'

The Kitty in front of her now reminded Lizzy of the eight-year-old version who would climb onto Jane's lap and ask for her to read another story on the stormy nights when she got scared. Lizzy held out her arm and Kitty fell against her.

'I'm sure Lydia's okay. She can be pretty scary and tough when she wants to be. Dad has just left to go find her. He'll bring her back.'

She felt Kitty relax.

'Hey, how come she was going to meet Luke?'

Kitty paused, then sighed. 'Lydia has the hots for him. That's one of the reasons she wanted to stay in Toongarrin in the first place. She went to parties hoping to run into him and said yesterday he'd finally been in touch after getting back from a job, and they organised to meet today. And then nothing.' Kitty moved so she could look up at Lizzy. 'Do you think she and Luke would have run off to get hitched or something?'

'Hm, Doubt it.' Lizzy felt a weird acid burn in her stomach. She didn't feel great about this whole Luke and Lydia situation at all. It felt off. 'They've gone off to a party together, that seems more reasonable.' Luke had shared family meals with them, after all. 'Let's just wait and see what Dad finds out.'

'Yeah, you're right.' Kitty sighed heavily. 'It's just, she's not as brave as she thinks she is.

Sometimes she does stuff that I know she's scared of.'

'Well, we're all a bit like that, sis.' Lizzy moved her arm and pushed Kitty upright. 'I better go see how Mum is. Jane will be home soon. She might make us her comfort pasta for dinner. I don't think Mum's up to cooking.'

'Oh, I love her special pasta. All that cream and bacon. Fixes everything.'

Back in the lounge room Margaret was asleep, so Lizzy went outside and sat by Pippa on the back verandah.

'Thanks girl,' she said as Pippa shimmied closer and rested her head in Lizzy's lap. She didn't settle long, though, before she sat up and barked as a car arrived.

'It's okay, it's just Jane.'

Lizzy got up to go meet her, but as she rounded the corner of the house she skidded to a halt. It wasn't Jane. Before her stood a man.

That man.

Will Darcy.

24

'Lizzy, we need to talk.' His face looked grave and his hair was ruffled as if it had been a rough night. 'There are things to say.'

'No, Will. Now's not the time for any of this.' Lizzy tried to step around him but he stood in her way again. She put her hand on his arm, hoping to move him aside but he was like a tree with his roots firmly planted, and she could feel his muscles under her hand resisting her. 'Please, Will.'

'I won't leave. I said things wrong last time. I've been thinking about it and about what you said.'

Lizzy grunted as she tried to budge him again. 'I can't deal with this, Will. So much is going on at the moment.'

'Lizzy, please hear me out.'

Lizzy stepped back and threw her hands up and only just refrained from stomping her feet. 'I can't,' she growled. 'Lydia has gone missing and may be with Luke Wickham — '

'Luke Wickham is a dickhead and a waste of perfectly good air,' he said gruffly, cutting her off. 'Didn't you read my email about him?'

It was like a shock of cold water, her mind suddenly derailed. 'Your email was about Luke?' she said, confused. Lizzy paused and focused on his eyes. 'I know you hate him.'

'Hate him? I despise him,' he spat. He stepped

into her personal space and rested his hand on her shoulder. 'Look Lizzy, I should have told you earlier about Luke, but I don't like people knowing our business. But I can see that not telling you hasn't helped either. And seeing as you didn't read my email, best I tell you what it said.'

She tried to focus on what he was saying and not the tingling warmth radiating from his hand on her shoulder. His touch was nothing like Luke's, she now realised. Will had never done anything untoward or inappropriate and she felt that she could trust him. He was arrogant but he was a respected man who wouldn't take advantage of a woman.

'It's true, Luke and I grew up together, but I found him a hard kid to like. He lied and stole, and he became very good at both. After my dad died and I came back I caught him stealing fuel and a phone, he made up some lame excuse and we left it at that. A few other things went on but he always had a story to explain things away. Then after a party for Paddy's birthday I went looking for Georgie.'

Will paused, he looked physically pained as he closed his eyes. Her heart began to race as she tried to swallow all he'd said, and fearing what was to come.

'If I hadn't gone looking for her and heard her scream . . . well, I just can't imagine what I'd have done to that prick,' he growled as he shoved his hands onto his hips. 'I arrived before it went too far, but that image will never leave me.' Will let out a shaky breath. 'He's lucky I didn't wring his bloody neck.'

'Oh my god. What did you do?' She had seen Will with Georgie, the depth of his feeling for her. Lizzy could imagine what he would be willing to do to protect her. She was starting to understand the man he was and he was truthful. She didn't hesitate to believe him.

'I sacked him and sent him packing. Told him I never wanted to see his face anywhere near Pemberley, near me or especially near Georgie. If I hadn't grown up with him, seen him fighting his own demons, I probably wouldn't have been so lenient, but Georgie didn't want anyone to know. So, for her sake we dealt with it quietly.'

Lizzy felt sick, her belly rolling in waves of horror and rage at what his young sister had endured. And her heart was heavy, she felt so much pain and sympathy for Will that it shocked her. It was like her brain was finally realising what her heart had known all along, that she wanted Will. Did she love him? She didn't want to and had tried so hard to fight him even after what he'd done to Jane.

Urgh! Lizzy shook her head, now wasn't the time to understand her heart.

'Poor Georgie. I can't even fathom how she must have felt, how awful. Oh my God.'

Luke was not the man she thought he was at all. How wrong she'd been, so easily fooled by his charms. She bowed her head and held her belly as the humiliation grew. To be fooled so easily. Will must have thought she was ridiculous, hanging from Luke's arm at the rodeo and saying how much better a person he was than

Will. Lizzy moaned with regret. 'I've been so stupid.' Her words were whispered.

Will had every right to agree with her, and she expected more words as such. But they didn't come.

'Don't beat yourself up,' he said softly. 'Luke is a master manipulator. How were you to know? If I'd not been so proud trying to keep it quiet about Georgie then I could have warned you all.'

'No Will, it's okay. I understand why you didn't. You were protecting Georgie.'

They stood staring at each other, breathing heavily.

'So Luke's always had problems?' she asked.

'Well, he was drunk when he . . . when . . . that night. He likes to drink and use whatever drug is going around. But growing up with me I think he always felt he deserved more. He was never happy with his place in life. My dad was really good to him and his dad, but it was never enough for Luke. He always thought he was hard done by. Thought everyone owed him something. Took what he wanted — still does from what I hear, robbing the people he works for. He just keeps moving to the next place.'

He bowed his head. 'It's not easy to talk about but you deserve the truth, Lizzy. I'm sorry I didn't tell you sooner. Luke is not a man to be trusted. Just be thankful he's not around here anymore.'

Lizzy felt a jolt of adrenalin as his words sank in. Luke had kissed her. They had been right near the spot where she now stood with Will.

She thought back to his smooth words, the way he'd spoken about Will. She grabbed her elbows as her skin crawled. She'd believed every word.

But even worse was the possibility that Lydia was with him. 'Oh no.' Lizzy put her hand over her mouth as a sudden wave of sickness shot through her.

'What is it? Are you okay?' said Will, his brow creasing.

'Lydia's been missing since yesterday, and . . . the last person she was known to be with was Luke. Oh Will, what if . . . ?' Lizzy squeezed her eyes shut trying to block out the images of Luke forcing himself on Georgie who then morphed into Lydia. 'Lydia's only fifteen!'

Lizzy was pulled into his strong embrace. It was calming and warm and if her mind hadn't been racing so much she might have realised Will was also gently rubbing her back. She wrapped her arms around him, hanging on as if it would stop the world from spinning, the feel of his constant heartbeat against her chest slowly soothing her.

'Try not to worry,' he said gently. 'Where was she last?'

'Toongarrin. Luke was there working for a contractor driving trucks. She wanted to meet up with him.'

Before Lizzy could say any more a car pulled up and Jane was standing nearby. Lizzy hadn't even noticed her coming.

'Lizzy, is everything all right? Hi Will.'

Will stepped back from Lizzy but kept a

steadying hand on her elbow until she nodded she was okay.

'Lizzy will explain,' he said. 'I've got to go. Look after her please, Jane? Bye.' With a last glance at Lizzy he left.

'Well, that was strange. Did I interrupt something?' asked Jane curiously. 'Why are you so pale?'

Lizzy hugged Jane. 'I need to tell you what Will told me about Luke. I think we better sit.'

Together they headed to their old two-seater swing hanging out the front from the big lilac tree. The wooden seat and old rope still held both their weights even though they weren't ten year olds anymore.

'I can't let Mum overhear this,' Lizzy said before repeating all Will had said.

'Oh no. We had him in our house, treated him as our guest. Do you think he stole from us too?' she asked, looking shocked.

Lizzy shrugged. 'Can't imagine we'd have much of value, but who knows.'

'What a jerk. What are we going to do about Lydia? Is there anything we *can* do?'

'I think we talk to Kitty and call all Lydia's friends. I'll keep trying Luke but I guess he might never answer. Hopefully Dad is having more luck.'

'I just feel so sick.' Jane was as white as a sheet, so Lizzy gently told her of her suggestion of pasta, if nothing more than to keep Jane occupied.

They didn't hear from their father until they were seated at the dinner table. Bowls were still half-full of pasta and there was an eerie quiet around the table. When the phone rang it was like a starting gun; they all jumped up to answer it.

'Let Lizzy get it,' said Margaret, but they all stood and moved to circle around her as she picked up the phone. It only took minutes to learn that John hadn't found Lydia but he had been told by 'someone in town' that she was seen getting into a ute with Luke Wickham early that morning.

'Dad's going to go to the police to try to get his ute rego to see if they can find them,' Lizzy reported as they all sat back at the table.

'But that might take ages! Why didn't she take her phone?' said Kitty. 'I need ice cream,' she added and headed to the fridge.

Lizzy stood closer to Jane. 'I couldn't tell Dad about Luke without everyone hearing.'

'Do you think we should? Might it make the police try harder? She probably hasn't been gone long enough for them to even do something. It's night-time, Lizzy! Where are they staying?'

Jane's face said so much more than her words. It was exactly what Lizzy had been thinking. Luke and Lydia alone all night.

'I don't know, Jane. I might call Dad back later and let him know but I don't think we need to worry Mum.'

'I agree,' said Jane. 'Maybe I should close the day-care centre tomorrow.'

'No, don't. There's nothing we can do, we just have to wait. Besides, so many people rely on you, Jane. I'm here if anything needs doing.'

'Yeah, I guess you're right. I just hate feeling helpless.'

★　★　★

The next morning everyone staggered around the house like zombies, dark rings around eyes and tousled hair from a restless night. Kitty stomped out in her blue pyjamas with bright yellow smiley faces on them, her face anything but.

'Any news?' she asked hopefully.

Lizzy shook her head slowly.

Kitty sighed, her eyes simmering with tears as she turned and shuffled back to her room.

Lizzy was putting on her work boots to head out to spend time with Pippa when her phone rang. A number she didn't know.

'Hello, Lizzy?'

A wave of relief crashed over her at the familiar voice.

'Lydia, is that you? Are you okay?' She pressed the phone harder to her ear trying to hear the quiet voice.

'Can you come and get me, please?'

'Where are you? What's happening? Is Luke with you?'

'I'll tell you when you get here. I'm fine. Please, can you just come?' she said with childlike urgency, reciting the name of a town three hours north of Toongarrin and telling Lizzy she was waiting in the local park on the main street.

295

'Okay, I'm on my way. Whose phone is this?'

'It's a new one. I'll explain later. Just hurry, please.'

Lizzy darted back inside. 'Lydia just called. I'm off to pick her up. Can you call Dad and tell him to head home and that she's safe.'

'Oh thank god!' said Margaret dropping the towel she was trying to fold. 'Where is she? What has she been doing?'

'How about we wait until I have her home before we start interrogations. I'm closer to Lydia than Dad, so tell him just to head home. We can sort the rest out later.'

Lizzy grabbed her wallet and headed for the door while Margaret, still with a hand on her chest, staggered to the phone. The relief was immediate but Lizzy still wouldn't feel good until Lydia was safely back home. She called Jane, who was at work, and left a message telling her the good news as she headed to her ute.

'Sorry Pip, best you stay home. I'll be back soon.'

★　★　★

When Lizzy pulled up outside the small park she spotted Lydia straightaway. She was sitting on a bench seat under a gazebo, her legs drawn up and her head was resting to the side like she was sleeping. The sight of her filled Lizzy with warmth and she smiled, then as she climbed out of the ute she had to force down the anger. It would only make Lydia want to run, and the main point was she was safe. Lizzy kept repeating it over and over in her mind. *Lydia is safe*.

Lizzy stood in front of the small form, shading her from the midday sun. Lydia opened her eyes, looking tired and so childlike. She also had red scratches on her cheeks.

What the hell? Lizzy forced herself to stay in control. 'Hey you. Ready to come home?'

'Lizzy!' Lydia jumped up and hugged her tightly. 'Yes, I want to go home. I'm sorry. I bet everyone is pissed off.'

Lizzy took a deep breath as she held her back so she could see her face. 'We're all just happy you're safe. Come on.'

She tucked her little sister under her arm and led her to the ute. The sun through the windows warmed up the small area, making Lizzy feel cosy as they sat quietly in silence. She saw relief on Lydia's face.

After chewing on her bottom lip for a moment she turned to Lizzy and asked softly, 'Why aren't you yelling at me?'

'We have a long drive home, plenty of time for me to talk. And besides, I don't think yelling would help.'

Lydia dropped her eyes to the floor as Lizzy started the ute. 'We'll stop in and have lunch at the next town. Looked like a good roadhouse.'

Lydia's head snapped up. 'No, please don't. Can't you just go to a coffee shop?'

'Um, I can,' she said frowning. 'But why?'

Lydia turned and stared out her window while Lizzy waited, ute rumbling and radio barely audible.

'Because I'm too embarrassed to go back there.' She swung around. 'But I had no idea, Lizzy, honest. I didn't do anything wrong except be stupid. I thought Luke was good, he was your friend, after all.'

Yeah, some friend. Lizzy breathed through her nose, trying to let her anger towards Luke and Lydia subside. Yes, she felt betrayed by her own sister but now was not the time to dwell.

It wasn't only Lydia who had been gullible except Lydia had to find out the hard way, it seemed. 'How about you start from the beginning?' she said, keeping her voice calm.

Lydia picked at her carefully ripped jeans, her painted nails chipped and chewed. 'I met up with Luke at a party, and he said he was leaving town that night. I didn't want him to go, I'd only just got to see him.'

She shot Lizzy a sideways glance as if waiting for a lecture on parties and boys, but none came, so she continued.

'Luke asked me to go with him. He talked about us having an epic adventure, and it sounded so good. Leaving the world behind and exploring. He made it sound so good, I didn't think, I just wanted to go, so I snuck off to meet him.'

'But it wasn't so good?'

She shook her head slowly. 'No. For a start I forgot my phone. When I realised I'd left it in my swag at my friend's place Luke wouldn't go back. He said he couldn't go back. But he said that was what being free was like and he talked me round. I didn't think our adventure would be a long one. I don't know, I didn't really think at all.'

Her face grew pink and her shoulders drooped.

'At our first stop Luke asked me for money. He spent my last twenty dollars on beer. It wasn't until he sped off after getting fuel later at another roadhouse that I realised he had no money. At one point he pulled into a farm off from the main road and I'm pretty sure he stole tools and drills from the shed. I knew then that he wasn't the guy I thought he was. I was too scared to call him out on what he was doing. I didn't know what to do.'

'Well, don't feel too bad, I just found out that Luke's not who we thought he was. It's easy to be fooled by people. Another reason you don't run off with a near-stranger.'

Lizzy went on to tell Lydia about Georgie. By the time she'd finished Lydia was as white as a ghost.

'Oh my god. Oh Lizzy, I got that vibe. Luke said that we'd camp on the side of the road and that he'd light a fire and I could share his swag.'

Lizzy turned off the idling ute — there was no way she could start driving home now — and stared at the steering wheel. 'Lydia? Did anything happen?' she asked her question very carefully.

Her sister shook her head. 'No, I freaked after he said that. He had this look in his eye that I didn't trust, but I didn't know how to get away. Then when it started to get dark he pulled into a bare patch on the side of the road and pulled out his swag. He said to go get some sticks for our fire and then the party would start. I was just trying to look calm while inside I just wanted to run.'

'What did you do?'

'I went into the bush for sticks but I just kept going. I tried to stay parallel to the road, or at least where I thought the road was. I could hear Luke calling and searching but I just kept moving through the scrub scared out of my wits. There was some moonlight; not much, but it was enough as I felt my way around. I was so scared.'

Lydia pulled up her sleeves and revealed more red marks on her arms. She stared at her hands, at her scratches. 'At times I'd stop and just listen, in case he was coming but my heart was beating so hard I almost couldn't hear. I was sure he'd find me.' Her voice was so low with the hint of a shake.

Her eyes were wide, her face still pale.

'It was like a horror movie. My mind probably made it way worse than it was, but still . . . scurrying around the scrub . . . I didn't even feel the scratches. I was just so scared.'

Lizzy only just held in a shiver at the thought of what could have happened. 'So, what did you do? Did you just stay in the bush?'

'Yeah. I walked till I was too cold, felt like I'd been walking all night. At one point I found a spot under a bush and curled up and cried. I felt something crawling on me and I freaked out and ran off until I calmed down and found another spot to sleep. I was so exhausted. When I woke in the morning I was frozen stiff, and I had no idea where I was. I came across a fence and followed it to where I thought the road was, and it worked.'

Lydia smiled then, as if amazed at her own courage and perseverance.

'Good girl, I'm impressed. So, you found the road?' Lizzy was hanging off every word.

'Yeah, but then I was too scared to walk along it in case Luke came past. So, I walked off to the side so any time I heard a car I could hide. I heard one coming around seven-thirty and got closer to the road — but it was Luke. Man, I've never felt so sick in my life. I just hit the dirt and lay in the tall grass hoping he hadn't seen me. I even let a bug crawl over my hand; I was too scared to move and ruffle the grass. But he just kept going, and then after about five minutes I felt safe enough to get up. I walked along the road a bit more, and then . . . that's when Will turned up,' she ended brightly.

Lizzy felt like she'd been slapped. 'Will?'

'Yeah, Will Darcy.'

'What was he doing there?' Lizzy frowned.

Lydia smiled, her eyes shining. 'He'd been looking for me. Saw me on the side of the road and pulled over. He said he'd seen a camp fire and wondered if it had been us. I told him how I'd run off. He said I was a clever girl.' She grinned.

'And?' Lizzy hurried her up.

'Well, then he drove me here, bought me a new phone and breakfast then he waited until I called you. I told him how Luke had been stealing, but he already knew. Will said he'd been and paid the places Luke stole from. That's how he knew which way we were going.'

'Is Will still here?' Lizzy glanced around. The strongest surge of admiration shot through her body. The thought and care, the lengths he'd gone to. Lizzy felt a warm buzz of gratitude. She wanted to see him, to thank him.

'No. I told him about the farm Luke stole from and we tried to find the place on Google so he could go back and repay them. He waited with me for a bit before giving me some money and leaving me to wait for you while he went off to follow Luke. He said he had unfinished business.'

Lizzy's heart was pounding, and her mind was focused on Will. How had he suddenly become her knight, saving the day and making her swoon? When exactly had her feelings for him changed? She shook her head as she stared at her hands.

'You are so lucky he came by. I hope you thanked him.'

'Yes, Mum, I did,' Lydia said sarcastically and then smiled.

Lizzy almost laughed; there was the Lydia she remembered. 'I'm glad you're okay. We all are.' Lizzy pulled her into her arms and they hugged for the longest time.

25

It was pandemonium when they arrived home. Everyone came rushing out of the house. With Pippa barking and all the cries from the Bennet women it was like a New Year's Eve celebration minus the fireworks.

'Oh my Lydia, come here, baby,' crooned Margaret. Then in the next breath. 'Silly girl! I could throttle you for almost giving me a heart attack. Be thankful I don't lock you up and throw away the key.'

Lydia hugged Margaret even tighter. 'I'm sorry, Mum.'

It turned Margaret to butter as tears sprang from her eyes. John stood nearby with a smile on his face and a hand on Lydia's back.

Jane, Mary and Kitty group hugged Lydia before Kitty started slapping her arm.

'You are the worst sister ever! Never, ever do that again,' said Kitty giving her one last half-hearted slap.

'Come on inside, I've baked scones, and the cream is freshly whipped,' said Margaret.

John led the way inside, followed by the Bennet women.

As Lizzy went to move, Jane stopped her and dragged her across to the seat on the back verandah. Pippa took up her usual position by Lizzy's feet and lay down with her head on her paws.

'You'll never guess who called,' she said trying hard not to smile.

At first Lizzy didn't have her head in the right spot after their crazy return but then it clicked. 'Charlie?'

'Yes. He rang not long after you left to get Lydia. He said he's missed me like crazy and wants to see me. Wants us to be together again.'

Jane's hands were clenched in her lap but they shook as if she were stopping herself from clapping with excitement.

Lizzy smiled; the joy on her sister's face was infectious. 'You're going to? After all that happened?'

'Lizzy, he told me he loves me and only broke it off because of things his sister said and because of Will.' She shrugged her slim shoulders. 'I believe him. He said he's been miserable.'

Leaning back Lizzy grimaced. 'He told you about Will?'

Jane nodded. 'Will even called afterwards to apologise. He wanted me to understand he was just looking out for Charlie. I get that. At least it wasn't something I'd done, or worse — that Charlie just didn't want to be with me.'

Will was making amends. Lizzy couldn't stop the warmth that spread across her skin. She reached over and held her sister's hand. 'Charlie loves you. That's huge.'

Jane's eyes sparkled. 'I know. I love him too,' her voice bubbled.

She was so blissful. Maybe now was the time to come clean. The truth that Lizzy had been keeping from her sister suddenly welled up inside her. 'Jane, I have to tell you something.'

Jane frowned yet somehow nothing creased, only her brows rose.

'I found out that it was Will who talked Charlie into leaving. I feel bad for keeping it from you but I wasn't sure how you'd take it and I was so angry with Will and then he asked me out,' Lizzy said in a rush.

'What? He *asked you out?*'

A flush crept up Lizzy's skin as she nodded.

'When?'

Lizzy gave Jane a condensed version of the events at Pemberley, finishing with Will's declaration in Wayne and Joy's shed. 'But I turned him down. After what he'd done to you I was so angry, Jane. And hurt. Only . . . now I realise I've been at fault too. I decided straight out that Will was a rich snob because I didn't like what he'd said about me. But . . . I misjudged him. He's actually loyal, honest and caring. Jane, he went above and beyond, he went looking for Lydia. He found her and brought her back to us and fixed up the mess Luke left behind. I feel awful about how I treated him.'

Jane smiled. 'It seems to me that maybe you're both even, and maybe more alike than you first thought.' Jane stared at Lizzy for a moment before saying, 'Charlie said he's coming to Charlotte and Ken's engagement party so we can catch up. Maybe Will will be there too?' she said hopefully.

Lizzy sighed. 'I doubt he'll want to see me.'

'Seems to me that he might. Who else would

go chasing after a missing sister?'

'I think it was maybe a sore spot because he didn't tell us about Luke earlier and then he felt responsible for Lydia.'

That's what Lizzy told herself, but deep down she felt a little flutter of hope. A yearning to see his face again. He evoked so many emotions, and he challenged her. He was a strong man with ideals, morals and a big heart. He had offered that heart and Lizzy had rebuffed him. But just a small part of her wondered if there was any possibility he might give her a second chance.

★　★　★

The next morning the Bennet household was back to normal. Kitty and Lydia were gossiping about a reality TV show, Mary was trying to tell Jane about her upcoming piano exam, Margaret was going on about a CWA crisis meeting for the bake sale event and John was trying to read his paper and drink his coffee while pretending to listen. Lizzy leaned back in her chair and smiled. Something so normal, and usually taken for granted, could be one thing she treasured most.

'John, did you hear me? I said they want me to make butternut snaps. The cheek! They know my scones are the best. John?'

'Yes, dear, your scones are the best.' He folded his paper. 'Well, Lizzy, I think it's time we got to work,' he said with a conspiratorial glance in her direction. 'As much as I'd love to stay and listen to the great scone debate.'

'Righto, Dad,' Lizzy replied. 'You go ahead. I

want to go over the budget and farm plan before James gets here.'

'Ah yes, James. I forgot about him.'

'I didn't.' Even with the recent household dramas, she knew this day would come. They couldn't avoid the bank manager forever. But she wasn't upset by her father's lack of interest. He'd handed over the farm reins a few years ago and she didn't need her name on the deed to feel like it was hers. John seemed quite happy taking a back seat and letting her lead the show.

'Best we get the house cleaned up,' said Margaret standing up. 'Come on girls, finish up. I need all hands on deck to tidy up and get morning tea sorted for James. Chop, chop.'

'Thanks, Mum,' said Lizzy as she headed to her room while her dad — he detested the farm bookwork — snuck out the back door like a robber in the night.

James arrived right on time two hours later. He was a tall, lanky man whose shirt was always tucked neatly into his belted jeans. His deodorant was strong, like Old Spice, but he was only fifty-two. He'd been their bank manager for the past three years, when things were cutthroat. He'd seen the Bennets at their worst, and Lizzy had had many calls and meetings with him since taking on the books.

'James, nice to see you,' said John, coming in the back door. 'I heard you pull up.'

The rest of the family remained out of sight as Lizzy, James and John settled at the dining table. Lizzy took James through the budget and projected outcomes she had poured hours into while John sat at the end of the table and listened. Any time she'd asked her father for his opinion he always just smiled and told her to go with her gut. 'All my ideas are outdated, Lizzy,' he once told her. 'No point me trying to hold onto the reins with my old traditions. Better to have you at the helm with fresh ideas and energy.'

'Do you want to come outside now and see how the crops are looking?' Lizzy asked James as she stacked up all her paperwork into a neat pile.

'Sounds good. Thanks Lizzy, I'm impressed,' he said. 'She was born a farmer I'd say, John.'

John smiled and nodded. 'More so than I ever was.'

These words filled her with a sense of pride and elation. It felt good.

'Another coffee, James?' asked Margaret from the kitchen bench, her pink frilly apron sitting over her blue linen dress.

'No thanks, Margaret. I couldn't possibly fit anything else in after all those scones.'

Margaret laughed. 'James, you didn't have to eat them all.'

He stood up and rubbed his belly. 'Oh yes I did. Best part of my day,' he said with a smile before following Lizzy and John outside.

Lizzy didn't take James to all the best parts of their crops, instead she gave him a real overview of the good and the bad.

'I don't know about you, John, but I'm not seeing too much of the bad,' said James holding a head full of wheat in his hand.

'Best I've seen our crops in a long time,' said John.

James glanced at Lizzy. 'I've been with you guys through the ugly and watched as you've worked hard to bring this place back. I'm pleased to say that the bank will be extending your overdraft should you need it and that you are out of the danger zone,' he said with a grin. 'You've been heading in the right direction recently but after going over your paperwork and your projected plans I can definitely say that you have the bank's continued support. I won't be peering over your shoulder anymore,' he said with a smile.

Lizzy glanced at her dad and when he smiled she hugged him firmly. 'Great news, hey Dad.'

'Yeah, well, I can't say I've had much to do with that. It's been all Lizzy. She has a head for this stuff and isn't afraid of learning. She's saved us loads by figuring out how to fix things herself and learning about soil health and the like. Farming's so different from what I learned from my dad and I'm too old now to change. Lizzy has been a great manager, I have complete faith in her. She's a smart one,' said John.

Lizzy clamped her lips together as tears welled in her eyes. She wiggled her nose trying to fight off the tingling of emotion. She'd never heard her dad openly speak about her like that. Oh, she knew he was proud and happy with how she ran things, but to hear those words was more than memorable.

'I know. We've noticed. It shows in just how good your progress has been. It was touch and go there for a while but Lizzy has implemented some gentle but beneficial changes that are really starting to take hold. Also, the Coodardy Farmers Association have a few empty seats on their board and I put your name forward, Lizzy. I'll email you the details but I think you'd be a great asset to have on the board.'

'On a board? I don't know if I'd be any good at that.'

'Sure you would be. You're young, smart and open to ideas and changes. I think you're just what they're looking for. I can help you. The board can even sponsor you to do a Leadership Masterclass if that makes you feel a bit better.' He put his hand on Lizzy's shoulder. 'Please think about it. Anyone who can turn a farm around like this is worth listening to. Congratulations,' he said, shaking their hands. 'I'll see you next time.'

As they watched James drive away Lizzy felt a flutter in her chest. It was a little bit of pride and a lot of nerves. Could she take on a board position? Did she want to? Already she knew the answer to that.

'My girl the mover and shaker and farm saver,' said John as he put his arm around her. 'I know I don't say it enough, but I'm super proud of you.'

He kissed her cheek and Lizzy felt the swell of emotion again.

'Thanks Dad.'

'Let's go have lunch,' he added, rubbing his belly.

'Oh, I'm too full of scones. I might head to

town and get those overnight parts from the depot.' And maybe find a quiet spot at the library to read for a little bit as a treat.

They'd been so careful with how they spent money these past years, and it had paid off. Hopefully the lean years were behind them. Jane could move out without feeling like she was abandoning everyone, and Margaret could start up accounts again in town without fear of not being able to pay them.

In town Lizzy had a sudden brain wave, turning sharply she parked in front of the Rustic Barn, a local shop filled with furniture and decorative pieces, including sculptures by a local artist, one of which Lizzy knew that Lottie had been eyeing off. It was a rusted-metal-and-wire chook, and it would be the perfect engagement gift.

She bounded through the white French doors and stepped into the shop with a spring in her step. Past photo frames and wall hangings to the last aisle containing most of the larger sculpture items. Her large energetic steps faltered, however, when she saw the chook in the hands of Caroline Bingley.

It was like hitting quicksand, her legs went heavy and her body slowed. Her great mood was instantly gone.

Caroline's willowy frame in linen slacks and a blue silk blouse with matching high heels was out of place in this quirky, rustic shop.

'Hi Caroline,' Lizzy forced herself to say.

Caroline made a face as if she didn't recognise Lizzy but then she sighed and put down the metal chook that Lizzy wanted.

'I'm trying to decorate Netherfield, but I think I'd have more luck online or bringing a truck load from the city.' She dusted off her hands.

Lizzy didn't bother replying, instead she reached for the chook Caroline had just put down and quickly tucked it under her arm. 'I find everything in here perfect.'

Caroline stared at her from head to toe, blatantly and unashamedly. 'Lizzy, tell me, I heard a rumour that Will asked you out.' She paused for a second, her face trying to crease in displeasure. 'Now, I'm sure it's just hearsay but if he ever *were* to show interest, I know you'll do the right thing in declining.'

Lizzy's eyebrows shot up, a little in disbelief at what was coming out of her mouth. Caroline looked at her nails as if she were discussing the weather.

When Lizzy couldn't fashion up a reply Caroline continued.

'You see, Will is a very important man. He's well respected in social circles and it's very important for him to have a partner who reflects this, and even improves it. Flannel is not a fashionable look, especially with some of his big clients. He has an image to uphold. You do *not* fit that mould. You understand what I'm saying? Put Will first and do what's best for him.'

Lizzy didn't know whether to laugh hysterically or console Caroline for being so ridiculous. 'Firstly, if Will has or does ask me out, that's none of your concern. And secondly, no I will not decline him.'

Caroline looked as if she'd been slapped. Her painted mouth moved like a big groper abandoned on the beach. Lizzy tried to keep her smile hidden.

'You'll ruin him. He needs a beautiful, sophisticated woman not some . . . hillbilly.'

Lizzy laughed. 'Oh Caroline. You're wrong. You don't know me at all, and I have no intention of justifying myself to you. And as for Will? If you think he's just looking for a bit of bling to hang off his arm, you really don't know him either.' She glanced down at her chook. 'Now if you don't mind, this hillbilly has a chicken to buy. Goodbye Caroline.'

Lizzy gave her the fakest smile she could muster, then turned on her heel and headed to the counter. 'Just the chook please, Sasha,' she said with a satisfied smile. 'And two of your lemon myrtle soaps. I love that stuff.'

'Goodo, just made them up yesterday. The myrtle is strong in this batch,' she said, wiping her hands on her calico apron. Her long braid hung over her shoulder and had a fresh picked daisy in the tie at the bottom.

Caroline's heels click-clacked their way through the shop as she breezed past them and out the door wafting her expensive perfume in her wake.

'You rightly told her,' said Sasha nodding to the door. 'She's been in here twice and just complains about the lack of taste. I'm thinking of locking the door next time I see her headed this way.'

'Not a bad idea,' said Lizzy. 'Thanks Sash, see you later.'

With her chook under her arm and soaps in her hand she headed outside. On the footpath she saw Caroline sashaying down the street with her shoulders back and head held high.

26

'Congratulations! Happy engagement,' said Lizzy, holding out the metal chook with its pretty yellow ribbon bowed around its neck.

'Oh my god, you got me Henrietta!'

Lottie had even named the chook but never bought it because she didn't think it would suit her room at the pub, but Lizzy knew she had a fitting home for it now.

'This is the best gift ever, thank you.' Lottie kissed the chook and then showed Ken who stood by her side smiling as his future wife explained the story of Henrietta. 'I would go in and talk to her, let her know that one day I'd buy her.' She hugged Lizzy again. 'I'm so glad you guys are here.'

'Jane owes me five dollars. I bet her that you'd be in tights and she didn't believe me,' said Lizzy, holding out her hand for Jane to pay up.

Lottie slapped her hand. 'You cheeky devil. Don't knock them until you've tried them. But come in, come and get a drink and see how all our hard work has paid off.' Indeed, the shearing shed had come to life magnificently, the blue-and-black colour theme and fairy lights offsetting each other to perfection. Even though they'd helped Lottie set up earlier it still was awesome to walk in and see it again, completed.

'Am I overdressed?' asked Jane as she glanced

down at the claret-coloured silk dress.

'No. It's perfect,' said Lizzy. She loved its low front with a sash that tied around Jane's waist. Her sleeves were long and flared slightly at her wrists; the skirt had the same gentle folds. She'd teamed it with cream heels and a simple gold necklace, and her blonde hair cascaded in curls around her angel face.

Lizzy glanced down at her own outfit, again hoping her white lace off-the-shoulder playsuit wasn't sliding down too far. It looked like a dress but was actually a one-piece with shorts and like Jane's it had a waist tie. The see-through lace sleeves went to her elbows and flared slightly. Jane had let her borrow her neutral wedge high heels, and dramatic gold hoop earrings dangled from her ears.

Again Jane had done her make-up in soft bronzes, and her tanned skin made the white lace pop. She felt like a fish out of water, making her nerves worse but she really wanted to look more than plain tonight.

The girls moved through as more people arrived.

'Oh look, there's Mum and Dad,' said Jane waving.

Lizzy was pleased to see Kitty and Lydia dressed in clothes that didn't reveal excessive amounts of skin. 'You both look lovely,' she said, meaning it.

'Best we could find so the mozzies don't eat us,' said Kitty, rolling her eyes.

'Good job, Mum,' said Lizzy with a laugh as she hugged her hello.

'Do me a favour and mention the mozzies from time to time, will you?' said Margaret as she watched the youngest two head inside the shed.

'Will do.' She gave her an in-the-know look and then hugged her dad. 'Hey Dad. Looking swish. New shirt?'

'No, just one I found at the very bottom of the cupboard that I haven't seen in years,' he said with a chuckle. 'You girls look so beautiful. Make a dad proud as punch.'

'Aw, thanks Dad,' said Jane.

Lizzy noticed Jane's body stiffen as if she was holding her breath and a dreamy look came over her face. Charlie must have arrived. She had a sudden feeling she was being watched, and glancing around she saw Charlie and Will walking towards them. Her heart lurched into her throat as she just stared at them. At Will.

He wore dark pants and a dark patterned shirt open at the front, making his skin glow like a golden sunset. His hair was stylishly tousled and his dark eyes were trained on her. They never left her face and it set her pulse thumping through her body and made her knees start to weaken. She couldn't deny that attraction, felt hopeless in the pull to this man.

She heard an intake of air and then Jane's arm brushed against hers. Charlie was in dark pants and a dark grey shirt. His blue eyes were vibrant as his steps quickened to reach Jane, leaving Will a few metres behind.

'Hi Jane.'

'Hi Charlie.'

Both spoke at the same time and then laughed nervously.

'You look so lovely.' Charlie reached out and took her hands in his.

Jane was beaming up at him. 'I'm so happy to see you, Charlie.' Her cheeks blushed as she dipped her head a little. 'I've missed you,' she added at a whisper.

'Shall we go for a walk?' he asked.

She nodded and moved towards him, then paused as she glanced back at Lizzy.

'Go, we'll be all right.'

They darted off like two teenagers up to no good. Lizzy was watching them but her whole body was in tune to the fact that Will was standing right beside her making her skin tingle and her breathing strained.

'They look happy,' said Will.

She smiled. 'They do. I'm glad. Jane has been a nervous wreck today. Counting down the minutes like a kid waiting for Christmas.'

Will chuckled. It was deep and infectious. 'Charlie's been no better.'

Lizzy finally turned to face him, but when she met his eyes her thoughts vanished. It felt like minutes went by before she remembered.

'I must thank you, Will,' she started. 'One, for getting them back together again. Jane said you called her.'

He looked to the ground as he pressed his lips together. But his gaze returned to her just as quickly. 'I had an apology to make and things to set right. I own up to my mistakes. Thanks for helping me to see what was right. When I

318

stopped and really saw Charlie, I realised how much he was suffering. It was all my fault, he did it because he believed me. Yet, I was the blind one.'

His warm slow smile set her body on fire. How had she handled standing so close to him before? She took a deep breath and cleared her throat. 'I think we can all be a little blind at times,' she said softly. 'Thank you anyway. And for what you did for Lydia. I can't imagine what might have happened if you hadn't found her.' Lizzy reached out and touched his arm. Her fingers tingled as if zapped by static. 'Our family owes you a great deal, Will. To go and find her, to look after her and fix the mess she was a part of . . . Well, I don't know how to explain just how grateful we all are.'

She frowned, thinking.

'What?' he asked.

'Lydia said you had unfinished business with Luke?' She narrowed her eyes, trying to interpret his expression.

Will smiled. 'Don't worry, he's not buried in a shallow grave somewhere. Although the thought was tempting. I helped lead the police to him and gave them all the evidence of his thefts. It's about time he paid for his sins.'

Lizzy sighed with relief. 'Oh, that's good. I feel stupid having believed him.'

'Don't,' he said softly. 'He's the idiot.'

Her hand ran down his arm to his hand without realising. Will glanced down and she quickly withdrew it and clasped her hands together to try to control the throbbing sensation.

'Lizzy?'

She licked her suddenly dry lips as she met his gaze.

'I did it for you,' he said softly. 'I found Lydia for you.'

Lizzy's breath faltered and her knees felt like they were about to give way when a voice startled her.

'Will, so wonderful of you to come,' said Ken as he strode towards them holding out his hand. 'Did Charlie come too?'

Lizzy stood mutely while her mind rolled Will's words over and over again . . . *I did it for you.*

'Is Caroline here?' Ken asked, still shaking Will's hand.

'No, she's back in the city but she sends her apologies,' he said. 'She's in a bad mood because someone said something to her that she didn't like.'

Lizzy's eyes shot to Will and she found he was staring right at her.

'I had to hear it from Charlie but nonetheless it was entertaining.'

He gave her a warm, sexy smile that caused shivers to shoot down her spine.

'Well, come on, Will. I'll get you a beer, and you must come say hello to Charlotte.'

Will opened his mouth to speak but Ken had put his hand on his back and was leading him through the shed. Lizzy watched him go, feeling suddenly alone.

It grew dark outside as the party began. Will was a popular guest, and Lizzy had trouble getting near him because Lottie wanted her by her side. All she could do was meet his gaze on occasion, and they would both hold it for a beat longer than normal, his eyes sparkling beneath the fairy lights.

At one stage as she helped bring out the plates for dinner she brushed against him to get to the table. She wasn't sure if it was her imagination but it felt as if he'd leaned back to make sure there was a touch. It was electrifying, as if the party was put on pause and only they were able to glide through time experiencing every nanosecond. Lizzy had never been so aware of anyone in her life. At all times she knew where Will was in the room; she could feel his presence as if it were her sixth sense.

Every time she caught his gaze her pulse jumped.

'Lizzy!'

Jane grabbed her hand and pulled her close. She was glowing, her smile wide and her lips plump and slightly bruised. Jane hugged Lizzy and they swayed to the music.

'I love seeing you so happy,' Lizzy said, feeling thankful.

Jane put her lips by Lizzy's ear and whispered, 'Now it's your turn. Go make it happen.' Then she pulled back and smiled. With a nod she let go of Lizzy's hands and headed off to Charlie, who was clearly waiting for her. He hadn't let her out of his sight all night.

Lizzy swallowed the lump in her throat as she zeroed in on Will. Maybe Jane was right. Maybe it was her turn. She was feeling a little courageous and impulsive, swept up in Jane's happiness.

She grabbed her glass off the table and downed the last of its contents before making her way through the talking, dancing crowd to Will.

27

Don't think, just do it!

Easier said than done, she thought as she drew closer and her nerves kicked in.

'I'm sorry to cut in, but Will is needed,' she said quickly as she reached for his arm.

His eyebrows shot up in surprise but he followed. 'Sorry,' he said to the group as she dragged him towards the shed door.

Lizzy didn't look back at him; if she saw any resistance from him she might just lose her nerve. She took him past the roaring bonfire where people were gathered by the heat, sitting on logs, hay bales and plastic chairs with drinks in hand. They continued towards the house but ducked around the front to the little arbour Ken had built with its climbing rose trellis sides and a bench seat beneath it.

'Please sit. I just needed some time with you, away from everyone else and where we can talk. We didn't really get to finish before Ken interrupted,' she said in a rush.

'No, we didn't.' He sat beside her, his leg jiggling on the spot. He watched her intently.

The moon was up and big and round. It hung like a low-voltage light, just enough to illuminate them with a silvery glow.

She stared at him, his eyes so mesmerising.

Now is not the time to lose your nerve!

He tilted his head a fraction. 'What is it you want to discuss?'

'Caroline,' she blurted.

His lips curled up teasingly. 'Ah. The bit about dating me? Yes, I was curious about that too. Did you actually say that? I wasn't sure if Charlie had it right.'

'I'm not sure what she told Charlie, but she did tell me not to date you, that I wasn't good enough.'

His brow creased and his eyes narrowed.

Quickly she hurried on before he brought a storm with his brooding. 'Don't worry, I wasn't offended or put off. I told her that I wouldn't turn you down if you asked me out.'

Will was quiet for what seemed like an eternity. Lizzy wasn't sure how long she could hold her breath for.

'I see. That bit did interest me.'

'Well, it seems only fair considering I knocked you back once before. But please know that back then I didn't have all the facts. Since then I've seen the real Will Darcy and . . . well, I've grown quite fond of him.' She sucked in a breath then rushed out her next words. 'Will, I want to be with you. Would you consider it even after everything we've been through?' The moment the words were out of her mouth she didn't regret them. She had to know now if she and Will had a chance.

He breathed in slowly, watching her carefully. She felt like a bug under a microscope. *Say something!* Oh, this man was infuriating.

'You can take some time to think about it,' she said nervously.

'I don't need time,' he said flatly.

'Oh.' Lizzy's mouth dropped open a fraction, unable to hide her disappointment as she glanced down at her hands making balls in her lap. She prepared herself for his answer, then glanced up to find his lips inches from her face.

Then they were pressed against hers and his hand was threaded into her hair. That leathery fresh masculine scent that she adored engulfed her as Will deepened the kiss.

She kissed him back, her hands reaching for his chest then up to his neck to pull him closer. Warm electrifying lips, his kiss was magically sweet yet so powerful that her body was trembling.

When they parted, breathing heavily against each other's lips she whispered, 'Is that your answer?'

Her lips tingled with need. She ached for more.

Will pressed his forehead against hers. 'I'm crazy about you, Lizzy. I wasn't game to ask again, but after Caroline's rant to Charlie I thought just maybe I might have another chance. But you beat me to it,' he chuckled, voice husky and raw.

He caressed her face and met her eyes with complete seriousness. 'I was wrong to say that about you when we first met. But it didn't take me long to see how similar we are, the passion we share for farming and our families. Lizzy, you've challenged me like no one ever has, you've surprised me and you've made me see things from a different perspective. I've never met anyone like you before. I want to be with you, Lizzy, always.'

His words rippled to her heart like the gentle caress of a wave.

'Hm, and you still haven't given me your answer,' she said playing with the hair at the nape of his neck. She felt like she was floating, like a bird soaring over the land. Heady on the excitement, her body felt alive.

'Oh, I did. Obviously you need to hear it again.' And with that he moved his mouth to hers, his lips parting as he kissed her again. And again.

It wasn't until she shivered that they came up for air.

'You're cold? Let's head back to the fire. This breeze is like ice,' he said, pulling her against his chest and rubbing her arms.

'I guess we should head back anyway,' she said sadly. 'I don't want to leave your side.'

'No one said you had to. I don't plan on letting you out of my sight tonight.' He dropped a kiss on top of her head and she sighed.

'Sounds fine by me.'

They got up, stretching before he snuggled her into his side again and they walked towards the shed.

'Lizzy, darling. We were wondering where you'd got to,' said her dad as they met near the house. His eyes took in Will and their embrace, and John narrowed his eyes. 'I thought you didn't like this man?' he said firmly.

She felt a chuckle rise up from Will's chest, glad he wasn't offended by her dad's frank comment.

'Not at first,' she said, glancing up at Will. 'But it turns out he's one of the good guys, Dad. I do like him. A lot.'

Will looked steadily at her before holding his hand out to her father.

'I'll look after her, sir. I promise. She's very special.'

John eyeballed him for a moment before taking his hand and shaking it. 'I wouldn't give my Lizzy up for anyone unworthy. But I trust her judgment. Come around for dinner soon.' He turned towards the house. 'Have fun, kids,' he added into the night.

'Well, that wasn't so bad,' said Will, kissing her.

Lizzy liked that he wanted to keep kissing her and wasn't afraid of who might see. And as if to prove himself he held her closer as they entered the shed. Many eyes turned to them and then did a double-take as they saw them with arms wrapped around each other.

Jane was sitting with Charlie on a hay bale and when she saw them together she yelped and jumped up to run straight over.

'Oh my god, for real?'

Lizzy just smiled. Well, she hadn't stopped smiling since Will had first kissed her. It was damn impossible not to. 'For real.'

Jane hugged Lizzy, pulling the lovebirds apart but Charlie wasn't far behind her, shaking Will's hand and then doing a man's half-hug-half-slap-on-the-back thing.

'This is the best. Wait till Mum finds out,' Jane whispered.

Lizzy glanced around the shed until she saw her mum sitting in the corner watching them. She had a hand to her lips and her eyes were glistening with tears. She dropped her hand and smiled, nodding her head a fraction.

'I think Mum is delighted,' said Jane as Charlie pulled her back against his chest as they stood there.

'Do I pass the test?' asked Will, his lips close to Lizzy's ear.

Lizzy turned, lifting her hand to his cheek to study his gorgeous face. Her heart could burst it was so full of desire for this man. It was the stirrings of love, she had no doubt. She was falling, and she was falling hard.

Suddenly there was an extra person draped around them. Charlotte was squeezing them and beaming.

'Oh my god. Love you,' she said, kissing Lizzy's cheek.

Lizzy looked up at Will, who was smiling. He looked as happy as she felt and it warmed her to know she was the cause.

'Remind me to text Georgie, she's going to want to know everything,' he said, adding flair to the last word.

'Maybe we can call her together?'

'Perfect.'

Amy Shark's 'All Loved Up' began to play, drowning out the voices in the shed.

'Would you like to dance, Miss Bennet?' Will

asked as he tucked her against him.

'I thought you didn't dance?' she teased but let him lead her in time with the song.

'For you, always.'

Acknowledgements

As a big fan of Jane Austen's *Pride and Prejudice* and all its retellings I've been thinking of this Australian version for many years. So it's a big thanks to Rachael Johns for giving me the encouragement to finally write it and to Rebecca Saunders for believing in it. Also a big thanks to Alex Craig for stepping in while Rebecca made a gorgeous baby. I'm very lucky to have such wonderful people to work with. Claire de Medici, thank you for your amazing edits. Also the rest of the fab team at Hachette, especially Karen Ward and Klara Zak, thank you, thank you. To Lyn Tranter, my long-time agent, thank you for continuing to be there in any time of need. To the best parents a girl could want, thanks Mum and Dad. Especially Mum, who helps out when I need a hand at events or just need my work read or ideas bounced around. Thank you to my supportive friends and family. Sometimes elements of your stories, lives and events tend to end up in my books, so thanks, for the ideas and creative use. Thank you to the readers, who are still with me ten years on. I love to tell stories; thank you for reading them.

We do hope that you have enjoyed reading this large print book.

Did you know that all of our titles are available for purchase?

We publish a wide range of high quality large print books including:
Romances, Mysteries, Classics
General Fiction
Non Fiction and Westerns

Special interest titles available in large print are:
The Little Oxford Dictionary
Music Book
Song Book
Hymn Book
Service Book

Also available from us courtesy of Oxford University Press:
Young Readers' Dictionary
(large print edition)
Young Readers' Thesaurus
(large print edition)

For further information or a free brochure, please contact us at:
Ulverscroft Large Print Books Ltd.,
The Green, Bradgate Road, Anstey,
Leicester, LE7 7FU, England.
Tel: (00 44) 0116 236 4325
Fax: (00 44) 0116 234 0205

Other titles published by Ulverscroft:

THE SADDLER BOYS

Fiona Palmer

Schoolteacher Natalie has always been a city girl. She has a handsome boyfriend and a family who give her only the best. But she craves her own space before settling down into the life she is expected to lead. When Nat takes up a posting at a tiny school in remote Western Australia, it proves quite the culture shock, but she is soon welcomed by the swarm of inquisitive locals, particularly young student Billy and his intriguing single father, Drew. As Nat's school comes under threat of closure, and Billy's estranged mother turns up out of the blue, Nat finds herself fighting for the township and battling with her heart. Torn between her life in Perth and her new community, Nat must risk losing it all to find where she truly belongs.

THE FAMILY SECRET

Fiona Palmer

Kim Richards is a creative woman of the land, a rural ambassador who is renowned for her contribution to her community. But deep down, she is lonely. She's already watched the man she loves marry someone else, and her dream of starting her own family feels like it's slipping through her fingers. Enter Charlie Macnamara, an older corporate man who has arrived in Lake Grace on business. Sparks fly between Kim and Charlie, but he seems to have a hidden agenda and a past life he's trying to hide. They're both drawn to local hermit Harry, a Vietnam veteran still haunted by memories from the war. What ties these three lost souls together? Can they solve a long-held family mystery, and can new love heal old fractures of the heart?

THE SUNNYVALE GIRLS

Fiona Palmer

Three generations of Stewart women share a deep connection to their family farm in western Australia, but a secret from the past threatens to tear them apart. Widowed matriarch Maggie remembers a time when Italian prisoners of war came to work on their land, changing her heart and home forever. Single mum Toni has been tied to the place for as long as she can recall, although farming was never her dream. And Flick is as passionate about the farm as a young girl could be, despite limited opportunities for love. When a letter from 1946 is unearthed in an old cottage on the property, the Sunnyvale girls find themselves on a journey across the world to Italy. Their quest to solve a mystery leads to incredible discoveries about each other, and about themselves.